The Sister Behind the Berlin Wall

Also By Cynthia Anderson

The Pilot's Wife

The Sister Behind the Berlin Wall

Cynthia Anderson

embla books

First published in the UK in 2026 by

embla books

An imprint of Bonnier Books UK
5th Floor, HYLO, 105 Bunhill Row,
London, EC1Y 8LZ

A CIP catalogue record for this book is available from the British Library.

ISBN: 9781471419065

Also available as an ebook and an audiobook

1

Typeset by IDSUK (Data Connection) Ltd
Printed and bound by CPI (UK) Ltd, Croydon CR0 4YY

MIX
Paper | Supporting responsible forestry
FSC® C013604
FSC www.fsc.org

The authorised representative in the EEA is Bonnier Books UK (Ireland) Limited.
Registered office address: Block B, The Crescent Building, Northwood, Santry, Dublin 9, D09 C6X8 Ireland
compliance@bonnierbooks.ie
www.bonnierbooks.co.uk

For my family, with love and appreciation

Prologue

November 1989

My dearest sister,

After all these years, this is such a difficult letter to write, but I must try, even if it never reaches you.

You're probably wondering why I never tried to get in touch before. I've waited a long time for my freedom. For too many years, I haven't been able to speak. Now I want to talk until my voice turns hoarse. I have forty-five years of explaining to do.

Let me start by apologizing for my silence. A silence born of regret for what I did.

I had an impossible decision to make, a choice that tore me apart, and I will never forgive myself for what happened. I know that I have hurt the people I love the most—and who loved me.

My only consolation has been the image I've carried all these years of you, Josef and little Katya leading a beautiful, happy life. Tell me about her. I can't believe she's older now than we were when she was born. And not a day goes by when I don't think of you both and wish that things could have been different.

At last, the wall is being pulled down. Come to Berlin. I'll be there the first week of January. We can meet at the place we went to before everything changed. Kaffee Post?

I'll be on the corner of Unter den Linden, where it used to be, waiting for you. Please, please come.

I long to see you again, to hold you and tell you everything.

With all my love,

xxx

PART I

Autumn 1942

Orléans, France

1

Rose

September 1942

Rose crouched on Quai du Châtelet, pencil poised between her fingers, and sketchbook balanced on her lap. Her hand darted across the paper. It had taken nearly a week to draw the Georges V Bridge—the principal crossing connecting the historic heart of Orléans with the Loire River's southern bank.

Today, she focused on the metal deck covering the bridge's missing arch, hatching fine lines and softening them with her finger to add texture and depth. It was when she was drawing that she felt truly alive. She carried a sketchbook everywhere, just in case something caught her eye. Léa, her elder sister, often remarked that Rose not only had talent but also the rare ability to detach herself from what was happening around her. For Rose, it was simple: if she was drawing, she was happy.

For the next hour, she captured the autumn light's long silhouettes and the golden glow on the bridge's metal deck.

A spear-like shadow fell across her sketchbook. Startled, she looked up. A German soldier, his figure looming large, stood over her.

"*Verboten*," he said, pointing at a sign not far off.

It was written in both German and French—*Quai fermé. Accès interdit*. "Embankment closed. Access prohibited". A wave of confusion ran down Rose's back. Every day this week, she'd come to the riverbank to draw the bridge, but this was the first time she'd noticed the sign. Had it been put up this morning?

"*Militarboot*," he shouted, turning to the barge docked at the embankment and the men unloading it.

Rose stared at the soldier's face, shaded as it was by the dark peak jutting out from his stiff cap. He stepped closer.

"I'm not drawing the boat, but the bridge," she said, her hand shaking as she lifted the sketchbook to show him.

"*Verboten*!" he repeated, his voice harsher. "*Fräulein ist eine Spionin.*"

Two years into the Occupation, her German was good enough to catch the accusation that hung in the air like a noose around her neck. His black-gloved hand reached for her arm.

Rose jumped back. A bolt of panic shot through her as she hurled the pencil case at his face, buying a few precious seconds to stand and run.

"*Halt, halt!*"

She darted up the steep embankment, heart pounding. Slipping on the cobbles, she lost her balance and the sketchbook fell from her hands. There wasn't time to stop. At Rue au Lin, she raced past the female workers leaving the vinegar factory. She didn't need to turn back to see if he was following—she heard the clip of the metal tips on his boots on the pavement close behind. Her adrenaline surged. If caught, she'd be thrown in prison for spying. She ran faster until she was nearly out of breath and a stitch formed in her side.

"Café du Marché," a man's voice called out. "Kitchen exit."

Up ahead on her left, the green sign for the Café du Marché swung above a door. With no time to hesitate, Rose entered. The soldier's footsteps faded.

Inside the restaurant, she avoided eye contact, swerving around the half-full tables. At the far end, red double doors swung open and a waiter, carrying a tureen of soup, appeared. She wove her way to the kitchen. Hit with the odor of fried onions and liver, the clanging of copper pans and the oppressive heat from the ovens, she felt a headache pulse behind her eyes. Where was the door? Léa always said not to trust anyone. Sweat slid down Rose's back. What if there wasn't another exit and the man on the street had set her up, leaving her trapped?

A draft of cool air rushed in and she maneuvered around the ovens to the rear of the kitchen, where a door stood ajar. She looked out to make sure the German soldier wasn't in the alley behind the restaurant. But the alley was blocked off from Rue au Lin with a single opening to a road farther along. The only way for the soldier to find her would be if he'd seen her enter the café and followed. Whoever had told her to come this way knew what he was doing. She stepped outside and walked briskly away.

Trying to appear calm, though her pulse raced and her nerve endings buzzed, she strode on. There was still a chance she might run into the soldier. Rose hadn't been this frightened since that terrible day two years ago when the French army blew up all the bridges in a desperate attempt to prevent the Germans from crossing the Loire and advancing deeper into France. The memory remained etched in her mind like one of her drawings—dive bombers screeching overhead as she and Léa raced to the bunker below the Dessaux vinegar factory, where they huddled underground, fires raging above. After ten long hours, they emerged to a new world: German soldiers patrolled streets of rubble and dust while fires burned for three more days. In an instant, their old life had disappeared.

The farther Rose walked, the more her thoughts drifted back to the man who had guided her to the safety of the café. Léa constantly drilled into her head that since the Occupation, trickery and deception had become part of daily life, what everyone called System D for *se débrouiller*, or getting by no matter the cost to others. Any sense of *fraternité* was lost.

And yet, someone *had* helped her. She wished she could thank him, but she'd been running too fast, all the faces she passed a blur. Now there was no way to find him, just like there was no way to retrieve the sketchbook that meant everything to her. She froze. The sketchbook had her name and address written on the back. If the soldier found it, he could track her to Madame Martin's boardinghouse, where she and Léa shared a room. Rose considered returning to the quai to look for it, but if the soldier was still there, he'd see her. She couldn't risk it.

* * *

As Léa undid her braids later that evening, Rose sat on the bed and told her what had happened at the quai.

"How could you not see the sign?" Léa brushed Rose's long brown hair. "You should be more—"

"I was there every day this week, and there wasn't a sign, or at least I don't think so . . ."

Léa put the brush down. "You were lucky. Be careful and stay out of their way. The Germans don't trust us. If we aren't working, then they think we're up to no good."

"But to accuse me of—"

A knock on the door. Léa went to open it. Madame Martin, the owner of the boardinghouse, stood in the corridor, hands crossed at her chest.

"A gentleman came by this evening asking for your sister," she said.

A terrible kick of a feeling lodged in Rose's chest—the soldier must have found the sketchbook, tracked her here and was now outside. She hadn't told Léa about her name and address on the back. She pinched the skin between her thumb and forefinger.

"Who came to see Rose?" Léa asked.

"Don't play dumb with me." Raising her voice, she pointed a stubby finger at Rose. "You know the rules. I won't have men coming here to call on you or any of my boarders. It's not permitted. That type of behavior leads to trouble, and I don't want my establishment's name sullied. Did I not make that clear when you moved in?"

"Yes, you did," Rose said, pinching her skin harder. "It won't happen again."

"It better not. I'm giving you a warning this time, but if another man comes around asking for either of you, then I'll make sure you're both gone by the end of the day."

Léa stiffened. Rose didn't like the condescension in Madame Martin's voice either but she felt a sudden sense of relief at the realization that the soldier couldn't be outside. Madame Martin would have dragged Rose downstairs and handed her over to him. She was always trying to please the Germans. But if he hadn't come asking after her, then who did?

"Did he give a name?" Rose asked.

"He wouldn't say." She made a disapproving click of her tongue before reaching for something out of sight. "He did leave this for you."

The sketchbook! Rose's head spun. She thought it was lost forever. "Thank you," she said, taking it from her.

"Remember—you only get one warning," Madame Martin said, her voice as sharp as a dagger.

Léa closed the door. "You didn't tell me you left your sketchbook on the quai."

Rose sighed. "I meant to. I forgot."

"Who would have brought it to you?" Léa asked as the mystery of the stranger's identity hung in the air between them.

"I don't know." Rose opened the sketchbook, and a note tumbled out. Léa picked it up. The sisters read it together:

You left this on the quai. I found your name and address written on the back cover. I'll be at Place du Martroi, near the statue of Jeanne d'Arc, every day this week at noon. How was Café du Marché? André

Rose smiled. It was the man who had guided her to the safety of the café. And now, he'd saved her by keeping the sketchbook out of the hands of the German soldier and bringing it back to her.

"Who is André?" Léa asked.

"The man I told you about."

Léa narrowed her eyes. "You said you passed him on Rue au Lin—how could he have seen you leave your sketchbook on the embankment, unless he'd been watching you earlier?"

"I don't know." Rose turned the pages until she came to the sketch of the bridge. The paper was slightly torn on the edges, but the drawing hadn't been damaged. She looked at Léa. "But what does it matter? He might have walked along the quai, seen me, then gone up to Rue au Lin. Why are you always so suspicious?"

"He's a stranger." Léa flashed her a pointed look. "Who is his family? Where does he live? He hasn't been introduced to you by someone we know and trust. Maybe you shouldn't—"

"Meet him? He helped me; that's kindness." Wasn't it enough?

Léa went to the window. Rose could hear the rattle of the glass pane as the tram passed in front of the boardinghouse. She'd always looked up to Léa, seeking her approval in everything she did. After their mother caught pneumonia in the winter of 1939 during the so-called fake war before the Occupation, and died the following year when Rose was sixteen, Léa became her guardian. She was grateful Léa had fought to keep her, and she hadn't been sent to live in a home for orphans. Rose wondered if she would have been as self-sacrificing as Léa had been with her. But sometimes Léa's caring could be overprotective, even oppressive. Now that Rose was eighteen, she needed to make her own decisions. She fell silent and waited, hoping Léa would give her blessing to go and meet André.

Léa turned around. "I'm sorry, I've got a lot on my mind. There's no harm in meeting him in the middle of the day in a public square. Just promise me you'll stay away from any German soldiers."

Rose nodded and went to embrace her sister. "I promise."

* * *

The next morning, Rose took special care braiding her hair. She even debated whether to wear it loose. But then she thought how ridiculous it would be to have long strands flowing in her face as she cleaned the school.

What was wrong with her? She didn't even know what André was like. She'd been too frantic to notice anyone while running away. He might be old enough to be her father. She had no memory of Papa—he'd died a few years after Rose was born—only the old photo of him in uniform before he was sent to fight in the Great War.

She looked down at her hands. This morning, she'd be careful to wear gloves while cleaning the classrooms. Normally, she couldn't be bothered, but since Savon de Marseille could only be bought on the black market, she had to use a soap with a harsh industrial odor, and she didn't want the smell to linger on her fingers for the rest of the day.

At noon, she walked along Rue Royale on her way to Place du Martroi, a ripple of excitement coursing through her with each step. The September sun shone bright, softening the crisp air. Brown and russet oak leaves lay scattered on the ground. It was all so strange and new—going to meet a man for the first time, someone who had saved her from prison or worse. And yet she had no idea what he looked like. How would she recognize him? Of course, she didn't have to. He already knew her.

As Rose reached the square with the statue of Jeanne d'Arc atop her horse, she was struck by how empty and desolate this part of town remained after the German bombing. She remembered the first week of the Occupation when she and Léa stayed in the boardinghouse, too frightened to leave. Eventually, they had to return to work or risk losing their jobs. Léa was a typist in Maître Mallon's notarial office; Rose cleaned a primary school. Each morning, she woke early, cleaned the school, then returned to the boardinghouse to feed the chickens and sweep the coop. In the afternoons, she searched for odd jobs—asking at hotels and inquiring among the women in the laundry for any extra washing or ironing tasks. If she earned a few rutabagas or potatoes, even an old sheet that she and Léa could turn into dresses, she'd find a quiet place to sit and sketch.

The square had an eerie, ghost-like quality. In the two years that had passed since the bombing, nothing had been rebuilt. Where apartments and stores once stood, only stacks of salvageable stones and bricks remained. With nothing to block the view—it was almost like standing in an empty, gray field. Why, she wondered, had André chosen this place for their meeting?

"*Bonjour, Mademoiselle* Rose," a man's voice at her side.

She turned. "André?" He was handsome and young. Her heart tightened.

He nodded. "How are you after yesterday? I was worried about you."

The only people who had ever worried about her were Léa and Maman. "Yes, thank you for—"

"I was lucky to be there. Usually, I avoid the center of town. Too many people."

"Is that why you wanted to meet here?" She motioned to the empty square.

"I hope the rubble doesn't bother you. German soldiers don't patrol here as much. Isn't that good? Let's walk."

"I don't mind the rubble," she said.

As they strolled together, she couldn't help but steal glances at him. The sleeves of his crisp blue shirt were rolled up to his elbows, revealing tanned forearms. His dark hair was cut short, the skin at his collar browned by the sun. Hands tucked in his pockets, he moved with an irresistible lightness, and she wondered how to capture such motion on paper. And then she remembered the sketchbook, and a swell of gratitude rose within her.

"Thank you for bringing my sketchbook to the boardinghouse. How did you know I'd left it on the quai?"

"I'd seen you coming every day that week, drawing the bridge. Since you didn't have your sketchbook when you ran past me, I figured it must be back at the embankment." He angled his head into the sunlight; his black hair softened, and the light turned some of his strands brown. "I hope I didn't cause you any trouble with your landlady. She wasn't happy that I came asking for you. She demanded I give her my name, but I wouldn't. She's not very friendly, is she?"

"She's always like that, insisting men shouldn't call at the boardinghouse. Don't worry—I'm used to her."

The sound of footfalls and men's voices came from across the square, drawing their attention. Two French gendarmes, tall and imposing in their blue uniforms, entered Place Martroi.

"Look, Rose, I must go," he said, stepping away from her. "Tomorrow, we could meet at Quai du Roi. Same time." He raked his fingers through his hair, revealing a slight scar on his forehead. "Bring your sketchbook."

Rose glanced at the gendarmes, their heavy boots echoing on the cobblestones. "I'd love to," she said, turning back. But André had already gone.

2

Léa

September 1942

"I've written a letter of recommendation," Maître Mallon said, shadowy rings like half-moons under his eyes rising through the lenses of his glasses. He lifted a paper from the desk drawer. "It should help you get a new position."

"Thank you," Léa said, reaching for the letter. Though under enormous pressure himself, she knew he'd done all he could to keep her. At eighteen, she'd started as an intern typist at Mallon Notary, and though her dismissal was expected, it still hit with unexpected force. An autumn wind blew through the open window, riffling the papers on his desk. She got up and put them back in order.

Maître Mallon waved his hand, signaling her to stop.

Léa felt a tightening behind her eyes and turned away. Knowing this was hard on him, she didn't want to make it any worse. She glanced at the wooden desk in the corner where she'd spent long hours hunched over a pale gray Hermes typewriter, the four rows of white letters on black keys imprinted in her mind.

"Maître Dupont has plenty of business. Go see him with my letter. He will take you on."

She turned back, shaking her head. "How can I?"

He removed his glasses and rubbed his eyes. "I've done you a disservice."

"I'm glad I know."

Even if he hadn't told her about the camps, she would have figured it out after typing his response to the Parisian notary. Maître Mallon had been assigned the task of visiting three camps—Beaune-la-Rolande, Jargeau and Pithiviers—on the outskirts of Orléans to obtain the signatures of the men sent there from Paris. He'd done as the Parisian notary asked, but in speaking to the men, discovered they were doctors, dentists, professors, and some had even fought for France, like her father, in the Great War.

Léa remembered the afternoon he returned, sitting in silence, staring out the window. She'd asked what crimes they were being held for, and he shook his head in bewilderment. "They themselves do not know, only that they are all Jewish, though most do not practice or attend synagogue." He'd straightened his back and looked her in the eye. "I will try to help them. I'm afraid my profession is actively stripping these men of their property and if I cannot stop it then at least I will play no part in it."

She'd typed the letter he'd written back to the Parisian notary. The Association of Notaries responded a week later, warning he would never work again, but Maître Mallon held his ground. "If I refuse, maybe it will give others the courage to do the same."

A year later, all his clients had switched their business to other notaries. Now, Maître Mallon had no choice but to close his office.

It was likely the last time she would see him. She wanted to part on a hopeful note. "Perhaps I can make more shirts for the men. Winter is coming and they will need extra layers." With the old sheets from the hotel laundries, she and Rose had made shirts to get the men through the winter.

He shook his head. "Thank you, but they're no longer needed."

She leaned forward, not understanding what he meant.

"The men have gone."

Surely they'd returned home to their families in Paris? She smiled at the possibility that his stance had helped them. He must have read her thoughts as his eyes, solemn and sullen, locked on hers. "Over the summer, they were shipped by train to Poland."

"Poland?" Her heart sank. She couldn't imagine what they would do there, and if their clothes hadn't been sufficient for the winters in Orléans, how would they manage farther north in Poland?

"I'm afraid that's not all," he continued. "They filled the empty camps with their wives and children."

A shiver ran through Léa. What sort of sick person could come up with such a plan? Separating families, sending the men away first, then interning the women and children who would have no one to defend them. She was almost too afraid to ask what had happened to them. "Are they still there?"

"Last month I went to visit . . ." His voice turned hollow. "French gendarmes were forcibly separating the children from their mothers and then loading the women onto trains also destined for Poland."

Anger burned in her chest. Why did it seem that Maître Mallon was the only one who didn't go along with the sorting and shipping of people as though they were packages and not human beings? She imagined the tears and cries of fear as the children were torn from their parents and then sent away on a train. "And now the children are alone?"

"Yesterday, they too were sent East by convoy."

Shame for her country flooded through her. She couldn't understand the cruelty that existed in the hearts of the men who carried this out. She looked at the letter, which once would have made her proud, and tore it in two. "I'm sorry, but I will never work at another notary office. Never."

"You shouldn't—"

"I'll become a cleaner like Rose." Some of the women at the boardinghouse had urged Rose to join them at the Salbris arms factory because the salaries were high and the hours good, but neither she nor Léa could bring themselves to work for the enemy.

"Léa," he said. "You're an intelligent young woman with your whole life ahead of you. You have more to offer . . ."

She sighed. The Occupation had woven a thread of greed through society. Everyone was out for themselves. She didn't know how it would end or what they would all become when it did.

"Cleaning is work I can be proud of," she told him. "I will never have anything to do with disposing of and selling innocent people's property and then shipping them out of the country." Everyone said that bad things occurred in Paris or Lyon, the big cities, not here—they were lying to themselves. Their eyes were open, but they didn't want to see what was happening in front of them, because it would mean they were a part of it.

"I'll write another recommendation letter, in case you change your mind."

"No. I'll be fine." Her voice softened. "Thank you."

He looked at her over his glasses. "I respect you for the kindness you show others, your discipline and work ethic." He drew a breath. "But war hardens people. Difficult times expose who people are at their core. You must be realistic. Things will get worse before they get better."

"How can they get any worse?" She sounded like the eighteen-year-old she'd been when she first stepped inside his office.

"Because one side will eventually win and the other will lose, and there will be much suffering in between. Think carefully about your next steps. Do what is best for you and Rose." He stood. "If you are in trouble, come to my home and I'll do what I can to help."

"Thank you." Léa embraced him quickly, turning away and thundering down the stairs so he wouldn't see the emotion welling up in her chest.

It was dark as she rushed along the sidewalk, tears streaming down her face. Their discussion had delayed her departure and left her feeling confused and disoriented. She had always admired Maître Mallon, seen him almost like the father she'd lost when she was just a child. He'd told her of his own struggles, how he'd come from a broken family and worked hard to achieve success as a notary. He'd been a beacon, reassuring her that there was order to the world and if she applied herself, she too could attain a better life.

She couldn't stop thinking about his warning—that times would get more difficult and that she must protect Rose. Léa thought of her mother's refrain whenever Léa came to her with a problem or had lost patience with Rose. *Keep a good heart.* That was her challenge—how to get through the war and keep her heart good. She would find a way to do that—she had to, not just to honor her mother but to be an example to Rose.

Léa wiped her nose with her sleeve and stopped to tie her shoelaces. Then, tightening her collar against the cold, she felt the change in the air. Last winter there hadn't been enough coal to heat the boardinghouse, so she and Rose huddled at night under one blanket, their bodies warming one another. If she didn't find work, how would they get through this winter? Madame Martin had already raised the rent, which the other women could pay with their higher salaries. Léa negotiated, in lieu of the extra francs, that Rose would tend the chickens. But what if she raised the rent again? Léa bit her lower lip. She'd been trying to hold things together, but as she passed the dusty, bombed-out streets, she suddenly felt like her world was splintering, and who would help her hold it all together?

The moon shone a gritty light on the boardinghouse up ahead. Waiting for the tram to rattle over the tracks, she wondered what to tell Rose.

As she crossed the street, stepping over the metal rails, Léa decided she would wait to tell her sister she'd lost her job. After what had happened at the quai, Rose didn't need another thing to worry about. All Léa had ever wanted was for Rose to be able to pursue her drawing. At first, it was for practical reasons: it was easier to give Rose a pencil and paper when her mother asked her to look after her, and she'd be content and still. But when Maman got sick, Rose had been the one to sit next to her, filling sketchbooks with her mother's fragile hands and face, including sketching her through tears on the day she died. Under the bed, Léa kept the four sketchbooks from that time of all the things they both treasured—the memories of the last weeks of their mother's life.

Sometimes Léa would take them out and look at them. She'd seen the improvement in Rose's skill, how she captured not only her mother's likeness but her spirit. How had she done it? Léa knew Rose had talent. She'd promised their mother that she would do everything to help her sister's dreams come true. Once the war was over, Léa was determined that Rose would attend the L'École des Beaux-Arts and become a professional artist.

She'd saved enough cash to cover next month's rent. She'd find a job and figure a way out of this just as she had every problem she and Rose had faced. With every bone in her body, she wanted to shield her sister from the reality of the war, while keeping a good heart.

3

Rose

Carrying the sketchbook under her arm, Rose shaded her eyes with her hand as she walked by the canal that ran along the edge of the Loire on her way to Quai du Roi.

She hadn't been this far east of Orléans since before her mother got sick. She, Léa and Maman would often come to this part of the river on weekends, lifting their skirts to tuck the ends in at their waists and removing their shoes to wade into the shallow water and onto the sandbars. Holding narrow fishing poles, they'd muddy the water with their feet to attract *goujons*—the tiny whitebait no bigger than her thumb. They'd spend an entire afternoon filling a bucket with the fish that their mother would later dip in milk and flour, then deep-fry in oil, serving it with fresh lemon squeezed on top and homemade *frites*. It was a favorite childhood memory, which made Rose's mouth water.

By the time she reached Quai du Roi, the noises from the trams and buses in the center of Orléans had receded into a distant hum. Sunlight shimmered on the sandy riverbed, making the water sparkle.

André, seated on a bench along the embankment, saw her and smiled, waving at her to join him.

"I'm glad you came. Sorry about having to rush off yesterday."

"Was it because of the gendarmes?"

He shrugged. "No one wants to be around those guys."

Rose didn't press him.

Pointing at the sketchbook on her lap, he said, "We have that in common."

"We do?" She edged a little closer to him. "Tell me what you draw."

"Anything, but mostly buildings. I studied architecture at L'Ecole des Beaux-Arts for a while. Shall we introduce ourselves properly? I'm André Simon. And you are?"

"Rose Cotillard."

"Rose Cotillard," he repeated, bowing his head slightly. "*Enchanté*."

She felt her cheeks flush with heat at how he said her name, soft and slow like the patter of rain. She wondered if he was the same age as Léa—twenty-two. But then he would have been drafted at the start of the war and sent to Germany. He had to be Rose's age, or maybe a year older.

"May I look at your sketches?"

She handed him the book and watched as he turned the pages. He smiled at the chickens pecking the ground outside the coop, the large plane tree with its broad leaves in the school playground, and Léa's portrait.

"Who's that?" A tuft of hair fell across his forehead.

"My sister."

"I can see she resembles you a little, at least from what you've drawn. What does she do?"

"She's a typist in a notary's office."

He continued to turn the pages, stopping at the boat she'd drawn two weeks ago. "You have a good eye, but—"

"What?"

"Can you see what's wrong here?"

Rose leaned forward. "Wrong?"

"Forgive me, I don't mean to offend you—"

"Oh, I'm not offended. I sensed something's off—the sail?"

"Yes. You see how it's too wide in relation to the hull? The perspective is wrong." He pointed at the river, where a similar boat was docked. "There's a technique for checking perspective."

She had always guessed the distance between things—the sail, mast and hull. She didn't know how else to do it.

"I can show you if you'd like." He lifted a pencil from his shirt pocket. "May I?"

"Yes."

"The key is to measure the distances between objects before you draw." He turned to an empty page. "Let's take that boat on the river. Use a pencil by holding it with your thumb at the midpoint, like this—" Extending his arm, he placed the top of his thumb about a third of the way down from the tip of the pencil. "Then position the boat within the pencil section above the thumb and close one eye." She raised an eyebrow. "It avoids distortion from double vision." He handed the graphite back to her. "Your turn."

She did as he said and closed one eye. He moved closer to see from her angle, and she caught a sharp and wild scent in the air, the way the river smells early in the morning before the sun hits the water.

"Now make two marks on the paper corresponding to the top of the pencil and one at the tip of your thumb." Rose made the marks. "That's the length of your object." He pointed at the dots. "Tilt the pencil sideways to get the width, and mark the paper."

She continued, and it reminded her of a puzzle drawn on the blackboard at the school, where the children had to find their way out of a maze of dots. "It's a grid."

"Exactly. Every time you draw something, start with the proportions, measure with your eye, marking them so you have a grid to follow."

"Thank you."

"It's nothing."

"How long did you attend L'Ecole des Beaux-Arts?"

"A year. I wanted to be an architect, but then the war started, and Papa was mobilized. I gave up studying to work and provide for my mother and younger brothers."

"And your father?"

"He's a prisoner of war in Germany. Maman sends him food when she can."

Rose wished she could say something to lessen the weight of the war, but the right words didn't come to her.

"What about your father?" he asked.

She looked at the river. Léa had made her swear never to reveal they were orphans, not even Madame Martin at the boardinghouse knew. Léa told everyone their father was a prisoner of war in Germany when the truth was he'd died in a boating accident a few years after Rose was born. Rose didn't want to deceive André after all he'd done for her; it felt wrong. She didn't understand why Léa insisted on lying, especially when she criticized others for doing the same. Léa didn't trust anyone.

"I was very young when Papa died. Maman passed away not long after the war started. It's only me and my older sister."

He seemed to withdraw, looking down at the ground. As the silence stretched, a ripple of uncertainty flickered in her chest. Had she been wrong to tell him the truth? She didn't know how to read people the way Léa did. She preferred to keep them at a distance, observing them as if they were objects to draw. It was safer that way, less chance of a misunderstanding. After an extended silence during which Rose had not dared to move, André finally looked up.

"I'm sorry about your parents. It must be hard on you and your sister."

Relief flooded her body. At least she hadn't said the *wrong* thing. The pencil slipped from her fingers. As André leaned down to pick it up, his hand brushed her skin and a strip of heat, like a fever, surged along Rose's arm. "It's your turn to draw," she said, wanting this time together to last.

On an empty page, he sketched the stone wall between the canal and the embankment. His lines were straight and solid, fast one moment, slow the next. In the lift of his arm, there was that lightness again, reminding her of the skaters who came to the river in winter, weaving gentle arcs across the glassy ice. Her drawings seemed clumsy and heavy in comparison. He drew the bridge that crossed the canal and the wide steps leading down to the river. And then, he looked at her.

"I hadn't realized . . ." he said, smiling. "Let me see how . . ." he turned back to the paper where he'd begun to sketch her face in the corner. "Your forehead and the distance between your eyes, the proportions of your face are lovely."

It made her dizzy to hear him talk like that, and it was the first time she could get a good look at him—his blue eyes beaming warmth and light, the slight curl of his hair and his mouth opening and closing as his hand skated over the paper. There was so much she didn't know about André, but in her heart, she felt the core of him revealed to her in this moment. She sat still and quiet, taking him in. When she glanced at the paper, she was stunned to find her face staring back at her. He'd somehow seen inside her, too. The moment was sharp and tense, but she sensed it coming to an end, like holding her breath—it couldn't go on, even though she wanted it to.

The bell tower on the church in the nearby village rang the hour. André's hand went still and a flicker of hesitation crossed his face. He closed the sketchbook and gave it back to her. "I've got to go. I'm expected at the vineyard."

"Is that where you work?"

"Yes, for the moment. It's the *vendange*, harvest time, so I'm staying there to help out." He smiled. "Next week, I can get off early on Monday. Shall we meet at the cathedral at three o'clock?"

"I thought you didn't like coming into town."

"I don't." He grinned. "But for you, I'll make an exception."

"See you then," Rose said, tucking the sketchbook under her arm. As she left the bench to head back to Orléans, the light on the river had changed, becoming softer and warmer. Shadows from the poplars along the bank stretched across the water. She felt different, too. She held the sketchbook close, recalling André's hand gliding over the paper, drawing her face. With every step, her heart climbed and her pulse quickened.

* * *

The rest of the week seemed to drag on forever, but finally, Monday arrived. Rose, filled with anticipation, brought her sketchbook—she was excited to show André how she'd used the perspective technique he'd taught her while drawing the statue of Jeanne d'Arc in Place du Martroi. She arrived at the cathedral fifteen minutes early, giving herself plenty of time. Knowing that André worked on a vineyard on the outskirts of Orléans, she didn't expect him to be waiting for her like last time.

As she stood before the cathedral's main doors, the bright sun warmed her shoulders and memories of her mother came to her. A devout Catholic, she'd insisted that Rose and Léa start catechism classes at the age of six. Maman, a seamstress, had sewn a white dress for Rose to wear the day of her First Holy Communion. Overwhelmed by the sweet, heady scent of white lilies and the light streaming in through stained-glass windows, splashing color on the stone columns, Rose had to be nudged by the girl beside her to move forward when it was her turn to take the Eucharist. Though her mother struggled to earn enough money, Rose carried fond memories of her childhood. She'd been happy then. Life was simpler than now. Entering the cathedral, she wanted to light a candle in remembrance of her mother and all she'd done for her.

When she came back out, the bells rang three times, but André was nowhere to be seen. Hadn't he said three o'clock? Maybe he'd been delayed by work at the vineyard.

Another fifteen, then thirty minutes passed. The bells rang once to mark the half hour, and still she stood alone, waiting. Looking out at Rue Jeanne d'Arc with grand buildings on either side and gendarmes patrolling the shops, self-doubt crept in. Maybe now that he'd met her, she was a disappointment. Their conversation on Quai du Roi kept spiraling through her mind. The moment she'd told him she was a cleaner and he'd seen through her sketches that she didn't know basic drawing techniques. Surely, he realized she was uneducated and socially inferior to him. Rose had never studied at L'Ecole des Beaux-Arts. And she never would. How could she have let herself believe that they were at the same level?

By the time the bells rang four o'clock, Rose had convinced herself that he wasn't coming. Not now or ever again. She'd let her mind run away with all sorts of ideas about him that weren't grounded in reality. He'd decided she wasn't the one for him, and she'd been foolish to think otherwise. When he'd seen her at the embankment drawing the bridge, he'd either imagined a version of Rose that didn't exist or was simply trying to do a good deed.

She descended the limestone steps, their midpoints rounded like spoons from centuries of use. The sun no longer warmed her shoulders; instead, it's reflection off the stone blinded her. She turned away from the main road onto a smaller one that would lead to the boardinghouse. She kept moving. It was the only way to handle the turmoil inside.

"Rose . . ." André said, running alongside her.

"André?" She was so surprised by his presence that she couldn't speak.

"I'm sorry. I couldn't go to the cathedral." He was slightly out of breath. "There were gendarmes patrolling nearby . . . I've got a confession to make."

She rolled her eyes, readying herself for an excuse of why they couldn't meet again. "I've got to go," she said. Keep moving. Don't get hurt. Be more like Léa.

"Can you stop and give me a chance to explain?" He touched her hand with gentle hesitation, bringing her to a stop. He let go, but his warmth lingered. "I'm on the run. I didn't realize the gendarmes would be around the cathedral. I couldn't risk them seeing me. I wanted to—"

"Why are they looking for you?"

"A month ago, I was called up."

"Called up?"

"*Service du Travail Obligatoire*—my generation's military service."

Rose recalled a poster in the train station: red as blood, and in the center, a soldier with a helmet, below him, men in suits. Bold black type at the bottom: *They give their blood. Give your work to save Europe from Bolshevism.*"

"Will you be sent to Germany?"

"Not if I can help it." He folded his arms over his chest. "I received the letter at my mother's address last month."

"What did it say?"

"It ordered me to report to the German Employment Office."

She'd seen other posters around town seeking volunteers to work in Germany, promoting high salaries and good working conditions, and how it would help bring French soldiers held as prisoners of war home through an exchange. "Can they force you to go?"

"Yes. But I don't want to go. I won't answer the letter."

"Won't they find you?"

"I've been living at the winery. Even my mother doesn't know where I am. As long as I'm off the books, working for cash, my name stays out of the files. They don't know where to find me. The winemaker is part of a network I'm in. He doesn't have enough labor, with so many men still held in Germany as POWs, especially now with the harvest. It works well for both of us." His face hardened. "How can they send me to work in the country that imprisons my father?"

"I'm sorry," Rose said. "I thought it was because of me."

"What?" He shook his head.

"Because I'm just a cleaner." Rose felt herself shrinking and lowered her eyes.

"You're an artist." He touched her chin, coaxing her to meet his eyes. "You've got talent. A good eye. To clean is not to be a cleaner. Do you understand?" He withdrew his hand. "Tell me again what you do?"

"I'm an artist," she said, smiling brightly.

"And to prove how much I believe that . . ." André pulled something from the pocket of his jacket ". . . I've brought you a gift."

"Me?"

"Close your eyes and hold out your hands." She obeyed, feeling a weight in her palms. "Now, open your eyes."

Her breath caught at the green ribbon tied around the package's brown paper. It had *Pastels Girault* printed in white ink—the art supply shop in the medieval part of Orléans. Every time she walked by, she would stop and stare through the window at the treasures on the other side of the glass, dreaming of what she might have, or could become, if she kept drawing. Her eyes flew up to meet his.

"Open it."

Unwrapping the brown paper, she found a white rectangular box of twelve pastels. Her breath hitched as she slid the tray out, revealing indented rows holding individually wrapped crayons in exquisite colors. "*Mon Dieu*. The blues. Three shades. Each has its own number."

André grinned. "There's a world of difference between number three hundred and fifty-three blue and number two hundred and eighty-eight blue."

Tears gathered in her eyes. Léa had given her charcoal and graphite, but no one had ever given her color. "I've never used pastels."

"They're meant to make you happy, not sad." He pointed at the box. "They have a soft, chalk-like feel, making them easy to blend and layer."

"How do they make the colors so vibrant?" She lifted one from the tray; it was like holding a bolt of light.

"They have a higher concentration of pigment and much less binder. And with the softness, you can produce a broader range of expressive strokes."

"I don't know how to thank you." She worried he had spent money on her that he didn't have or should have spent on buying food for his mother and brothers. "Are you sure you want to give this to me?"

"Only if you promise to draw something for me."

She studied his face—would she start with those blue eyes that made her melt, his long lashes like black ivy? Or maybe she'd commence with his square chin, the dimple in the middle, the playful smile on his mouth. Perhaps the lovely dark curls in his hair.

"I'll draw you."

"Not me." André laughed. "I'd much rather see the world through your eyes. Show me what I haven't seen before, and I will be a happy man." He leaned in close, then pulled back. "I'd like to meet Léa. Why don't you and your sister come to the vineyard on Saturday? I'll be working on the harvest, but you two can join in, if you'd like. I'll show you how to pick the grapes, and we can have lunch together with the family."

"That would be nice. I think Léa would like it, too."

He smiled. "Let's meet again at Quai du Roi at nine in the morning? It's in Combleux, a twenty-minute walk from there." He stepped back, turning away.

"André, thank you again for the pastels. And please be careful—I don't want them to find you."

"Don't worry. They won't."

4

Léa

The stench of boiling cabbage reached the boarding-house's upper rooms as Léa scanned the help-wanted ads in *La Feuille Libre*, Orléans' local paper. Madame Martin let the cabbage cook all day, adding water, salt, sometimes a rutabaga or turnip, and if the boarders were lucky, a sliver of *lardon*. Léa swore that after the war was over, she'd never eat cabbage again.

Most of the official notices were from the government, requesting volunteers to work in Germany or in war-related industries in Orléans, which promised good salaries and better housing. Léa glanced through them. They weren't for her. She would never allow herself to stoop so low to assist Germany in continuing the war.

Despite being turned away from the sugar refinery and vinegar factories, Léa hadn't lost hope. She'd weathered hard times before and refused to let these setbacks deter her. Determined to find a job, she considered applying for domestic service positions, cleaning or childcare, even if it meant working for the wealthy. A knot of tension formed in her back. These were the people profiting off the war. Still, she recalled Maître Mallon's advice: *be realistic . . . do what's best for you and Rose.* Léa had to compromise, balancing what was right with what she needed to survive, especially after her exchange with Madame Martin this morning.

The floorboards in the hallway creaked; every move echoed through the boardinghouse's old beams and rafters. It must be Rose returning from work. Léa couldn't delay sharing the news of her job loss with her sister any longer. She didn't want to trouble Rose but it was no longer something she could hide.

The door opened. Rose, beaming, entered.

"You seem to have had a good day," Léa said.

"I met André." Rose removed her shoes. "Look what he gave me." She pulled a box from her bag.

When Léa saw *Pastels Girault* printed on the ribbon, she couldn't believe André had that kind of money. Hadn't Rose said he was responsible for his mother and siblings? She felt a pang of worry that he might be engaged in something illegal to afford such a gift. But she didn't want to say it yet. She had enough bad news to deliver without adding more. "He's very generous."

"Yes. He's invited—"

"Sit down for a moment." She needed to say it right away so she wouldn't make the mistake of holding off any longer. "I lost my job."

Rose sank onto the bed. "But you're Maître Mallon's best typist."

"He's lost his clients."

"I don't understand. You were always there late finishing his files." Lifting her knees, Rose placed her chin on them, her wide eyes staring at Léa. "He must have had so many clients."

"He's an honorable man." Léa took a breath. "But in France, at the moment, the people who are in power and those who work for the government aren't honorable at all. They only care about enriching themselves. Even if it makes the country poorer." Rose stood and came by Léa's side. "They've made an example of him to deter others. I was the last typist he let go. There is literally nothing for me to type."

A look of despair showed in Rose's eyes. "I'm so sorry."

Léa took her sister's hand. "Unfortunately, I have more bad news. Madame Martin dropped a bombshell today. She's increasing the rent in October." Despite her determination to remain strong, her voice cracked. "I've saved enough to cover the one hundred and fifty francs for October, but we can't pay more." She shook her head. "We won't be able to stay." The weight of these words hung in the air. A shadow fell over their future.

"I'll sell the pastels on the black market—will it be enough?"

Tears pricked Léa's eyes. "No, I don't want you to do that." She twisted her finger around the edge of her sleeve, shame burning inside. She was the one meant to be providing for them.

"You've done so much for me," Rose said. "How much more does she want?"

"One hundred and eighty francs."

"So we need thirty francs. I'm sure the pastels—"

"And then what do we do for November? And afterwards? She's so greedy that in another few months, she'll raise the rent again." Léa pointed at the paper. "Women are making good salaries working in German arms factories. They can afford to pay these prices." She shook her head. "But we can't."

Rose pressed her lips together as if she didn't know what to say or do. There was a solution Léa had considered before, but feared it was the first step in a downward spiral that the sisters couldn't escape.

"We could move to a cheaper boardinghouse. Find a room for seventy to ninety francs a month without meals—"

"But we're already skipping lunch. Will we have to drop dinner?"

"We'll manage." Léa had no idea how.

"I hate this war. All it does is destroy." She went silent for a moment. "It's not fair. We should be in love, raising children, and happy. We can't let this war destroy us, too."

"We won't." Léa feared it would but she didn't want to tell Rose that. "We don't need to have all the answers now. Something will fall into our lap. Everything will work out. Tomorrow, I'll go around to the boardinghouses to see if we can find a cheaper one. Now, tell me about André. You were saying that he's invited you somewhere."

Rose smiled. "*Us*. He's invited us to come to the vineyard on Saturday, where he works. He wants to meet you."

"Me?"

"I told him all about you. And I think they need extra hands to help with the *vendange*. I'm so excited to spend a whole day with him. Please come?"

Despite herself, Léa nodded. "Of course. I want to meet him, too." She forced a tight smile. It would be an opportunity to find out more about André and what he might be involved in. Rose was too young and inexperienced to realize the dangers circling them. "And maybe getting out of Orléans for a day is just what we need to figure out what we do next."

* * *

On Saturday morning, there was a chill in the air, but the sun was out and fishermen crowded on the embankment. They passed a large outdoor market with stalls set up along the river. Léa couldn't believe the prices for carrots and onions—nearly double the cost since the war had begun—and there were only two stalls selling them. A breeze blew, and a few leaves, brown on the edges, tumbled along the ground as the sisters headed east and away from Orléans.

André was waiting next to the bench on Quai du Roi, two bicycles at his side. Last night, Rose had sketched him from memory. Léa had encouraged her to use the pastels, but Rose refused in case they would need to sell them. Still, she'd captured his likeness so much that Léa recognized him now immediately.

"*Enchanté*." André held out his hand to Léa. "Rose speaks so highly of you."

Léa smiled, shook his hand, relieved that he seemed genuine and down to earth. "I'm glad to meet you."

"I've brought an extra bike. It will save us time getting to the vineyard. Rose, you can go on my handlebars, and your sister can take the other one."

Léa hadn't ridden a bicycle in years and felt a surge of excitement. She trailed André down the towpath beside the Loire. She'd forgotten the pure thrill of wind streaming through her hair as she pedaled faster to keep pace.

Stopping momentarily on a bridge, he pointed to the locks filling with water as they prepared to lift a boat to the next level. Farther on, the towpath turned into coarse, chalky gravel.

On the left, they passed the white limestone tower of Saint-Jean-Baptiste Church, where the towpath split into upper and lower routes. Léa felt her shoulders drop, and the tension in her neck ease. Escaping the crowded city streets and the rubble marring the city center was a relief. She followed André onto the path toward the quiet village of Combleux. After passing the town square, they cycled up a gentle slope into rolling hills striped with vines.

They came to a farmhouse with thick, pale stone walls set in a horseshoe shape. Dense lavender bushes, their blooms long gone and now silver-tinted, grew along a wooden fence with a gate off its hinges. André cycled into the courtyard and dismounted, leaning his bicycle against the wall. Léa did the same.

Purple cyclamen and white crocus carpeted the ground. Léa carefully stepped around the tiny blossoms on the slope that led up to the vines. A yellow-haired dog bounded down the hill, barking furiously until it spotted André, then wove between his legs for a good stroke on its back and belly.

A middle-aged man came down the path between the vines. "André, that was fast," he said, shading his eyes from the sun.

"I brought an extra bike. Let me introduce you to Léa and Rose Cotillard." André turned to the sisters. "This is Édouard LeBlanc."

"Hello, and welcome." Édouard smiled at them. "André thought you wouldn't mind helping us out today with the *vendange*." His arm swept up to the vineyards. "We've got a lot of grapes to pick. Do either of you have any experience picking grapes?"

"No, sir," they both said.

"André, go down to the *chai* and find two of the smallest overalls and boots for these city girls. They can't be working in dresses. Straw hats, too. Then you and Rose can work on the red grapes on the other side of the house, and I'll keep Léa with me, showing her what to do. How does that sound?"

André gave a thumbs-up to Édouard, then took Rose's hand, and together they went down to the farmhouse's eastern wing.

Léa felt a jolt of surprise at André's intimacy with her sister—it was as if they'd known one another for years, not just a short amount of time.

"Don't worry—it won't all be work," Monsieur LeBlanc said. "My wife and daughter are tending the vegetable garden, and they'll have a nice lunch ready for us in a few hours!"

"That's a good incentive." Léa smiled. "Is it hard for you to make ends meet with all the rationing and higher prices?" She wanted to probe a little and see if she could get a reaction. "I suppose the vegetables grow as well as vines in this soil, and that helps."

"Actually, they don't. We have a saying in the business: vines grow best when made to suffer, but vegetables need to be pampered." He smiled. "The soil is too rocky for most of them, but my wife somehow makes them grow. It's because of her hard work that we struggle less than others."

When André and Rose returned with the overalls and boots, the sisters put them on, along with the straw hats.

"We're going to work on the red grapes," André said, picking up a basket. "Call us when lunch is ready!"

Édouard turned to Léa. "That boy is always hungry!" He slid the leather handles of a large wicker basket over his shoulders, and she followed him up the slope to the rows of vines. He stopped and put the basket down, pointing to the grapes dangling from thin shoots.

"Colors are key when picking—deep browns, yellow, transparent green. If you don't find those colors, leave them on the vine for the third pass." He wiped his forehead. "I used to harvest thrice. Now, with only André helping, I'm lucky to make two passes. But with this fine weather, the bright green ones can stay on the vines until early October. It will give them more time to ripen."

He walked to an adjacent row, cupping a cluster of clear grapes with a madder hue. "This color signifies a high alcohol concentration, giving the wine a rich taste. I don't want all the grapes like this, but a small amount is perfect."

He took a few steps farther along the row. "Now, do you see the dark brown lines running over these grapes?"

"The color is more like mustard than green," Léa said.

"We jokingly call those lines *le poil de lièvre*, the coat of the hare, because it resembles the stripes on a hare's fur. Pick them—they give a unique flavor."

Léa nodded.

"Finally, never pick bright green grapes; they must always have a yellow tint. If you find one side of the cluster bright green and the other yellow, leave them to ripen more. That's it." He paused to look at her. "Any questions?"

"So, I fill the basket—"

"Yes, drag it along the grass as you pick, but be careful not to damage the vine. We'll need cuttings for next year."

All morning, Léa picked grape clusters and put them in the basket. Monsieur LeBlanc stayed nearby, checking occasionally to make sure she chose the right ones. Sweat rolled down her back, and her legs ached from standing and bending to clip grapes. But the work wasn't hard, and it distracted her from their money troubles and worrying about where they'd live in October.

"Lunch," a woman called out.

Monsieur LeBlanc motioned that Léa should follow him to an open space where a blanket was set out on the grass. "Come, meet my wife and daughter."

They walked toward a pretty dark-haired woman and a young girl with blonde hair tied in two braids.

"Léa, this is Virginie," said Édouard, smiling between her and his wife.

"Thank you for coming to help today," Virginie said. "Where are you from?"

"I live in Orléans in a boardinghouse with my sister, Rose."

"Oh, yes, André's friend," she said, her eyes sparkling.

"And, this is our daughter, Paulette." Édouard winked at the girl, who glanced up from her basket.

"How old are you?" Léa asked.

"Eight." The girl grinned, showing a missing tooth.

"Paulette is a big help to me," Virginie said, lifting a bottle and a loaf of cornbread from a small wicker basket, along with tin cups. Paulette, carrying tomatoes and radishes in her basket, spread them on the blanket. Léa eyed the bottle; whatever was inside smelled sweet, like grape juice.

At that moment, Rose and André walked round from the other side of the house, and introductions were again made by Édouard.

"Have either you or Rose had *bernache* before?" Virginie asked.

"No," Rose said.

"I love it," Paulette said, beaming.

"Be careful, *ma puce*. Don't spill it all over you today like yesterday! It's the fermented grape juice before it turns into wine. Full of vitamins." Virginie poured a cup. "Here, have some. It's refreshing after all of your hard work."

The cool liquid on Léa's throat was welcome. It tasted like apple juice. She couldn't remember the last time she'd had fruit, maybe an apple in the spring. She looked at Rose to gauge her reaction.

"I can see why you love it, Paulette," said Rose. "The taste is thrilling. Does it contain alcohol?"

Monsieur LeBlanc laughed. "About two percent. This morning, I drew it out of the vat, so it's quite fresh. Enjoy." He raised his glass, and they all toasted.

Though Léa's shoulders throbbed from the lifting, she felt touched and grateful for their hospitality. Today was the first real lunch she and Rose had had in a long time. Maybe losing her job wouldn't turn out to be the end of the world, and something good would follow. For four years, all she'd known was Maître Mallon's office—narrow windows, the staccato click of typewriter keys, the sharp tangy smell of ink from the ribbons she constantly changed—Léa once loved it. Now, looking back, it seemed a much less pleasant way to spend her day than being out here. She took another sip of the *bernache* and placed a slice of tomato on the cornbread.

Rose huddled next to André. They looked so natural together. For an instant, Léa saw herself from a distance: a twenty-two-year-old woman looking at two people embarking on a romance, and for a split second, she wondered why she couldn't have the same life. Her father's voice came at her: "*Don't worry, Léa. I will always be here for you.*" But he hadn't been, and just when she thought life without him had stabilized, her mother fell ill and Léa struggled to earn enough money to buy medicine and pay rent. After she lost her mother, she decided she couldn't open herself up to anyone—the pain and heartbreak of losing someone she loved was too great. But every now and then, she wondered if she hadn't made that choice, what kind of woman would she be now?

"Would you like some more *bernache*?" Virginie asked.

"No, thank you." Léa heard the church bells ring the time. It was already late afternoon. She was rather reluctant to leave such a convivial atmosphere, and was reassured about the LeBlanc family. She'd seen nothing in her interaction with them to indicate that they might be doing something that could get Rose in trouble. "I think we've taken up enough of your time. Thank you for your warm hospitality."

As they said goodbye and cycled back to Orléans, Léa overheard André invite Rose to the cinema.

Rose hesitated. "I don't have money for a ticket."

"That's not a problem. My friend works as a ticket seller. If the seats aren't all filled, he'll sneak us in for free. Monday seven o'clock at Place Gambetta?" André turned to Léa. "Would you like to join us?"

"That's kind, André, but I have one or two things to do, so I will decline." It wasn't strictly true, but Rose and André didn't have much time to spend with each other and Léa knew she'd be the third person out. Her confidence in André had grown, though, and she trusted him to look after her sister. "Thank you for today—we had a lovely time."

* * *

At the boardinghouse, after the sisters had changed, brushed their teeth and washed their faces, they turned off the light and huddled close in bed. Moonlight shone through the thin curtains. Léa could see Rose's eyes wide open, fixed on the sky outside. She stroked her sister's arm. "That was a wonderful day, and the LeBlanc family was so welcoming."

"It was the best day of my life," said Rose.

"Because of the lunch?"

"Partly—the cornbread was delicious and the tomatoes were so fresh." Rose turned to her sister. "What do you think of André?"

"I like him. He seems genuine and kind."

"He is. Can I ask you something?"

"Sure."

"Have you ever been kissed?"

Léa sat up on one elbow. "Did André kiss you?"

"No. But I could feel he *wanted* to." She covered her mouth with her hand. "And I wanted him to kiss me too!"

Léa rested her head on her arm. Rose was growing up so quickly. "What do you mean you could feel it?"

She usually shut such thoughts away. Wanting to be kissed seemed pointless.

Rose closed her eyes. "It's like looking at the sky at dawn, all that color—yellow, orange, blue—it stirs your soul." She opened her eyes.

"Your soul?" Now, it was Léa's turn to giggle. "From the anticipation of a kiss?"

"Don't laugh! You'll know what I mean when it happens to you."

"You make it sound so serious." Léa smiled.

"Love is serious."

"I disagree." Léa suddenly stiffened. "Working, taking care of family, responsibilities, that is what's serious."

Rose turned to her. "But how can you do those things without love?"

Rose was right, in terms of family—Léa loved her sister, which is why she cared for her. But for her, love between a man and a woman was a choice, not a necessity. One didn't need it to lead a fulfilling life. Indeed, she feared it might only cause more trouble.

"I think love is hope," Rose said. "It helps you forget past sorrows."

Léa softened again and squeezed her sister's hand. "Whatever it is, I'm happy for you."

"One day you'll feel it, too."

"No. Romantic love isn't for me."

"Don't say that." Rose looked pained. "You simply haven't met the right man."

"I'm not intent on meeting a man." Léa sighed. "It's work I need to find."

"Do you know what André said?"

Léa could see her sister smiling in the moonlight. "Tell me."

"He wants me to draw so that he can see the world through my eyes."

"He's right. You should draw; you have talent."

"Thank you," Rose said, squeezing Léa's hand, "for listening."

"Time to sleep. You've got an early start."

Rose turned to the window. It didn't take long before Léa heard her sister's steady breathing—she'd fallen asleep.

But Léa couldn't sleep. Rose was eighteen and in love. She was happy for her sister. And now, a part of Léa wished she could experience the feeling of being in love or being kissed. She did remember what it was to be eighteen—the sense that the world was a magical, wonderful place and the future bright. But then Maman died and Léa had to grow up fast. She'd lost that sense of wonder overnight. She wanted Rose to hold on to the feeling as long as possible, though. To do that, Léa had to find a job and a new place for them to live fast. October was less than a week away.

5

Rose

André stood outside the cinema, hair slicked back, brown jacket over white shirt, shoulders hunched forward, eyes pinned to the ground. Rose sensed a sharp air of vigilance about him but the moment their eyes met, his demeanor softened and he approached her, hands at his sides.

"You look lovely," he said, grinning.

She wore her hair loose, a pin on the side holding it off her face. "Thanks." She'd wanted to look nice and was glad she'd worn the lucky blue dress her mother made for Léa's interviews, paired with a white cardigan for warmth. She pointed to the poster. "Are we watching *Remorques*?"

He nodded, unable to look away from her. She felt off-kilter, used to being the observer, not the observed.

"What do you think?" he asked.

"Wonderful, it's only my second time at the movies." Her first movie had been when Léa received two free tickets from Maître Mallon. "Will we be able to get in?"

"Wait here." He bounded over to the ticket counter. She looked at the poster. The illustrator had drawn Jean Gabin, Madeleine Renaud and Michèle Morgan against a backdrop of a boat battling rough waves in the sea. She noticed their eyes matched the blue of the water. She thought the artist had done a good job.

André returned. "It shouldn't be a problem. Let's wait across the street."

They moved away from the people gathered in a line, crossed the street and stood in front of a cobbler's shop.

"Thank you for Saturday," she said. "Léa had a wonderful time."

"The LeBlanc family liked you both. And they're grateful for all the work you did. I hope you'll come again."

"It's just you and Monsieur LeBlanc picking all those grapes?"

"Yes. He says the warm and dry weather has given us more time; we've probably got two more weeks until we finish."

A whistle came from across the street, and they turned to see a man signaling to them.

"The movie is starting," André said. "Shall we?"

He reached for her hand, filling Rose with a yearning she'd never known. It was as if she'd always been observing life through a glass door, never experiencing its warmth first-hand. But now André stood at the door, holding it open. Even if she and Léa hadn't sorted out where they would move to and Léa had yet to find a job, Rose wasn't troubled like she would have been before. André gently squeezed her palm, and she felt like the luckiest woman in the world.

Inside the cinema, the screen's light flickered over the red velvet seats. A few couples sat farther up; the cinema was less than half full. André held her hand as they took seats in the last row near the exit. A black-and-white newsreel played, covering Germany's advance into Russia and a Japanese offensive in Guadalcanal.

She turned to him. "Gua . . . dal . . . canal?"

"An island in the Pacific Ocean," he whispered, bringing her hand to his lips, giving it a gentle kiss.

As Rose watched the film, she found it hard to follow the action. Sensations coursed through her. André's touch was cool and sensual like bath water—comfort, joy, surprise. Did he feel it too? She wanted to remember every detail so later she could tell Léa.

On the screen, the tugboat captain stood alone on the beach. Rose didn't know what had happened to the two women in his life, but suddenly they were gone. Relaxed and at ease, she leaned on André's shoulder and closed her eyes.

"Are you tired? We can go early." His voice was like a warm breeze on her cheek.

She lifted her head and gazed into his eyes. His mouth opened, and their lips met. They kissed—cautious and tender—and a thousand spidery threads spun through every part of Rose's body. She gave up to him completely, not knowing that a kiss, her first, could last so long. *Let us stay like this forever*.

When the movie ended, the lights came on. Smoothing her dress, Rose felt changed. She was no longer the woman she'd been upon entering the cinema. André was still holding her hand as they stood. He hadn't let go of it, and she was sure he never would. Slightly jittery, she felt at peace. There was no one else like him, this man who had steered her to safety in the Café du Marché, engaged with her art, believed in her dreams, and respected and understood her closeness to Léa. The moment he entered her life, Rose's world changed. With André, she felt alive and able to see past the war's darkness to a brighter future together.

Hand in hand, they walked along the row. He went ahead, blocking her view of the aisle. She wanted to remember this moment, the feelings swirling inside. But then she felt him hesitate, and in the next instant, he let go of her hand.

At the door, two gendarmes were checking identity papers. André stepped away from her and, once he was free of the aisle, made his way to the emergency exit. Rose, sensing danger like a swift-moving storm, willed him to hurry, though knowing he mustn't draw the attention of the gendarmes. A swish of blue. Her legs shook.

"*Vos papiers, monsieur*."

Trickles of sweat slid down her back as she watched André pat his pockets. Surely, he wouldn't surrender his papers.

"*Mince*, looks like I've forgotten them," he said.

The gendarme whistled to his colleague, who came over and attached handcuffs to André's wrists. "Come to the station and we'll check your papers there."

A part of her wanted to believe he'd figure a way out, that he was too clever and strong, that he'd escape and be back with her tomorrow, but another part knew that the gendarmes had come to the cinema to hunt men like him. He was trapped.

In a way, it was her fault. She should have urged him to avoid the center of town; the risk wasn't worth it. He'd dropped her hand to protect her because whatever suspicion had fallen on him could pass to her if the gendarmes believed they were together.

Rose's chest burned but she forced herself to do what André would want—move forward and away from him.

"*Vos papiers, mademoiselle, s'il vous plait*."

She opened her purse, reached for her papers, and handed them to the gendarme.

"Who did you come here with?"

"No one," she said, swallowing. "I'm alone."

The gendarmes exchanged a look, and for a moment, she almost wished they wouldn't believe her and arrest her, too. At least that way, she could be with André for a few more hours, maybe days or weeks. But that wouldn't be fair to Léa—she had to help her sister. There seemed to be nothing she could now do for André.

"Let's bring him to the station," one of the gendarmes said, glancing back at André. "Put him in the back of the truck."

The gendarme, still holding her documents, pushed André out the door. Rose hesitated. She couldn't let her papers go. She tried to speak, but shock locked her in place. She stood frozen, her voice momentarily gone.

"Hold on," André said, turning back. "That young lady needs her documents."

The gendarme glared at him and then at Rose. "Do you know this man?" he asked her.

"No, I don't." She knew she had to sound confident, though it tore her heart. She could still feel André's imprint on her hand, giving her courage. "Please, can I have my identity papers back?"

The gendarme sighed and threw them at her, though they landed on the floor. Rose bent down to pick them up. "Thank you," she said.

In her heart, she'd spoken those words to André, and she was sure he knew that in the way he smiled as he looked back at her before he was turned to face the front. She lifted her chin, watching him leave, vowing to herself that this would not be the last time she saw André. That no matter what it took, she would find him again.

* * *

As Rose reached the boardinghouse, guilt and fear twisted through her body like a tangible force. She was eager to speak with Léa, hoping that Maître Mallon might know someone who could help André. She clung to the belief that this wasn't the end, that there was still hope of seeing him again.

She pushed the main door open and skidded to a stop, breathing hard as Madame Martin stood in the center of the corridor. "Is something wrong?" Rose asked.

"I don't know. That's what I've been waiting to ask you."

She wanted to push past her and up the stairs to Léa, but Madame Martin was planted in her way, blocking the narrow corridor so Rose couldn't get round her. "What is it that you want to ask?"

"Late for you to be out on your own, isn't it?" Madame Martin eyed her blue dress and loose hair.

"I was with a friend."

"What kind of friend?"

Rose heard the lock in the door upstairs click. Maybe it was Léa coming out to the landing to listen.

"I'm tired and I'd like to go up to my room."

"Not until you tell me where you got these." Madame Martin took an object from her apron pocket and held it up.

Rose leaned forward, disbelieving. "How did you get them?"

"That's what I want to ask you." She smirked. "While you and your sister were out today, there was a complaint by one of the boarders of a leak right below your room. Of course, it was my duty to unlock the door and check the sink to ensure everything was fine. Luckily, it was, and on my way out, I saw these."

Rose reached out. "The pastels are mine. A gift. Give them back."

"A gift? From whom?"

"None of your business."

"Since you live in my boardinghouse, I make it my business."

A lump lodged in Rose's throat as Madame Martin tightly gripped her beautiful pastels. She stepped forward, determined to take them from her.

"Not so fast," Madame Martin said, slipping the box back into her apron pocket. "You need to explain how, with your sister losing her job and you earning very little as a cleaner, you had the money to purchase a box of *Pastels Girault*? Because in my mind, it doesn't make sense."

"I told you, they were a gift," Rose said. "Please, give them to me. I want them back."

Madame Martin crossed her arms at her chest. "I'll tell you what I want. For you and your sister to move out. I don't allow thieves to rent my rooms or live under my roof. You two are a bad influence on the other women. You both better be gone tomorrow—do you understand?"

There were still two days left in the month and they'd paid the full September rent. She had no right to throw them out before then, nor to steal their personal items. Rose stepped closer and squared her shoulders, ready to fight for her pastels once more.

"Tomorrow morning," Madame Martin said, "I'll go to the gendarmerie and report that I found this box of pastels in your room. And unless you can produce the individual who gave them to you, I think you'll struggle to explain to the officers how you could afford to buy them." She smiled. "It's up to you. Explain yourself to the gendarme, or leave the pastels with me, and it will be our little secret."

Rose felt herself waver.

Madame Martin pressed two fingers to her lips. "I won't say a word."

Just a moment ago, Rose had been strong and ready to fight Madame Martin. Now, it felt like someone had hollowed out her insides and tipped all her strength out. She'd been set up, and there was nothing she could do. Léa was right—there was no longer any *fraternité* among people. Everyone was out for themselves.

She pushed past Madame Martin and made her way up the stairs, where Léa stood waiting on the landing, and together they entered their room.

"*Elle est une vraie pute*," Léa hissed. "I heard it all."

"She came into our room with the intention of stealing something." Rose's eyes filled with tears, her voice wobbling. "But something even worse happened at the cinema."

Léa stepped closer. "What?"

"The gendarmes were checking identity papers, and when André didn't have his, they took him away. He'll be sent to Germany." The weight of this hit her anew with all its unbearable force and her tears flowed freely. "I'll never see him again."

"Oh, Rose, I'm so sorry." Léa pulled her close and held her.

6

Léa

October 1942

The winery was their refuge. It was the only place they were welcome.

On the terrible night Madame Martin expelled them, the sisters decided they would go the next day and explain to the LeBlanc family why André wouldn't be returning.

The morning they arrived at the winery, Virginie stared at the suitcase in Léa's hand. When she asked where they were going, Rose had broken down in tears, saying they had no place to go, and that was when Édouard insisted they stay there with them. In return, the sisters would help with the harvest because André wasn't coming back.

Sweat gathered on Léa's back and legs as she steadied herself, hauling the straps of the basket brimming with grapes over her shoulders. After she tipped the basket full of grape clusters into the wooden crate, Léa returned to the row of vines where Rose was picking the grapes, Paulette by her side.

The little girl followed Rose like a faithful friend, carrying Rose's sketchbook so that she might have a chance to draw when she took a break. Léa was relieved. It seemed they'd made the right decision in coming to Combleux. A fortnight had passed since their arrival, and their old life seemed to belong to another world.

Neither sister missed the boardinghouse's meager dinners, Madame Martin's deceitful behavior, or the constant presence of German soldiers on the street. In Combleux, they worked hard, but there was more food—eggs in the morning for breakfast; fish once a week from the Loire; and on the last Sunday of every month, chicken from the brood that Virginie raised.

The war seemed distant, as if a hidden wall blocked it off from the farmhouse. However, Léa noticed Édouard's watchfulness, stopping to listen if a car approached, as if he was always on guard.

"Time for lunch," Virginie called out, coming up the hill carrying a basket and blanket. Paulette jumped and waved the pocket-sized spiral sketchbook in front of Rose. Édouard said that André had bought it, intending to give it to Rose as a surprise. "He traded it for a bottle of wine from my reserves," he explained after both sisters stared at him with wide eyes, knowing the cost of paper.

Rose carried it always, sketching some part of the vineyard every day at lunch: the oak tree, vegetables growing at the back, the rows of trellised vines, the stone farmhouse, lavender bushes, the nuts that had tumbled from the walnut tree, stray cats stalking mice through the tall grass, robins and blue tits and the occasional kite swooping in and, of course, the LeBlanc family. Paulette, mesmerized, would sit beside Rose, shifting her gaze from the object to the sketchbook, trying to decipher how she did it.

Today, Virginie had picked pears from the orchard surrounding the vines. They were ripe and glowed yellow-green with russet rims. Even before Rose finished eating, she arranged the pears and walnuts, opening some and placing the broken shells around the fruit. She added a ceramic pitcher, placing it to the right of the pears. Then she began to sketch. Paulette knelt down by her side, peering over Rose's shoulder.

Léa thought of the pastels taken by Madame Martin, and how perfect the green, yellow and red pigments would be for what she was drawing now. Since their arrival in Combleux, neither sister had spoken of that night. But the unfairness stung.

"*Voilà*," Rose said. "A still life with walnuts, pears and a pitcher."

"What's a still life?" Paulette asked.

"A still life—"

The rumble of a diesel engine drowned out Rose's voice. The women looked at one another. Only German officers drove vehicles. Sensing the mood had shifted, Paulette yanked on her mother's sleeve. "What's wrong, Maman?"

Virginie stood. "I'll take Paulette and Rose to the vegetable garden in the back." She held her arms out as if to gather them up. "Léa, please go and see if Édouard needs help."

An unspoken agreement existed between Virginie and Léa—both felt a duty to shield Paulette and Rose from danger. Léa descended the slope to the *chai*, the barrel and aging hall, where at the end of every day, she guided the donkey pulling the wooden cart loaded with grapes. She never entered, always leaving the cart outside for Édouard to bring in. The pale blue wooden doors stood open, flanking the stone walls like shutters. Hearing voices, she hesitated, then took a few cautious steps, inhaling the earthy headiness from the grapes fermenting inside.

"Herr LeBlanc, you test my patience." A man's granite voice echoed off the domed ceiling. "Have my orders not been clear?"

"But last year—"

"It's not your business to remind me of what happened last year."

"My family can't survive if we aren't allowed to make wine."

"And our army can't win without fuel and oil. Your family made it through this year."

Léa positioned herself behind one of the tall concrete vats. She counted six fermentation vats, each with a large stainless-steel plaque and spigot on the front. On the plaque on the vat opposite, she glimpsed the blurry reflection of a gray uniform, black boots and SS runes.

"That's because I sold off the previous year's wine. But if you again requisition all my production, I won't have anything more to sell."

The man's reflection disappeared from her view. "Winter is coming. I must supply the solvents and anti-freeze the army requires. All production will be distilled into fuel and industrial alcohol. Now, open the doors on these vats."

"Why? The fermentation is proceeding. Your fuel will be ready in another week," Édouard said, a tinge of panic in his voice.

"I order you to open the doors on these vats."

"Yes, Weinführer Brucker."

Léa crept to an alcove off to the side so she wouldn't be seen. Since this was the first time she'd been inside the cave, she couldn't quite figure out what was happening, other than the distinct splash of liquid being poured into the vats.

After some time, silence returned. Léa left the alcove, inching her way back to the vat.

"That should take care of any plans you have to siphon off wine." A sharp click of boot heels sent a shudder through her. "I'll be back at the end of next week to collect the fuel. Make sure it's ready."

"Yes, Weinführer Brucker." Édouard's voice fell flat as if all the life had been sucked out of it.

Léa didn't dare move again until she heard an engine outside clatter to a start and drive away.

"What was that all about?" she asked, finally stepping into the open.

"You heard us?" he said.

"You aren't making wine but fuel for the German army?"

"Weinführer Brucker's orders." Édouard did not meet her eye.

"Who is—"

"He manages the Loiret wine region and has the power to decide our production." Édouard sat on the stool, hands on his thighs, casting a despairing gaze over the vats. "Some winegrowers only have half of their production requisitioned, but he *steals* all of mine." His face hardened.

"Surely he pays you for making fuel."

He shook his head. "Requisitioning production for the German Wehrmacht is always without compensation."

Léa wished she could do something to help. "What did he pour in the vats?"

"Heating oil. The wine is ruined."

She drew back, her cheeks burning with anger. She'd mistakenly lulled herself into believing the farmhouse could be a safe harbor to ride out the war. The reality was that everyone faced trouble, whether in the city or the countryside. It was the first time she understood the extra burden she and Rose placed on Édouard and Virginie by being here. "Rose and I shouldn't be here. We're a burden you can't—"

"No," he said, standing. "Virginie and I are grateful for your presence and help. With André gone, we wouldn't be able to make the fuel without your labor, not to mention the wonderful companionship Rose provides for Paulette." He smiled, seemingly wanting to reassure her. "You mustn't worry. I knew this day was coming. I have a plan. Everything will work out." He took a breath. "Don't say anything to Paulette or Rose; they're both too young to understand. I'll tell Virginie later." He tilted his head toward the window, and sunlight flickered across his face. "Do you understand?"

Léa nodded, though doubt churned inside her. She couldn't imagine how Édouard could fight back after the Weinführer had tainted all his wine. "You've done so much for us. If I can help—if you need anything—please ask."

"Thank you, Léa."

* * *

That night, Léa struggled to sleep. She didn't know if it was because of the soreness in her limbs—she'd worked all day until it was no longer possible to see the grapes in the darkness—or if it was the conversation she'd overheard between the Weinführer and Édouard.

Next to her, Rose dozed peacefully. Léa didn't want to disturb her sister, so rather than tossing and turning, she decided to go to the kitchen and drink a glass of water, hoping it would soothe her mind and help her return to sleep.

She slid out of bed, the cold floor shocking her bare feet as she tiptoed across the room. She went through the open door to the corridor and into the kitchen. After filling a glass from the ceramic pitcher of water on the counter, she drank the cool liquid. Moonlight shone through the window, casting an ivory teardrop on the counter. She looked out the window: a light burned in the *chai* on the other side of the courtyard. It had to be Édouard. But why was he working when he should be sleeping?

Leaning close to the window, she saw a single silhouette cross the light. By now, Léa was wide awake. Why was he being so secretive—hiding the Weinführer's visit and now working in the middle of the night? She put the glass down, went to the main door, slipped on her boots and crossed the courtyard.

Entering the vaulted *chai*, she inhaled the heady smell of grape must. From the drops of liquid on the ground and the small wooden ladder in front of one of the cement vats, she realized Édouard had been checking the fermentation. Where was he?

Léa advanced farther. In the corner near the rear wall, where she'd earlier seen a desk and chair on top of an old carpet, the carpet was now rolled up and placed on the table along with the chair and pushed to the side, revealing a stone that had been lifted from the floor. She crept closer and saw a narrow wooden staircase leading to an underground hatch. Was he in there? "Édouard, it's Léa. Are you down there?"

Édouard appeared. "Why are you here?"

"I couldn't sleep."

"Go back to bed, Léa. You shouldn't be here."

"But I'm already awake."

"This isn't something you need to get involved in. André wouldn't want that for you or Rose. The less you know, the better. Now, go."

Defying him, she put her foot on the top step and crouching low, descended to the bottom rung. She could stand upright because the ceiling was high enough. The walls were a mix of dirt and chalk, like the soil. "Has this level always been in the house?"

"Yes. My father brought me down here for the first time when I was a boy. And his father did the same. Winemakers need good storage, and the limestone makes digging and hollowing out easy."

She glimpsed four oak barrels stacked on their sides. "You're making wine?"

He nodded and pointed to the other side of the stairs, where demijohns full of wine lined the floor. "I made two hundred bottles of wine last year under Weinführer Brucker's nose without him knowing and sold them all." He grinned. "Now, all that's left is to deliver the demijohns to the black marketeer. I ran out of bottles, but he's willing to take the jugs and do the bottling himself."

Léa didn't know what to say.

"Keep it to yourself. Not a word to anyone. The Weinführer already suspects I'm making wine on the side but he has no proof."

All she could think about was the risk he was taking. What would happen to him if he were caught? What would happen to them all if he were caught?

His gaze was locked on hers and despite her unease, she nodded. "Of course. I won't tell anyone."

Édouard motioned to the stairs. "Go back to the house. You don't need to be a part of this."

"Is anyone helping you now that André's gone?"

"I can get by fine on my own." He smiled. "This vintage is some of my finest with caramel and smoky notes from the oak barrels. I got three times the pre-war price!" He laughed. "I tried to act disappointed when the Weinführer poured the heating oil into the vats so that he wouldn't be suspicious."

Léa sat down on a low stool.

He scratched his forehead and shrugged. "I guess you're not going back to the house?"

"I want to help you, the way André did."

"All right then." He sighed. "Let's get to work."

"What's down there?" Léa asked, pointing at an opening farther on.

"A tunnel that leads nearly to the river, a little over 500 meters. When I was a boy, my father used the tunnel to move the wine in barrels rather than going through town to reach the transport boats on the Loire. At one time, a train ran through Combleux."

Léa walked over to the tunnel, which had a thick layer of dust on the ground and cobwebs across the opening. "What's at the other end?" She tried to imagine a door, but to where?

"There's a metal ladder at the end, which you can climb to reach a metal hatch that opens to the outside. We keep it sealed to prevent flooding. That's why the tunnel doesn't go up to the river. Before the locks and canal were built, Combleux had its fair share of flooding."

She noticed a key hanging on the side wall and pointed to it. "What's it for?"

"It opens the metal hatch at the other end. I don't like going in there. The ceiling is low, and it gives me an uneasy feeling."

She could understand that and wouldn't want to go in there either. "What can I help you with?"

"I need to put the labels on the demijohns. If you can cut them off the printed sheets," he said, motioning to paper on the ground under the stairs, "then I'll show you how to stick them on with a brush of water."

Léa smiled. "Yes, I can do that."

He brought the labels out from under the stairs and handed them to her. At the top was printed *Édouard LeBlanc*, and below it a cluster of grapes hanging from a vine, followed by *1942*, and the grape variety, *Sauvignon Blanc*. Léa settled on the ground and began cutting through the open spaces between the squares with scissors.

"Make sure you cut off my name. Only leave the year and the grape variety."

She nodded.

"You've not spoken of your parents. How long have you been without them?"

"Maman died in 1940 before the Occupation started, Papa a few years after Rose was born. She doesn't remember him."

"And you raised Rose after your mother passed?"

"Yes, as best I could. I should have done more for her."

"What do you mean?"

"She had to quit school at fourteen to become a cleaner. My salary wasn't enough to support us."

"Well, I think you've done a fine job. Rose has real talent. And you've encouraged that." He placed a cup with water and a brush next to the demijohns. "You both can stay here until the war ends and longer after that, if you'd like."

"You're very kind. But we're a burden."

"No. Having you both here makes me feel more at ease."

"Why?" She thought it would be the opposite.

"We can't guess what the future holds. But knowing that you and Rose will be here, safe . . . Never mind," he said, "let's get these labels on."

7

Rose

The next morning, Rose winced as Léa braided her hair.

"Ow," Rose said, lifting a hand to her head, "you're pulling too tight."

"I'm sorry," Léa said, "I'll redo it."

"Is everything all right?" Rose studied her sister's reflection in the mirror. Dark circles rimmed her eyes. Maybe she was tired. Léa was often short-tempered when she was tired. But something seemed different about her today. And then Rose noticed the light coming in from the window, the glow of it on the mirror like a drop of water gleaming on a blade of glass. And all she could think about was how to recreate that light on paper.

"We need to finish the harvest today," Léa said, carefully plaiting Rose's hair.

"Why today?"

"The authorities will come in a week to collect the wine." Léa pursed her lips. "If we work through lunch, do you think we can finish today?"

It was the one day during the week that Paulette had no school. She would be following Rose around, asking questions, trying to get her attention. "I think we could, but I need to give Paulette a task to keep her busy and out of our way."

Léa slid Rose's two braids forward over her shoulder. "Then you must do that," she said.

At breakfast, Paulette was still in her pajamas, one of the perks of not having to rush out to school. Rose smiled at her. "I hope you're planning on getting dressed. I need your help today."

"Oh?" Paulette's hands clapped and her legs swung under the table.

"Léa and I must work throughout the day, with no time for lunch, to finish the harvest." At Paulette's frown, she added, "But when I finish, I would like to draw a still life, one that is different from any of the others I've done."

Rose smiled as her mind jumped back to those first days in Combleux. Rose had been cleaning the dishes after dinner in the kitchen and Virginie had come alongside her. "I have something I'd like to show you," she'd said, clutching a leather-bound book against her chest. "Leave the dishes for me to finish later."

Rose had dried her hands and followed Virginie to the two chairs near the window. The cost of electricity had gone up so much that the lights were never turned on in the main house and reserved only for the *chai*. The autumn days were shortening. Virginie lit two candles and placed a book on the table.

"This book belonged to my father," Virginie said softly. "He was a shopkeeper, but his passion was painting. In his free time, he studied the old Masters." She handed the book to Rose. "You might enjoy looking through it, as the book has all the old Masters who were Papa's favorite painters. Keep it for as long as you're here. Maybe it will inspire you."

"Thank you, this is so kind of you to share," Rose said, wanting to ask if Virginie's father had also been a painter, but upon opening the book, she was drawn into a riveting image that took her breath away. A wooden table set against a gray wall, a green velvet cloth covering all but the edges of the table. On the cloth, objects were arranged: opened oysters glistening on a silver platter, walnuts with fine lines like an old woman's face, cracked hazelnut shells with edges sharp as a knife, a half-peeled lemon's stippled rind curled like a cat tail on another silver platter, a clock, a gold key attached to a sky blue velvet ribbon, an engraved silver dish with a stem, and shimmering glass goblets half filled with wine. Rose inched closer, hardly believing what she saw.

Inside the goblets, floating in the wine and at the upper rim of the glass, were windows. She squinted, sure that inside the windows another reflection floated—was it the painter? Her gaze shifted to the lemon's golden light reflected like beams of the sun on the silver platter. It was all light and reflection, gorgeous soft and hard light that seemed to reach back to eternity, doubling and tripling on itself in the images on that table and in the room—the room that wasn't in the painting and yet present, as if the windows were open and she could feel a warm breeze entering from outside. Magical. But how had the painter done it?

She searched for a name and found it not in the lower right-hand corner but in the book. *Willem Claesz. Heda*: *Still Life with a Silver Tazza*. What is a tazza? Her gaze shifted back to the painting, and through a process of deduction, she figured that one unfamiliar object, the one she couldn't attach a name to must be the tazza—a wide silver dish tipped over on its side, the light from the invisible window glinting like a sword on its rim, painfully hard so that she wanted to look away.

Rose then lifted her head from the book and realized that Viriginie had returned to the kitchen because she could hear the water running in the sink. She stared at the window, where the fading sun cast a faint glow and darkness blanketed the ground. Inside, the air shimmered with the flickering light of the candles. Light, she thought, is the key. The element she'd tried to capture on the bridge the day the German soldier chased her. She never truly understood its significance until she set her eyes on the painting by a man who had lived three hundred years ago. A man, what was his name—Heda—who could bring light, through a window only visible in a reflection on a glass, into a room which changed everything it touched: the sharp glint on the silver dish, the soft sunny bounce on the peeled lemon, the warm golden glow inside the glass of wine. Remarkable.

That night, she carried the book with the three-hundred-year-old still life to bed. She felt as if Virginie had handed her a sacred stone. Not just a work of immense technical proficiency that she couldn't even begin to do with pencil and paper (if only Madame Martin hadn't taken her pastels), but something of profound insight. Now, she had a path, one that felt true to her original intentions—sketching objects rather than people because the former were predictable; they didn't die, steal or disappear like her mother, Madame Martin and André all had. With the book next to her, Rose had fallen into a deep slumber.

Paulette clapped her hands, bringing Rose back into the moment. "What do you want to draw?" she asked.

"That depends on you," Rose said.

"Me?"

She nodded. "You will be the one to collect the items for my still life." She stood and pulled down a rattan basket hanging on the wall. "You will have the whole day to find the right ones but there is one condition."

"What's a condition?"

"It's like a rule," Léa explained.

"You cannot include anything that I've already drawn."

"Oh," Paulette said, looking around the kitchen. "No grapes?"

"No. You have my sketchbook. Study the drawings carefully, make a list of every object I've sketched, and then you will be able to check that what you put in the basket is correct."

"I will get your sketchbook now," Paulette said, jumping down to the floor.

"No, you won't." Virginie pointed at her chair. "Sit down, Mademoiselle LeBlanc. First you will finish your breakfast, get dressed, complete your homework, then help me with some laundry, and once that's all done you can carry out Rose's task."

A little petulantly, Paulette returned to the chair. "How many objects should I find?"

"As many as you want," Rose, said, before realizing that the task was meant to keep Paulette occupied for most of the day. She corrected herself. "But the basket must be full, you could even bring me two baskets."

"Two baskets?" Paulette's eyes widened.

Rose nodded.

"And for me," Léa said. "I want you to write down the name of every object in your notebook, with correct spelling and accents."

"Oh no, I can't spell." Paulette shook her head.

"That is exactly why you must do it," Léa said. She turned to Rose. "Let's get started. We have a full day."

Once the sisters were outside, they shared a laugh.

"Do you think we overdid it with Paulette?" Rose asked.

"Not at all. She needs to practice because apparently the marks on her *dictées* at school aren't good. Come, we've got four rows left to harvest. If we each do one in the morning, eat a quick lunch, then one in the afternoon, we'll be done by the time Paulette comes out of the house with her baskets!"

The sisters went into the *chai* to put on their overalls. Édouard was inside crushing and removing the skin from the grapes they'd picked the day before. Édouard never had breakfast with them—he was always up before dawn and working while everyone was still sleeping.

"Good morning," Édouard addressed them. "Today we finish the harvest. I can't thank you both enough."

"Rose, you go ahead," Léa said. "I'll join you outside shortly."

Rose nodded, lifting the overalls and a hat from the peg on the wall. She went outside and hauled a basket up the slope to the vines. What did Léa want to speak with Édouard about in private again? Was Léa keeping secrets from her?

The yellow-green grapes glistened with the morning dew, and Rose thought of the still life by Heda. She would never be able to recreate that light without color. Maybe it had been wrong not to stand up to Madame Martin to get her pastels back. And then she thought of André. Though she didn't speak of him, he was always present, like a bit of light inside her, keeping her company during the long hours of bending over the vine trunks to pick the grapes. She could hear his voice and feel the warmth of his breath on her neck. A flicker of doubt crossed her mind—was it foolish to cling to these memories? When would she see him again? More than anything, she wanted to know that he was safe.

Léa walked up the slope. Rose could see by how she held her arms tight to her sides that something was on her mind. Rose wished that Léa would stop trying to protect her from the truth. But Léa set about picking the grapes and didn't say a word.

By the time the sun was high in the sky they'd both finished an entire row. When the church bell rang the noon hour, they took a break, drinking water and eating cheese. Rose tried to get her sister to talk a little.

"Is everything all right?" Rose asked.

"Yes."

"You look tense, not like your usual self."

"I'm fine. Let's get back to work."

Rose's fingers ached from holding the cutters in her palm all morning but when she snipped the final cluster off the vine a few hours later, she raised her hands in the air and shouted, "I'm done."

"Bravo," Léa said.

At that moment, Paulette came out of the farmhouse carrying a basket overflowing with items. The sisters looked at one another and smiled.

"I completely forgot," Rose said.

"Look, look!" Paulette ran up the slope nearly tripping over herself, weighed down by the objects clinking against the side of the basket. "I did what you said. Made the list and see—nothing in the basket is in your sketchbook."

"Well done." Léa clapped her hands.

"I wrote everything down—do you want to see my list?" Paulette asked, excitedly. "Or are we going to do the drawing first? Can I help you put things on the table?"

Rose wanted to draw even if her fingers were sore from gripping the cutters all day. "Let's see what you've collected for me."

Paulette jumped up, excitement rippling from her small body. She pulled out a paper from the basket and handed it to Léa. "With Maman's help, I checked all the spelling."

"Bravo." Léa bent down, took the paper and kissed her on the cheek. "I will look these over carefully." Then her gaze shifted to her sister, who was removing a silver platter from the basket, turning it one way and another to catch the falling sunlight. "Did your Maman agree that you could take this?" she asked, a note of worry in her voice.

Paulette nodded. "She said every still life has a silver platter."

Rose, remembering the paintings in the book, smiled. "Your mother is a wise woman."

"Can you teach me how to draw?" Paulette suddenly asked, her eyes flashed with joy.

Rose looked at her, nonplussed. "I've never taught—"

"Please, please—"

"Paulette," her mother said, coming out from the house. "Are you pestering Rose again?"

"I want to draw like Rose. She can teach me."

Virginie clapped her hands. "Oh, I see."

"You want to, don't you?" Paulette pleaded.

"Of course," Rose said. "I just don't know how."

Virginie smiled. "Just tell her what you do, that might be enough."

"Please. I promise to be good," Paulette said.

"All right, we can try. Let's start by bringing the basket inside and arranging the items on a table until we get the right composition."

"What's a composition?" Paulette asked, jumping up and reaching for Rose's hand.

"I'll explain it once we're inside." Paulette's small hand inside her own made Rose's heart swell. Paulette was so young, Rose hoped that she would always be protected from the danger lurking all around on account of the war, just like Léa had done for her. Rose glanced at her sister before gathering up the basket.

That evening, Virginie allowed Paulette to skip her chores of peeling the potatoes and setting the table so she could help Rose with the arrangement of the still life. Virginie had given her permission to move the chairs under the window, placing a wooden table there instead. Paulette had found a blue velvet cloth in the attic upstairs and she and Rose had brushed the dust off it outside. Now, they draped the velvet material over the wooden table.

"It's the color of a *mésange bleue*, isn't it?" Virginie said, entering the room and staring at the table. "Come, dinner is ready. You two can work on the still life tomorrow."

"But I have school." Paulette frowned.

Rose gently pinched Paulette's nose between her first and second finger then withdrew, showing her thumb. "I caught your nose." She laughed.

Paulette shrieked and touched her nose. "No, you didn't."

"You can help me after school. I'll wait for you."

Paulette smiled, took Rose's hand and together they followed her mother into the kitchen.

8

Léa

Now that the harvest was complete, Léa spent more time in the *chai*, helping Édouard. The most pressing problem was to find containers for the ethanol. Since Weinführer Brucker had returned only a handful of the steel gas canisters from last year, Édouard decided to fill the old oak barrels from previous vintages with fuel. But as he'd stored them outside under a tarpaulin, first, they needed to be cleaned and checked for leakage.

Léa helped him roll the barrels on their side into the *chai*.

"Can you see that?" Édouard pointed at the bung hole at the head of the barrel where lumps of white fungus grew. "We will need to brush that off and then clean it with hot water to kill the mold."

Léa brushed the barrels, then carried the hot water Virginie had boiled in a large pot from the kitchen to the *chai*. Once they were all cleaned, she rolled the barrels outside, and Édouard inspected the metal hoops. He replaced any that were warped. The final step was to fill them with warm water to kill any mold inside and check for leakage.

"Under normal circumstances, I'd dry the barrels completely before filling them." He sighed. "But there's nothing normal about this, is there?"

Léa nodded, yawning. Over the last two nights, while Rose had slept, she'd come to the *chai*, finishing labeling the demijohns, placing them in rattan baskets then stacking them in crates.

"Come on, Weinführer Brucker arrives in two days. We need to fill the steel containers and barrels with ethanol before then. I checked the vats this morning; the fuel is ready."

They had filled half the barrels when the sound of a diesel engine made them stop and look up.

"Could the Weinführer be early?" Léa asked, unease sweeping over her. She glanced at the corner, to check that nothing revealed the hidden hatch. Last night, they'd covered the stone entrance with the rug and placed the carpet, table and chair on top, as always.

Édouard straightened his shoulders and brushed dust off his hands. Footfalls crunched the pebbled path outside. They turned to the open doors, where the sun caught the long shadow of a person standing at the entrance. Léa's stomach tightened with alarm as she recognized the sharp-pointed boots as the ones worn by German soldiers.

"Herr LeBlanc, are you in there?"

"Who is it?" Édouard's voice was calm and steady.

"I'm Kommandant Abetz." He strode into the *chai*. "You're coming with me."

"What, why?"

"There's been a Resistance attack on the main cable leading from Combleux to Orléans. Partisans from Combleux destroyed it." His eyes darted from Édouard to Léa.

"I know nothing of it," Édouard said. "I've been—"

"We'll see about that."

"I have work to complete for Weinführer Brucker."

"The harvest is over." The Kommandant glanced around the *chai*. "What work?"

"My wine production has been turned into ethanol. Weinführer Brucker will collect the barrels the day after tomorrow. I have ten yet to fill."

The Kommandant stepped forward, his dark eyes locked on Léa. "And you cannot do this work on your own?"

Léa hesitated, her voice trembling as she searched for a way to persuade him not to take Édouard. "The barrels are heavy. I can't lift them to the spout to fill."

The Kommandant watched her with a calculating expression that made Léa feel as small as an ant he could crush at his will. Holding in her fear, she didn't dare look away. "Then I will send a man to help you." His gaze flicked toward Édouard. "You have five minutes to gather your things. Instruct your wife to bring your meals to the mairie every day. I'll be waiting for you outside." He put his hands behind his back and strode toward the door.

"What are we going to do?" Léa whispered, her voice shaking.

"It will be all right. Don't trust the man he sends here." A fierce light shone in Édouard's eyes. "You told me once to ask if I needed help—do you remember?"

She nodded.

"I'm asking now. Can you be a friend to Virginie and Paulette, protect them in case I don't come back?"

"You will return!" She gripped his hand. "Tell me you will."

He leaned in. "Finish the work I still have to do." Léa stiffened, remembering the demijohns in the hidden hatch. "Can I rely on you?"

"Yes," she whispered, heart pounding, unsure what she'd just agreed to.

* * *

The house that afternoon felt empty. Usually, Virginie went to fetch Paulette at school, but she'd sent Rose so that she and Léa could talk in private. They sat at the round table in the dining room as she told Virginie what had happened. Virginie didn't seem shocked, but concern filled her eyes. Léa felt a cold chill and cupped her hands around the mug of tea Virginie had placed on the table.

"We have a problem," Virginie said a little later.

"With the wine?"

"It's already been sold and the delivery confirmed for the day after Weinführer Brucker collects the ethanol."

"Maybe Édouard will be back by then?"

Virginie tented her fingers, elbows on the table. "We can't rely on that. We must be ready to deliver it without Édouard."

Léa remembered how heavy the four-liter demijohns were to lift into the crates. Could they move that many jugs without being seen?

Virginie's index finger slid like a silent blade along her neck. "The smugglers are gangsters. They won't hesitate to denounce Édouard to the Weinführer if we don't deliver."

"But isn't the smuggler also guilty?"

"He can lie, say that Édouard proposed meeting him, but he came to tell the Weinführer. He'll likely collect a reward, and he might even be given some of the cases."

Just like Madame Martin, Léa thought. "What was Édouard's plan?"

"He's arranged to meet him in the middle of the night. The smuggler will come by *péniche*—a motorized barge. Édouard intended on the donkey hauling the cart loaded with the crates to the river at a place where the embankment isn't too steep."

"Then we'll do the same."

"The trouble is, the donkey's frightened of her own shadow. She's terrible with strangers or sudden noises. Édouard knows how to handle her since he's raised her from birth. Without him to calm her, she'll bray all the way there, giving us away."

It was true that every time Léa had attached the cart to the donkey's harness and tried to guide her down the hill to the *chai*, the animal wouldn't budge. Even if she brought a carrot or apple from the orchard, the animal stubbornly stood still. The donkey moved for Édouard only. There had to be another way. "What if we bring the cases through the tunnel?"

"I've thought of that." She took a sip of tea. "But the demijohns aren't light. And then how will we get them from the tunnel to the river? It's another three hundred meters."

"If one of us can be in the tunnel and another one outside with the wheelbarrow at the other end, then we can place two or three crates on the wheelbarrow and bring the demijohns down to the river that way."

"Possibly. How many trips do you think it would take?"

"Depends on how many crates we can stack on the wheelbarrow—five? If we could get a second wheelbarrow, then we'll go faster."

The women sat in silence, running through the logistics in their minds. "Édouard will know if the tunnel is a good idea," Virginie said, shifting her weight in the chair. "We need to discuss it with him."

"How?"

"They won't let me see him when I bring the basket of food."

"Maybe I can try." Léa could see Virgine's eyes lined with exhaustion, strain or both. She'd promised Édouard that she would protect his family. "You will stay with Paulette. Rose and I can transport the bottles."

Virginie glanced sideways at the door. "I can't allow—"

"If we're caught." She didn't want to think that way, fearing she'd jinx it, but she was sure Édouard's instructions were clear and she'd given him her word. "You must say that you aren't a part of it and know nothing."

Virginie shook her head. "You can't take all the risk for me. It's not fair."

"I can for Paulette. She needs you to protect her. Who knows when the war will be over? Rose and I are adults; we can look after ourselves."

"No." She looked down at her hands. "Édouard wouldn't want that."

"Yes, he would. My sister and I are returning the debt we owe you for taking us in after we were kicked out of the boardinghouse."

"This is black market smuggling." She leaned forward, taking Léa's hand. "If you're caught, the consequences could be prison or worse."

Léa knew there was no other way.

The front door opened and the sound of footsteps racing over the stone floor echoed through the hall.

"Maman," Paulette ran to embrace her mother. "Rose picked me up from school! We sang my favorite song the whole way back."

Virginie lifted her daughter up on her lap. "Isn't that lovely. Let's go wash your hands and get you a *goûter*. There might still be a half slice of apple tart left, then you can start your homework."

"After I finish, can I help Rose?" Paulette pointed at the table with the silver platter.

"Yes, you can. Come along now." Virginie smiled at Rose, who had just entered the room. "Thank you for collecting Paulette. I'll bring an extra mug. There's more tea in the pot and it should still be warm. Paulette and I will be in the kitchen so that you and Léa can talk."

Rose glanced at her sister, who was staring at her lap. Virginie placed her hand on Léa's shoulder on her way out. "Thank you."

"Where is Édouard?" Rose asked.

Léa shook her head. "There's something I need to tell you."

Rose sat down, and Léa told her what had happened to Édouard and the plan she had talked of with Virginie.

Rose sat still in the chair, listening without saying a word. Finally, Léa leaned forward. "Will you help?"

"Of course." She took a breath. "It's just . . ."

"What?"

"Keep me out of the tunnel. You know how I hate cramped spaces. Promise?"

"I promise. You won't need to go in the tunnel. I'll do that part."

"All right. I'm happy to help." Rose glanced at the window. "I want to get back to the still life while the light's good," Rose said, standing.

Léa decided to go to the *chai* to run through her plan one more time just to be sure. Tomorrow, she would bring food to Édouard at the mairie, maybe her only chance to talk with him before she and Rose smuggled the wine.

At the *chai*, she found the door ajar, which surprised her because she thought she'd closed it. She stepped inside, heard noises at the back and hesitated. No one should be here. "Hello?" Her voice sounded sharp in the domed *chai*.

And then she saw him: a man, bent over what appeared to be one of the old barrels that she and Édouard had washed last week. With a crowbar, he was attempting to lift the barrel head. "What are you doing here?" she said, trying to sound less afraid than she felt.

He turned. "Get out."

"No. You get out," she shouted.

"Hush." The barrel lid popped off, and he put it on the ground. Next to his feet stood an open canvas bag. He turned to face her. "Édouard sent me. I need to move what's in this barrel. Now either help or leave me alone."

"Who are you? How do I know that Édouard sent you?"

"I'm a friend of his and André's. I've been instructed to move these." He turned back and lifted a rifle out of the barrel, holding it up. "Before anyone finds them."

"What are they doing here?" Léa moved from side to side, fear like an electrical current surging through her body.

He put the rifle in the canvas bag, then took out another. "Édouard's been storing them for us. He's a good man. We don't know how they caught on to him or why they picked him up. But now that he's in detention, we must get these out of here to protect his family and our network."

Léa's head spun. Worry gnawed at her, sharpening with every rifle he removed from the barrel and placed in the bag. "Are there other barrels?"

"Two more. Are you going to stand there staring or help?"

She stepped forward. "Who was Édouard working for?"

"The Resistance. Now, continue unloading this one while I open the other barrels. Once these are out of here, there's no reason for the Nazi bastards to accuse the family of any involvement. Everyone will be safe."

Léa wanted to believe him; logic told her that what he'd said was true. But as her hand gripped the rifle's cold metal forearm, doubt rose at the back of her mind.

9

Léa

November 1942

Léa avoided looking at the red and black banner with the swastika above the door of the mairie in Combleux. As she climbed the stairs, the basket of food in her hand, her heart pounded with uncertainty. From Virginie's visits, she knew the mairie had a side annex where prisoners were held under provisional detention. Still, she'd need a convincing reason to be allowed to see Édouard.

Léa hadn't told anyone at home about the rifles Édouard had been storing for the Resistance. She didn't want to alarm Virginie, and the fewer people who knew, the better.

Inside the mairie, she crossed the herringbone parquet floor, passing men and women sitting on wooden benches set against a wall with an old tapestry. They seemed to be waiting, and she noticed a woman with a basket, surmising she was also here to deliver food. At the far end of the room, Léa strode up to where a man sat behind a wooden table.

"I'm here with food for Monsieur. Édouard LeBlanc."

"Over there," the man said, signaling to the benches she'd seen earlier. "Wait until you're called."

Léa sat down, crossed her ankles and placed the basket on her lap. Virginie had packed fresh clothes, an apple, cheese and a bottle of beer.

German officers stomped across the parquet, engaging in a heated exchange. On Léa's right was a conference room. The doors were closed, but she could hear men's voices coming from the other side. Maybe Édouard was held in there with the others. The Germans had arrested many men. Some were kept as hostages to pressure the guilty into confessing. Léa hoped Édouard was one of these hostages and would soon be released.

Another German officer appeared. He stood in front of the woman with the basket. "Madame, I shall convey this to your husband."

Léa could see the disappointment on her face. "May I speak with him?"

"Discussions with saboteurs are not permitted. The men are kept in isolation." He clicked his heels and left.

The woman clutched her hands in front of her and padded across the hall to the door.

Léa gripped her own basket. How could she persuade them to let her speak with Édouard? The salon door opened, and a soldier emerged, striding over to her.

"Mademoiselle, papers please."

Léa reached for her identity card in the front pocket of her dress. His gaze shifted between her and the photo. "Why are you in Combleux? You should be in Orléans."

"My father and Monsieur LeBlanc were friends from school. Every autumn, we would come and help the family with the *vendange*." She cleared her throat. "Madame LeBlanc's daughter isn't well today, so she asked me to bring his food and clothing."

The soldier's eyes were as empty and black as a starless sky. Outwardly Léa met his gaze, but inside, every nerve in her body pricked. He yanked the basket from her, nearly spilling its contents on the parquet.

"I'll bring it to Monsieur LeBlanc," he said.

"Pardon, monsieur, but there is an important question I must ask Édouard LeBlanc."

"Not until after his release." He stepped away and it took all of Léa's control not to reach out and touch his arm to pull him back.

"It concerns Weinführer Brucker's orders . . ." He paused. "The Weinführer requisitioned the LeBlanc vinery's harvest for industrial alcohol. Monsieur LeBlanc had been in the final stages of production at the time he was arrested." She squeezed her hands at her sides, summoning strength. "I'm now in charge and there's an unusual smell coming from two of the vats. Fermentation seems to have stopped. If he can tell me what to do, I might have a chance to save the ethanol for Weinführer Brucker."

She was venturing onto dangerous ground. What if the officer checked the *chai* to verify her story? She'd be caught, and then who would deliver the wine to the black marketeer? As he studied her face, her muscles tensed and she felt like she'd run an enormous distance but still wasn't any closer to her goal.

He handed her the basket and proceeded to the salon. "Wait here. I'll bring him to you."

First step. Léa doubted he'd leave her alone with Édouard. She'd use a coded language.

A few moments later, Édouard, looking terrible, his face drawn and his eyes red with exhaustion, was escorted into the hall by the soldier, who stationed himself nearby to overhear the conversation.

"Léa, thank you for coming—and for the supplies."

Fearing she didn't have much time, she said, "Two vats have a strange odor and when I opened the doors, the bubbling ceased." She swallowed. "What should I do? I don't want to disappoint Weinführer Brucker with less ethanol than he's expecting."

Confusion shaded Édouard's face. *Please, Édouard, this is important.*

"Did you check the temperature?"

"Oh yes, it's . . ."

"Too low?" he prompted.

She nodded. Thank God. He was reading between the lines of what she was saying. "It all started the night the donkey brayed without stop. We considered taking him to the river, to cool him down but Virginie warned he was too stubborn to go."

The soldier looked at her, suspicion in his eyes.

"A slight change in air temperature can start the donkey braying. Maybe the animal senses a storm. But it often corresponds to a problem with the fermentation process. Have you stirred the lees?"

"What is that?"

"Sediment at the bottom of the tank. Stir it with the baton by the vats. The bubbling should return after a few hours."

"Thank you," she said, handing him the basket. "Virginie wants to know what you need. She's busy with Paulette. Rose helps me." Léa met his eyes. "She's the key."

He nodded and his eyes shone bright, perhaps with recognition of their plan to use the tunnel to transport the wine to the smuggler. "Tell Virginie that a book would be nice to read if she could include one next time. Oh, don't forget to collect the walnuts under the tree." He smiled.

"There should be plenty on the ground by now. Virginie can use the rail carts to store them, making it easier for everyone."

"That's enough." The soldier stepped forward, pulling Édouard away.

She wanted to tell him one more thing, hoping to ease his mind. "I cleaned out three barrels."

"Thank you, Léa, for everything." His eyes were full of sadness. "And tell my wife and daughter how much I love them."

Léa listened as his footsteps echoed across the parquet floor, trying to push away the thought that it might be the last time she'd see him.

* * *

"Rail carts?" Virginie frowned. "That was his message?"

Léa had told Rose and Virginie everything Édouard said, hoping there might be some hidden message that only Virginie would grasp.

"Are you sure he said rail carts?" She shook her head. "I have no idea."

"He said they could be used to collect the walnuts."

"Could my poor husband have lost his mind? We collected the walnuts last week." She held out her palms, the fingers tinged with dark brown streaks. "It takes weeks for the dye from the inner casing to fade. We peeled them all off, then arranged them on the greenhouse floor to dry."

"It must mean something," Rose said. "Why else would he mention it?"

"How did he look?" A crease of worry appeared on Virginie's forehead.

"Good," Léa lied.

A loud knock startled the women as they turned to the door.

"Who could that be?" Virginie advanced to the front of the farmhouse. Rose and Léa followed close behind.

"Madame LeBlanc?" A short man with a swarthy face stood at the threshold. He removed his hat and tilted his head down in a bow. "Paul Ferney. I've been sent by Weinführer Brucker."

"Oh . . ." Virginie hesitated, and turned to Léa.

"I'll show you around the *chai*," Léa said, stepping through the threshold to introduce herself. "That's where we need assistance." Léa strode across the courtyard.

"Are you also a winegrower, Monsieur Ferney?"

"I used to be in the textile trade, traveling salesman between Marseille and Orléans." He looked behind him and all around. "But that work isn't possible with the war."

"Were you not mobilized to fight when the war broke out?"

"You ask a lot of questions, young lady."

An awkward silence. The bluntness of his comment made her wonder if he was really here to help.

"I have three children and a wife with a heart problem, so I was exempt on compassionate grounds."

Léa pushed open the door to the *chai* and waited for Monsieur Ferney to pass through before closing it behind her. She continued to pretend there were fermentation problems, thinking the Weinführer might question Ferney about her that day. Ferney didn't seem to know about wine production; she wondered if he was searching for the rifles. "I think I've resolved the problem in two of the vats."

"What problem?" He strode around the room, looking behind the vats.

"The fermentation had stopped in two vats, but I did as Monsieur LeBlanc advised this morning, and it's working again. We can fill the barrels from the rest." She fetched two large leather aprons hanging on the wall. Returning, she found he was gone.

"Monsieur Ferney?"

"I'm over here," he called.

She walked past the vats to the back wall at the end of the *chai*. Her mouth dropped.

"You look like you've seen a ghost." He laughed. "Got something to hide?"

"Nothing to hide." She handed him one of the aprons. "I'll show you what to do after you put this on."

He leaned on the desk, his feet crossed on the carpet covering the entrance to the hatch.

"It'll protect your clothing while we fill the barrels. Come on, they're over here."

They worked in silence the rest of the day. Ferney rolled the barrels to the vats, lifting them onto the rack as Léa opened the metal faucet so that the alcohol flowed through the bung hole. She let it spill over, as Édouard had taught her, then inserted a metal spigot to drain off the alcohol before closing it with the wooden bung to seal the hole. It was laborious work. There was a sheen on his forehead and damp patches under his arms but he didn't complain.

"That's it for today," she said, wiping her forehead with the back of her hand. "Come after lunch tomorrow. The alcohol in the remaining two vats should be ready. And then we can fill the other barrels."

"The Weinführer gave me strict instructions," he said, removing the leather apron.

"Which were?"

"That I should come in the morning and remain all day." His eyes locked on hers.

"It's not necessary, but if that is what you like." She shrugged, trying not to show how uneasy his words made her. "There's always plenty of work at the vineyard. I'll ask Madame LeBlanc tonight about other tasks until the fermentation is complete."

"Tell me where to put this." He held up the apron.

"I'll take it."

"Why don't you give me a key. You can take your time with breakfast. I'll just let myself into the *chai* and sweep—"

"That's very kind of you to offer but that won't be possible. We only have one key to the door."

He handed her the apron. "See you tomorrow morning."

She hung the aprons on the wall. Her stomach twisted as she considered everything Ferney had said. She closed the door and locked it, relieved he was gone until the morning.

Léa entered the kitchen. Virginie was busy peeling the potatoes for dinner.

"How was Monsieur Ferney?" she asked.

"Very curious about the *chai*. Walked all around it, and he asked a lot of questions. Can you think of something for him to do tomorrow morning?"

"There's plenty of wood that needs chopping. The logs are around the back of the property, so he'll be out of our way."

"Good." She sat down. "Any progress on what the rail carts might mean?"

"No. It doesn't make any sense." Virginie wiped her hands on her apron.

Rose and Paulette entered the kitchen, their faces ruddy from the cold.

"How was school today?" Léa asked.

Paulette handed her a piece of paper. "I got ten out of ten on my *dictée*."

"Bravo! We must celebrate."

Virginie lifted her chin in the direction of Paulette. "What do you say?"

"*Merci*, Tante Léa for helping me."

Léa felt a swell of emotion in her chest. No one had ever called her Tante before. "Come here, I want a hug." Paulette leaped into her lap and wrapped her arms around her neck.

"There's something else Paulette has to tell you," Rose said. "We've been talking about games."

"A game with the rail carts," Paulette said, turning to Rose and smiling.

"Go on."

"Papa and I used to play *cache-cache* with them." She twirled a finger in the air. "Papa said I was the same size as his crates of wine. He'd attach all the carts together." She leaped off Léa's lap. "I'd hide in one, like this." She crouched low, grinning. "He couldn't find me!"

Virginie glanced at Léa, then came forward, kneeling at her daughter's side. "Paulette, tell us where those rail carts are now."

"He hid them."

"Where, *chérie*?" Léa could hear the urgency in Virginie's voice.

"Behind the greenhouse!"

"You mean under the tarp?"

"Yes. Shall I show you?"

"Oh yes," Virginie said, kissing her on the forehead. "Such a clever girl."

The evenings were shorter now, and as they made their way across the gravel path, past the vegetable garden, darkness fell fast. Léa looked through the greenhouse's glass windows, walnuts spread across the floor as far as the eye could see. Now, Édouard's mention of the walnuts made sense. She brushed past the weeds and purple and white cyclamen growing along the edge of the greenhouse as they advanced to the rear.

"There it is!" Paulette said, indicating a tarp covered with leaves and branches. "Papa keeps a lot of things back here." She stepped back. "Watch out because spiders make their webs under the tarp."

Léa pulled one stick and another out of the ground, and with Rose's help, yanked the tarp off. The sisters gasped at the carts stacked upside down and the four metal wheels at each corner that pointed toward the sky.

"The carts!" Paulette shouted, jumping with excitement.

"I don't think you can fit inside one now." Virginie laughed.

Rose came forward and pulled one out, flipping it around. Léa peered inside the hollow interior. It was just big enough to hold a couple of demijohns, maybe four, if they were stacked close and one on top of another. "How many carts are here?" she asked.

Paulette helped her count. "Eight, nine, ten," the girl said, a zing of pride ringing in her voice.

Virginie turned to Paulette. "Why don't we go back to the house and get the dinner ready while Rose and Léa sort through these carts?"

Rose turned to Léa. "How will these carts help us?"

"The wheels," Léa said. "See how straight they are? They're designed to run on tracks, not on regular ground."

"So?"

"There must be tracks in the tunnel."

"Was that Édouard's message?"

"I think so. He wants us to transport the wine through the tunnel."

"By using these rail carts?"

"If we can put all the demijohns in and make one trip, it will save a lot of time."

"Let's go back to the *chai* and check the tunnel to see if there are rails."

"I'm worried about Monsieur Ferney," Léa said, looking around.

"You think he's watching?"

"I think Weinführer Brucker sent him to watch us. Let's wait until later tonight, after everyone has gone to sleep. Then we can sneak into the *chai* and keep the lights off."

"But it will be too dark to come back here to bring the carts around. I say we move them now while there's still some light. We can stack them in the courtyard close to the *chai*."

"Good idea."

10

Rose

Two days later, Rose stood alongside Léa, waiting as Weinführer Brucker inspected the vats and the barrels to confirm the quality of the fuel. When he was satisfied all was in order, he instructed Monsieur Ferney to help the sisters wheel the barrels to the truck parked outside, where he lifted them onto the truck bed with the driver's help.

Returning inside to fetch another barrel, Rose noticed the Weinführer walking around the *chai*. She saw mud on the floor near the carpet, and smoothed her hand over her apron to stop it from shaking. They'd spent the last two nights bringing the rail cars inside, cleaning them out and hauling them into the cave. Then they'd swept out the *chai* so that there would be no trace of what they'd been doing—but clearly, they'd missed a spot. Would he notice? The Weinführer tapped his boots on the carpet, as if testing what was underneath. She held her breath, waiting, but he seemed satisfied and left.

That night, the sisters set out when the church bell rang at midnight. A full moon shone. At least it would make it easier for them to find their way to the jetty where the smuggler's boat would be waiting, but it might also make them more visible to passing patrols. Rose had an uneasy feeling. She wished André was here.

"That's it. We're done. Are you ready?" Léa asked after they finished loading the last of the wine into the tunnel.

"We could wait a few more days," Rose suggested, shuffling her feet. Maybe it was just the sense of being underground that gnawed at her. Moving away from the tunnel, she recalled how the Weinführer had tapped his boots on the carpet—did he know? "What if he's figured out what we're doing?"

"He couldn't have," Léa said. "Your imagination is working overtime. Good for art but not for practical matters."

"But I—"

"If we don't go, the smuggler will think Édouard kept the wine for himself. We have to move tonight. It's the only way to keep Paulette and Virginie safe."

That was the heart of it. Hearing it again gave Rose the impetus and strength to push forward. She recalled all they'd already gone through to prepare—walking to the jetty early in the morning, then meeting Virginie on the towpath along the Loire. She'd just returned from delivering the food to Édouard, and showed the sisters where the tunnel ended so they could trace their way from it to the jetty, which took less than five minutes. She could risk five minutes of her life to keep the LeBlanc family safe.

"How many trips do you think it will take us to bring all the wine to the jetty?" Rose asked.

"If we can fit two cases in one wheelbarrow, and we both have a wheelbarrow and go back and forth, three trips at the most."

"Less than thirty minutes and it will all be over," Rose whispered, trying to reassure herself.

"That's right. And you don't have to go in the tunnel."

"Good, because I'd never be able to."

"Come on," Léa said, let's get the wheelbarrows ready. "Are you sure you can wheel them on your own to the tunnel's outer door?"

Rose nodded. "I brought an old blanket to put on them to deaden the rattle of the glass. I'll be fine."

Minutes later, Rose was alone on the road, wheeling the carts through the darkness. A low humming sound broke the quiet—crickets—and hearing them made her less jumpy. She kept close to the side of the road, ready to steer the wheelbarrows onto the verge and hide in the darkness if she heard a bicycle or car. She thought about Léa underground, pushing the carts through the tunnel. Why wasn't her sister scared? Rose would never understand Léa—how she could be so brave and bold.

Plane trees dotted the road. Rose took in the moonlight shining on the yellow-brown leaves. She wished she could be back at the house, working on the still life she'd started a few days ago. She'd sketched the moonlight reflecting on the silver platter. She planned to leave a trace of herself in the reflection, just as Claesz and the other artists did. Then a shudder ran through her as she remembered the skulls from those paintings, how they sat like ticking clocks in the corners, reminding the viewer that time was short. Was that what she'd been feeling all day—a sign that something would happen to her and Léa tonight? No, she was thinking too much. One step after another and she'd soon be there.

When Rose reached the oak tree that marked the end of the tunnel, she put the wheelbarrows down and felt around in the grass for the metal door. Finding it, she knocked three times and waited.

The metal hatch creaked open. It took Léa a few pushes to loosen it enough to break the seal of weeds that had grown up around it.

"Léa?" Rose whispered.

"I'm here. Hold on, I'll bring up the first crate."

Rose placed the wheelbarrows side by side. Once Léa reappeared, she took the crate and put it in the wheelbarrow, and it went on like that until both wheelbarrows were full of demijohns.

"Perhaps we should bring the rest of the crates out and stack them on the grass?" Léa suggested.

"Yes. Hand them to me."

Once they had all the crates out, Léa left the hatch open. There was no handle on the outside, so closing it would mean she couldn't open it when they returned.

"Let's go." The sisters wheeled the barrels through the grass to reach the jetty. Virginie had said the man would be there at two in the morning, and just as they came upon the jetty, the church bell rang out twice. The *péniche* was waiting. They could see a man standing on the grass, smoking a pipe.

"Where's Édouard?" he said, his voice fraught. "I agreed to meet Édouard, not two women."

"He couldn't come," Léa said. "He sent us instead."

The man threw his cigarette to the ground and stubbed it out. "I don't like last-minute changes. Let's get this over with." He helped them unload the wheelbarrows, counting the crates as he stacked them on the boat. "Where's the rest?"

"Around the corner," Léa said.

"What? Sitting ducks get shot."

Rose's stomach clenched into a hard knot of fear.

"Come on, Rose," Léa urged. "We'll be quick."

"Get on, then," the man snapped, his voice sharp and impatient.

Rose's uneasiness surged and the anxiety that had simmered all day and night now crashed to the surface.

Hands shaking, she grabbed the other wheelbarrow and followed Léa.

"We'll load up the wheelbarrows with all the crates because I don't think he'll wait for another trip," Léa said.

Rose tried to keep pace with her sister, but she struggled, exhausted and out of breath. She'd stayed up late the night before, helping Léa load the crates into the rail carts. The church bell rang the half hour. Rose saw Léa already at the jetty unloading the demijohns onto the boat. She tried to pick up her speed but she worried that the demijohns would tumble out. Suddenly, the smuggler ran toward her.

"I've got this," he said, gripping the wheelbarrow, pushing her aside. Rose followed. She saw the plank of wood he'd placed between the boat and the shore. He didn't bother to stop and unload the crates; instead, he rolled the wheelbarrow across the plank and onto the boat.

"You ladies better go hide—now, now," he said, untying the ropes and casting off.

A rattling noise in the distance made the sisters turn. Headlights flashed in the darkness. Rose's knees began to shake. She felt Léa drop something into her pocket. "Run to the tunnel," her sister whispered urgently.

Rose stared into the darkness, as if she was in the tunnel and the walls were closing in, clawing at her throat, freezing her in place.

"Run. You've got the key to the hatch in your pocket. To the tunnel now."

The car was getting closer. She heard the gravel crunching under the tires.

"Close the hatch. Lock it with the key. They won't find you. Get to the farmhouse." She pushed her along. "Think of Virginie and Paulette."

"Come with me," Rose pleaded.

"Go now, before they get closer."

The car headlights beamed brighter, making Rose's heart thump.

"Trust me." Léa pushed Rose so hard she nearly fell. "Run."

Suddenly, the fear that had frozen her limbs shifted into panic. She ran. Her heart hammered and her chest burned. The sense of danger was so overwhelming her mind went blank. She reached the opened hatch and slipped inside. She could hear distant voices, shouts in German echoing with menace.

Rose closed the hatch. The voices grew muffled, like sinking underwater into darkness. She reached into her pocket for the key Léa had put there, her fingers trembling as she found the opening. She slipped the key inside, turned it clockwise until it clicked. Locked. She removed the key and exhaled.

And then, with a sudden piercing awareness, she realized that she was safe, but her sister wasn't.

11

Rose

In the darkness, it took all Rose's effort to hold back the panic churning inside her. She clung tightly to the metal rungs, terrified that if she moved her hands or feet, the walls of the tunnel would press in and crush her. Her palms grew sweaty, and her breathing became ragged and uneven. The darkness left her disoriented. But she had to force her way through it. Move. Taking a deep breath, she eased her grip on one rung, then another.

Something landed on her head. She shook her hair, fearing it was a spider, but it seemed to be a clump of dirt from the ceiling. And that's when she felt the vibration overhead.

Could it be Léa? Reaching for the metal rung, she climbed back up toward the hatch. She intended to unlock it so Léa could enter. But halfway up, more dirt rained down like fine dust, forcing her to stop. If it was Léa, wouldn't she knock on the hatch to alert Rose? Listening intently for voices, she heard none. A sudden realization hit her—Léa wouldn't be wandering back and forth; she knew the location of the hatch and would either knock on it or find another way back to the vineyard. Someone had taken Léa, and now they were searching for Rose.

Think of Virginie and Paulette. Her sister's last words echoed in her mind. If something happened to Rose, Virginie and Paulette would be left alone. With a steely resolve, Rose shimmied down to the rail carts, punching through the fear and keeping one hand on the tunnel wall to guide her all the way back to the opening.

As her fingers scraped the limestone, Rose kept thinking about Léa. Would they bring her to the town hall and put her in the same room with Édouard? It wouldn't take the authorities long to figure out Léa's connection to the LeBlanc family. Soldiers might arrive tonight to question them. Rose had to warn them. She wasn't worried about Virginie, but Paulette, out of fear, might reveal something she'd overheard, putting them all at risk.

Reaching the end of the tunnel, Rose rushed into the cave. Every minute was precious. She crept up the stairs and lifted the hatch door. She listened for a few seconds before deciding no one was there, and entered the *chai*, closing the door and replacing the rug and furniture to hide it.

Outside, the night was still and quiet. The full moon shone on the courtyard, casting eerie shadows over the farmhouse. From the kitchen, she hurried to her room, hiding her clothes at the bottom of the laundry hamper and putting on pajamas. She pulled back the sheets on her bed and ruffled the pillow before making her way to Paulette's room.

Moonlight shone in from the window, falling over the young girl's face. She was in such a peaceful sleep that Rose didn't want to wake her, but if her instincts were correct, then her sleep would soon be disturbed by loud knocking and shouting voices. There was no way to escape the impending danger.

"Paulette, wake up, it's Rose."

She turned to her side and opened her eyes. "Rose?"

"I need you to do something very important for me. Listen."

Paulette sat up on one elbow and rubbed her eyes. "Yes."

"Tonight, some men from the police will knock on the door. They will ask you questions. You must tell them only what I tell you. Do you understand?"

Rose made Paulette repeat it two times, then slipped into the bed with her, covering them both with the sheet. Rose closed her eyes, wishing she could fall asleep, but every fiber in her body was pounding like a wild animal waiting for the predator to pounce out of the deep blackness. Eventually, sleep must have overtaken her because she awoke to pounding on the door. She got up, went to the corridor, and saw Virginie opening the door.

"Is Rose Cotillard here?" a German officer demanded, pushing the door aside and entering the house.

"What do you want with Rose?" Virginie asked.

"Is she here?"

"I'm Rose," she said, stepping forward.

The German's eyes locked on her. He turned and signaled to the soldier at his side. "Take her to the station."

Virginie stepped in between them. "What for?"

The soldier grunted and pushed her aside with his hand. "None of your business."

"Of course it's my business. I'm a friend of her parents, and I'm responsible for her. I demand that you tell me what's going on."

"Her sister was arrested this evening for smuggling wine. We know she didn't act alone."

"Rose was here all night. You can't just take her away without evidence."

The two men looked at one another.

"It's true," Rose said. "I've been here all night. Paulette had a nightmare, and I heard her cry out. I went to her room, and she asked me to stay with her until she fell asleep."

"Where is Paulette?" the soldier asked.

"My daughter is in her room sleeping, of course." Virginie gave Rose a look of concern.

"I will ask her." He looked at Rose. "You stay here."

Virginie followed the soldier to Paulette's room. Rose stood still, waiting, hopeful but anxious that Paulette wouldn't let her down. When Virginie and the soldier returned, she held her breath, waiting for an answer.

"It's true. The child said the young lady was with her through the night." The soldier turned to Rose. "Who helped your sister bring all that wine to the river?"

She shook her head. "I don't know. She doesn't tell me anything."

The soldier turned to Virginie. "And you?"

"No, all the wine making and selling is done by my husband—"

At that moment, the door opened and Weinführer Brucker entered. "Good morning."

"Where's my sister?" Rose stepped forward. "Is she at the town hall with Monsieur LeBlanc?"

"No. Your sister committed a serious crime in assisting Édouard LeBlanc to sell wine on the black market. I warned them both and they didn't listen."

"Where is she?"

"I ordered her to be placed in the camp at Jargeau."

Rose drew back, confused. She'd heard that name before . . . It took a moment before she could figure out where—Léa had told her that Maître Mallon had gone to camps in Pithiviers to help Jewish families who were sent there from Paris. Jargeau wasn't far from there. Rose felt the breath go out of her and tears welling, but seeing Paulette standing at the threshold, she knew that crying would only frighten the child and wouldn't help Léa. As soon as the sun came up, she'd see Maître Mallon and ask for his advice. Maybe they could go together to Jargeau. "Can I visit her?"

"Yes." His eyes narrowed on Rose, making her turn away.

Virginie put her arms around Rose. "It'll be all right. We'll get them both back."

"I'm afraid you're wrong, Madame LeBlanc," the Weinführer said. "I've come to inform you that due to your husband's criminal behavior—not limited to black market smuggling but also stocking weapons for the Resistance—"

"I don't know who told you that, but my husband isn't involved with the Resistance." She squeezed Rose's hand.

"A very good source told us. He was condemned to death by a German Military Tribunal." He checked his watch. "And executed an hour ago."

Virginie drew in a sharp breath, her body shuddered as she buckled to her knees and a deep, desperate moan escaped her lips. She buried her face in her hands and sobbed uncontrollably.

Rose's limbs trembled as she rushed to console her. "Oh, Virginie," she said, tears in her eyes, throat raw. "I'm so, so sorry."

"Maman, what's happening?" Paulette called out. "Why are you crying?"

Rose's heart twisted at the alarm in Paulette's voice. She felt the weight of the poor girl's grief pressing down, knowing her world had shifted forever, just as it had for her and Léa after losing their parents. She knelt beside Paulette, wrapping her arms around her tightly, whispering, "Your Papa has gone away. I promise, we will get through this together and everything will be all right."

But deep in her heart, she felt the raw truth: nothing would ever be the same again.

12

Léa

That same night, Léa sat in the back of the police van, gripping the sides as it rocked over the uneven road. She'd thought they'd take her to the detention center in the mairie or the police station in Orléans, but they'd been driving too long for that. She couldn't imagine where she was going. She hoped that Rose had made it through the tunnel without being caught. Despite everything, she'd managed to keep her sister safe.

The back doors swung open the moment the van came to a stop. In the murky light, an arm reached inside and grabbed Léa, yanking her out. She stumbled as her feet hit the ground, landing on her knee. A sharp, searing pain shot up her leg. She pushed herself up, blinking back tears.

"Go to the gate," the gendarme shouted, pointing ahead. He'd left the engine running. The acrid fumes scratched her throat. Beams of light shone down from towering wooden poles, revealing the gate, wide enough for a car to pass, with military guards in front. To the side, barbed wire extended in all directions.

Léa limped toward the gate, trying to shift the weight off her injured knee. A guard pulled back the barrier, gesturing for her to pass through. Someone knocked on the door of a building next to the gate. It opened, and she went inside.

After crossing the threshold, she looked down at her knee. The skin was raw and pink. Blood trickled down her shin. One gendarme stood behind a desk, took her paper and read it.

"It's the middle of the night." He looked down at a book on the table, then eyed Léa. "You'll have to share a bunk in cabin F for tonight." He pointed to a door. "Through there."

She needed water, both to drink and clean her knee. Her mother's voice in her head told her that soap and water, applied to all wounds, no matter how small, stopped an infection.

"May I go to the toilet first?" She asked, pointing to her knee.

He glared. "This isn't a hotel. Toilets are all locked up until the morning."

Léa pressed her lips together. Her mouth parched, throat tight with dread. She could hold off until the morning. Maybe in the cabin she'd find water or a sink. She limped past the cabins and arrived at the one with a black F painted on a white square.

She opened the door. A single light bulb hung from the ceiling, and a stove was in the center of the room, with a table and chairs where a woman sat alone, sewing. Two corridors led off the main room—maybe there were more rooms in the back. She couldn't hear any voices coming from inside them, so everyone must be asleep.

The woman got up and approached Léa. "Who are you?"

"I was told to come here for a bed."

The woman scratched her head. "You shouldn't be coming here at this hour and we have no extra beds. Who sent you?"

"The gendarme said cabin F . . . Is there a toilet or a sink I could use?"

"Outside, but they lock them at night." The woman bent down, nodding at Léa's knee. "You're lucky I don't sleep. I've got some water to clean that. You're probably thirsty, too."

"Yes," Léa said, her throat cottony.

She motioned to a chair. "Wait here. I'll be back."

Léa thanked her and sat down. The woman returned with a glass of water. Then she brought a bowl of water, a bar of soap and a rag. Léa drank, the liquid cooling her burning throat. Then she set about cleaning her knee.

"You can share with me tonight," the woman said. "I'm Edith. What's your name?"

"Léa. Thank you for the water and for helping me."

"After you've rested a little, you'll need to find another cabin." Edith's brown eyes scanned Léa's face. "As I said, there's no room for you here."

Léa nodded, though in her gut, she suspected none of the other cabins would have room for her either. She bit her lower lip and told herself she'd figure it out.

"In the morning, go to the gatehouse and ask for another cabin assignment," the woman said, patting Léa's arm. "But for now, you take the left side, and I'll take the right. Come, let's sleep."

Léa followed her to one of the rooms off the corridor. Inside was pitch-black, so the woman took Léa's hand and guided her to the far end. Grimacing, she removed her dirty shoes and reached out her hand until she touched the bed's cold metal frame. She crawled on the mattress, careful with her knee, the straw filling poking through the thin sheet, rough against her skin. Edith's presence reminded her of Rose, though the sisters hadn't shared a bed since the boardinghouse, as they had separate rooms at the LeBlanc's home. She hoped Rose was safe, and neither she nor Virginie would be implicated in the smuggling.

Closing her eyes, she tried not to think about the future. It was too far ahead. She'd ask for another cabin at the gatehouse. Once she had a bed, she'd know what to do. In daylight, things would be clear.

* * *

Léa awakened to a bell clanking outside. She sat up. The room was empty, Edith gone. Rubbing her eyes, she carried her shoes and made her way out to the corridor and the main room she'd been in the night before.

The sun shone bright through the filthy window. She saw a few women sitting on a bench in front of the cabin. Not far from them, young children held hands as they spun in a circle, laughing. The barbed-wire fence stood in the distance like tiny cathedral spires.

She put on her shoes and opened the door; her knee throbbed as she went down the steps. She looked for Edith, wanting to thank her for last night, but couldn't see her. Walking away from the cabins and children playing, she got her first glimpse of the enormity of the camp and the strands of wire twisting in layers with barbs at regular intervals and supported by tall wooden poles with lights that she'd seen last night. At the far end, cordoned off with barbed wire, stood a building with women milling around outside.

Léa found the toilets, four stalls in a stinking wooden building behind the cabins, and waited in line until it was her turn. The stench in the stall made her retch. It was a simple hole in the ground, no plumbing. If the men also had only four toilets, that meant just eight latrines for so many people. They must know that this was insufficient.

At the front gate, people were waiting in line to speak with the guards. An older woman complained that the soup was too watery, and her daughter, six months pregnant, needed protein. A man asked for a pair of shoes because his had been stolen overnight. The guard shrugged and waved them off. Finally, it was Léa's turn. Straightening her shoulders, she advanced to the desk.

"I arrived last night and was assigned to cabin F, but it's full. Please, will you assign me to a bed in another cabin?"

"Cabin F?" He rubbed his chin, taking a ledger from the shelf. His index finger ran down the page until it came to a sudden stop, and the gendarme made a grunting sound. "Cabin M," he said, looking over the ledger to meet her eyes, "has become vacant overnight." He dipped his pen in ink. "Your name?"

"Léa Cotillard." She stood.

"Mademoiselle Cotillard." He snapped the book shut. "The food rations are slim, clothing is insufficient, especially in winter. And there's no point in complaining about anything." He cleared his throat, a lewd glint in his eyes. "But if you need special assistance, perhaps we could come to an understanding."

Léa blinked, fighting to keep the disgust from her face. She understood what he was intimating—and a surge of defiance made her want to tell him she wouldn't be coming back for anything. But she needed that bed, so she swallowed her pride and let it go.

As Léa approached the cabin, she saw a small group of women gathered outside, some of them crying.

"What's wrong?" Léa asked.

A woman, bone-thin, pointed at the stairs. Léa turned to see two guards carrying a stretcher with a body covered by a blanket.

"Poor Simone," the woman sobbed. "I thought she was tired and decided to let her sleep in, but when I came back with some bread from breakfast—" she sucked in a breath "—her body was cold and stiff. She died in the night."

"I'm sorry. Had she been ill for a while?"

"Ill?" The woman scowled. "It's been two months since we've had meat. The men are served meat every Sunday because they work outside the camp." She bowed her head. "Simone was twenty-two." The woman wiped a tear from her face. "It wasn't illness that killed her." Raising her shoulders and lifting her head, she seemed to arrive at a realization. "They'll kill us all."

Léa felt sick. Revulsion mingled with guilt as she instinctively stepped back, trying to separate herself from the grieving woman and the reality before her. Had Simone paid the price for not taking the gendarme up on his offer? Léa struggled with the thought of taking the poor woman's bed. It felt deeply wrong. Maître Mallon had said that war hardens people. Léa wondered if she needed to do the same, forcing herself to focus on what she needed tonight, not on who had slept in the bed before.

"Léa?" She turned to see Edith approaching, calling her name.

"Yes?"

"You're wanted at the gate."

She had a sinking feeling. "Tell the gendarme I won't go."

"But—"

"I went this morning, like you said and was assigned the bed of a woman who died in the night. The gendarme wants to see my reaction. I won't give—"

"You have visitors," she said. "It's not normally permitted, but your sister—"

"Rose?"

Léa sprinted toward the gate, her knee aching, but she didn't care. Bursting into the office, breathless, she called out, "Rose."

Her sister rushed forward, arms outstretched, and they embraced. For an instant, everything felt right.

A hand yanked her away. "No touching," a gendarme barked. "You may speak but not touch." He gestured to a table in the corner. "Ten minutes."

At Rose's side stood Maître Mallon. Shame, like a dark cloud, fell over Léa. "Maître Mallon, I'm sorry, I—"

"There's nothing to be sorry about. Rose came to ask for my help. Nothing else needs to be said." He gestured to the table, and they settled around it.

Rose crossed her legs, her gaze on the two officers rifling through her bag. "I brought you a few things," she said, a slight tremble in her voice. "Maybe it's not allowed."

It was almost as if they'd switched places. Rose had become the elder sister, bringing Maître Mallon to help Léa. She knew it couldn't be easy for Rose, who avoided conflict and tense situations, preferring to be alone with her sketchbooks. Though Léa loved Rose for trying, she knew there was nothing Maître Mallon or anyone could do to get her out of here.

"Thank you both for coming," Léa said, trying to put on a brave face.

"How are you holding up?" Maître Mallon asked.

Thinking of last night's struggle to find a bed and the young woman's body on the stretcher this morning, Léa tried to hold herself together. She hoped Rose wouldn't see the strain on her face. Wanting to lessen their worry, she chose her words with care. "The camp is complicated. There aren't enough beds or food. I don't know why they put me here."

"Maître Mallon knows," Rose blurted out, rubbing her hands on her thighs.

Lacing his fingers into a tight ball, Maître Mallon leaned forward. "After Rose came to me," he said, "I went early this morning to police headquarters. Your case is already closed. The black marketeer, in return for lenient treatment, pointed you out from the photo in your identification papers as the woman who helped him smuggle wine." He took a breath. "I'm sorry to inform you that Édouard LeBlanc was executed following a conviction by a German military tribunal. Weinführer Brucker recommended the Jargeau camp as a suitable place for you to serve out your sentence."

"Édouard's dead?" Léa bent forward, straining to breathe. Was it her fault? She looked at Rose. "Because of the smuggling?"

"They said he was working with the Resistance," Rose added.

Léa felt cold and numb inside. "He deserved a trial, a chance to defend himself. Poor Virginie and Paulette—tell them I'm so sorry."

"They're suffering terribly but they're also strong." Rose reached across the table and took her sister's hand. "And you need to be too."

"You said my sentence has already been decided."

Maître Mallon glanced at Rose, then turned back to Léa. "A year."

It suddenly felt as if all the air had been yanked from her lungs. But what had she expected? They'd murdered Édouard. Maybe she was lucky to get one year. She thought of Simone, the woman in cabin M, who hadn't survived six months. Could Léa endure a year? She pressed the heel of her hands against her eyes. *Don't cry. Never cry.* She'd said those words when her mother died. *Don't let Rose see you cry*. She drew a long breath, letting it settle, giving her time to put on the mask she always wore as a shield for both of them. She lowered her hands.

"I see," Léa said, her voice tight.

Rose fidgeted in the metal chair. "Maître Mallon has a proposition for you."

"There's a place you can go," he said. "It might be better than here. Not perfect."

Léa leaned forward. "Where?"

"A place where you'd be paid to work."

"A prison in another town?" Léa stared hard at him, trying to figure out why he was being evasive.

"Not a prison, but in another country. The German Employment Office in Orléans is actively recruiting women with criminal convictions to work in German factories."

Léa bristled. "No—"

"The conditions are—"

"I'd be working for the enemy!" She couldn't fathom betraying her country.

"Germany needs labor to run their factories," Maître Mallon said in the official, calm notarial voice that she'd always found reassuring, until now. "You will have a contract, be given food, medical care, a salary, a pension, and your criminal conviction will be wiped from the record."

"No, no, no. I've never worked for the Germans, and I won't start now." She folded her arms and looked at Rose, who stared back with confusion in her eyes.

"You don't have to do anything you don't want to," Rose said softly, her voice trembling.

"Think about it," Maître Mallon said. "The employment conditions are bad in France. The money men and women working in Germany send back is what keeps their families alive."

"But it keeps the war running too!" Rose burst out.

Maître Mallon had said from the beginning that she needed to harden herself and do what was right for Rose. Was he telling her now that going to Germany was the right thing for Rose? She couldn't make sense of it. And yet, if she went to Germany maybe she could provide for herself and Rose. The idea twisted inside her. Maître Mallon was a good man who'd tried to help others, even as he'd lost everything. Six months ago, his eyes shone bright, and he'd worn a well-tailored suit with a crisp white shirt and sharply starched collar. Now, she barely recognized him—his eyes were dull, his hair had thinned, hanging like threads around his face. Even his shirt was gray and creased.

"It's the politicians who fuel this war," he said, voice hard. "Pétain and Laval send our young men there instead of putting them in uniforms, but no one calls them traitors." He took a breath. "You're the one stuck in the crossfire—so you must choose what's right for you. And for your sister."

Simone's dead body being carried out of the hut flashed in her mind. Was he warning her that she and Rose might share a similar fate if she didn't find a way out?

He sighed, looking her in the eye. "Your sister said you risked yourself to help the winemaker's family. That's who you are. That's what will never change. Your heart is good, no matter where you end up."

Maman's words came to her: *keep a good heart*. It was all she could control. As long as she kept it as her true north, where she was sent didn't matter. She'd carry it.

"Maybe you're right," Léa said quietly.

Rose leaned forward, her eyes shining with sudden apprehension. "But you have to do it only if it's your decision. Don't do it because of me. I couldn't bear it if something happened to you over there, and it was all my fault." She glanced at Maître Mallon. "We don't know what life will be like over there."

He nodded, understanding. But Léa's mind was turning over. It was a difficult decision to make, and though she knew Rose now had misgivings out of concern for her, she must think with her head, not her heart.

"Believe me," Léa said, "if I stay in here, I know something terrible will happen to me." She shook her head. "War is about money and power in the hands of men. They don't care about us." She looked down at her hands, wishing the choice, the world and her country were different.

"Léa's right," Maître Mallon said. "I've lost everything for my principles. Now, I can't help anyone, not even myself. Principles don't feed you, and if you're not strong, you can't help others."

"Would you do it differently knowing what you know now?" Léa asked.

"In my profession, we swear an oath to uphold the laws of the state. What do you do when the state is wrong, seizing the assets of the innocent? I chose not to uphold the laws because I didn't want to hurt those families. But in doing so, I wasn't able to help them get their property back or prevent them from being sent out of the country." He shrugged. "I don't know if it was worth it. But your situation is different. You won't hurt anyone by working in Germany. You'll be sent under a legal contract for a year, and then you'll return."

"But she'll be helping the enemy," Rose said.

"Your sister will find a way to make up for it." He smiled. "Good always cancels out the bad."

Léa's chest tightened. She couldn't believe her future hinged on a choice like this.

"Does she have to decide now?" Rose asked.

"We'll need to act quickly. Germany will not want to accept a worker who has been in an internment camp for weeks or months. Your ability to negotiate for a better position is stronger now than it will be in a few weeks . . ."

Léa knew why he'd cut off what he intended to say—when she'd be weaker.

"Decide now before the chance passes," he stressed.

"Time's up," the gendarme said.

Maître Mallon stood. "We'll come back in a few days."

"I wish I had not returned in that tunnel, but stayed with you . . ." Rose's voice cracked a little. "Then we'd have been arrested together; we'd be in the camp together. We could help one another like we always do."

"Well, I'm glad you're not in the camp with me," said Léa. If she had done anything right, it was keeping Rose out of here. "Tell Virginie I'm so very sorry about Édouard, Rose, and give Paulette a big hug from me. I love you." She blew a kiss with her hand.

"I love you, too," Rose said.

As Léa watched two of the people who meant the most to her in the world leave, she felt torn between survival and loyalty. Her head told her that the only way to endure now was to cross a line she never thought she would. It didn't matter that notaries, government officials and the women in the boardinghouse working in German armaments factories were collaborating—they would say they had no choice and did it for France. But what would they say about Léa moving to Germany?

It would be a mark on her forever. She didn't know what to do. Her mother's voice came to her: *let it sit with you, and time will sort it out*. At least Léa could look forward to seeing Rose again soon—and that gave her hope.

13

Léa

Léa paced the camp, walking along the edge of the barbed-wire fence. She couldn't stop thinking about Rose and what would happen to her if she remained here. Now that poor Édouard was gone, Virginie would struggle to hold on to the winery. She might not be able to manage it on her own and Rose would have to find another place to live. Rose could always return to her job cleaning the school in the mornings, but the pay wouldn't be enough to cover a room in one of the cheaper boardinghouses. The only way to support Rose was to go to Germany, though it meant Rose would lose her sister, as well as having lost André, the man she was in love with.

Kicking pebbles, she struggled with the choices ahead.

"Just arrived?"

Léa turned. Behind the barbed wire stood a woman with sunken blue eyes. "It's the second time you've gone past this way," she said.

Behind her, a group of women sat on the steps of a barracks smoking and watching Léa.

"Yesterday," she said.

"Oh, that's why you're walking in circles." The woman laughed.

"Maybe," Léa couldn't help but smile. "And you?"

"A week." She looked beyond Léa, straining to see farther. "What's it like on your side?"

Léa shrugged. "Too many people, too few cabins. Not enough toilets. Cold nights." She shifted her feet, stirring dust in the rocky dirt.

"Same as here." She hugged her waist. "That's why I'm getting out."

"They're letting you out?" Léa's voice caught.

The woman looked up, her gaze drifting after a black bird slicing across the sky. Sunlight glared down and she made a visor with her hand. "A recruitment man came by. Wants us to work in Germany. Volunteers, he says. Did he come over on your side, too?"

"No clue." Léa nudged a pebble with her foot. It was true what Maître Mallon had said about recruiting women with criminal records.

"There's a one-thousand-franc bonus on departure." She rubbed one eye. "Says he'll send half my first month's money up front to my mother."

Léa angled her body away from the fence, wanting to keep walking.

"I need that money for my little boy, Raphael."

"You have a boy? How old?" Léa said, turning back to the woman.

"Three."

"Only three. It must be hard to be away from him?"

She nodded, her expression tense. "I'm not like the others." She glanced at the women on the steps. "After I had Raphael, I lost my job. His father is a POW in Germany."

"That must have been hard. What's your name?"

"Juliette. And you?"

"Léa." She paused. "Does your mother care for Raphael while you're here?"

"Yes, but she has no money. Papa walked out on her before the war." As Juliette spoke, Léa stared through the barbs in the fence—tiny metal crosses tilted sideways like mines sticking up in the air. "In Germany, I'll be paid to work. I'll be doing something I won't be ashamed of . . ." Her mouth tightened. "Using my brain and not my body." She looked at Léa, desperation in her eyes. "Do you understand?"

"Yes." Léa had heard that prostitutes were kept in a separate part of the Jargeau camp. She shuddered to think of the poor woman's choices: earn money as a prostitute in France or work in Germany. A bitter taste welled in her mouth. She would do the same for Rose.

"Even if they let me out in six months . . ." Her face changed. "There's nothing here for me. I don't want to be like them." She edged away from the barracks toward the fence. "Just so my baby can survive."

"How long will you be gone?"

"A year," she said, exhaling. "It's not too long, *n'est-ce pas*?"

"No." The little boy would be four. She was missing Raphael's first years.

"After the recruiter explained, I just blurted out *yes*. Now, it's sinking in." A shadow passed over Juliette's face. She twisted the edge of her blouse between her fingers. "Do you think I made the right choice?"

All Léa knew was that Juliette had made her choice for the right reason. Wasn't that the most important? "Yes," she said, "you're not hurting anyone but helping Raphael and your mother."

"That's what I think." Juliette smiled. "Thank you."

"Juliette, come back inside," a woman on the stairs called out. "It's cold, you'll get sick."

Léa watched the women stamp their cigarettes under their shoes, then tuck them into their pockets for later.

"I've got to go," Juliette said.

Léa didn't want her to leave. "When will you go?"

"Tomorrow." She stepped back from the fence. "Goodbye, Léa."

"Goodbye, Juliette. Good luck."

Léa walked. Something inside her galvanized. The last thing she wanted was for Rose to end up in a desperate situation, the way Juliette had. Alone. Without André or Léa. Her chest tightened at the frightening thought that Rose, left with no other choice, might fall into prostitution.

The farther she walked, the more her resolve hardened. Maître Mallon was right. Working in Germany—no matter the cost—would at least give her the means to keep herself and Rose safe. One year. She could endure it for her sister.

* * *

With each passing day, Léa's determination grew stronger. Seeing the terrible conditions in the camp and the bad luck that brought so many here, she realized that working in Germany was her only way through the war.

A few days later, she stood at the gate, tightening the collar of her coat against the biting cold morning, hoping that today Rose and Maître Mallon would return. She looked out at the thick chalk-gray fog, feeling the dampness seep through her clothes. She could only see what was in front of her because a gray haze muffled the distant shapes, making everything feel faraway and uncertain. Now that Léa had decided, each day that Rose didn't know felt awkward and strange, as if time had been suspended and wouldn't resume until they were reunited about the way forward.

The guards gave her sideways glances, making her uneasy. When the bell rang for lunch, Léa—concerned she might miss Rose—didn't want to leave the gate. But unable to ignore her growling stomach, she trudged to the canteen for the watery soup, her mother's voice reminding her she would need it to keep up her strength.

Returning to the gate, she continued to wait. The morning fog had now lifted, but there was still no sign of Rose. As the church bells rang the hour and the afternoon advanced, she paced, hands behind her back, doubts and worries swirling inside her. Had Rose stumbled into trouble, like at the boardinghouse?

"Léa," a man's voice called out.

She spotted Maître Mallon pushing two bicycles—one on either side of him—up the hill leading to the camp. Léa stretched up on her toes, looking for her sister. No Rose.

Maître Mallon leaned the two bicycles against a bench. He showed the gendarme some papers. Léa expected Rose to crest the hill at any moment. Then the gendarme motioned for her to go inside the office. She sat at the table across from Maître Mallon.

"Léa, we don't have much time," Maître Mallon said urgently, "there's something I need to—"

"Where's Rose?"

"Don't worry. Rose is waiting for you at the station." He lifted a file from his leather satchel. "She helped me organize your release. If you're willing. We took the liberty—"

"She agrees that I should go?" Léa leaned forward.

He nodded. "If that is what you want."

"Yes, it is," Léa said, relief flooding through her. What she dreaded most was that Rose wouldn't want her to go and they'd argue and part on bad terms.

"All you have to do is sign these papers, agreeing to the conditions in the contract, and then we'll go to Rose." He raised his hand to his face, wiping beads of sweat from his forehead. It wasn't like Maître Mallon to perspire, not in this cold. "There's been a slight change," he said. "I want you to understand completely before you sign."

She waited.

"The duration of the contract is no longer a year." He touched his collar. "It's until the war ends."

"How long could that be?" she asked.

"We don't know. You mustn't feel compelled—"

"What does Rose think?" Léa wanted to speak to her sister, get her advice.

"She says it's up to you and whatever you do, she'll support it."

"Is that what she said?" He nodded. Léa hesitated. "I need more time to think—"

He checked his watch. "The train leaves in three hours."

"For Germany?"

"Yes." He put the pen on the table and slid the paper over to her. "Read the contract. Ask any question, and I'll do my best to answer. Rose waits for you at the station—she went to pack a suitcase with your things."

She wished Rose was here so she could look into her sister's eyes and know it was the right decision. But in her heart, Léa felt she had no other choice. She flipped to the last page and scratched her signature above the line where her name had been typed.

"You must read it in full. Your future depends—"

"If you believe I should go, I trust you."

"Initial the bottom right corner of each page, confirming you've read and understood." He cleared his throat. "Léa, if you need to reconsider—"

"You said we didn't have much time." She initialed the pages, then handed him the pen. "Let's go to Rose. I have to see her to say goodbye before I leave."

Standing, he showed the contract to the gendarme. More papers appeared for them to sign.

"Now, we can go," Maître Mallon said, returning to the table after conversing with the gendarme. Maître Mallon glanced at his watch. "If we hurry, you'll make the train."

A slight panic at the back of her throat. "Rose is at the station?" She couldn't leave without saying goodbye to her.

"Yes."

She followed him out the door to the bicycles. He mounted one and gestured for her to take the other, and they pedaled side by side on the towpath along the Loire. The ride to Orléans took three quarters of an hour. They parked their bicycles at number 1 Rue Royale, where the German Employment Office was housed.

Slightly out of breath, she followed him up the stairs to the second floor. The interior surprised her with its grandeur. A chandelier suspended from the ceiling cast delicate light. Below it, a white and black marble fireplace anchored the room, its mantelpiece adorned with a gold-framed mirror. Wooden panels lined the lower walls; tapestry covered the upper.

"Have you made the arrangements I asked for?" Maître Mallon asked, arms tight at his sides.

"The upfront advance has been paid to Madame Virginie LeBlanc, as requested. And we've found a suitable factory outside of a big city," the man behind the desk replied. He turned to Léa and asked, "Madame Cotillard, do you have any questions?"

"No," she said quietly, wondering why the money wasn't going to Rose.

"Very good." He stamped the papers and returned them to Maître Mallon. "One of my men requested a visit to see a sick family member in Berlin, so I've arranged for him to act as an escort to Paris, then on to Germany. All the tickets are in the envelope." He tapped a metal bell on his desk. A man in uniform opened a side door and saluted the man at the desk.

Maître Mallon placed a hand at the edge of Léa's elbow as if to reassure her. "Rose wanted the money to go to Virginie. She'll explain it all to you at the station."

The man at the desk stood. "We'll take over from here." He signaled to the soldier to escort Léa out the door.

Léa had the strange sense of the walls closing in on her and her legs went weak. Maître Mallon kissed her on both cheeks.

"You'll do fine," he said, seeming to sense her doubt. "I have full confidence in you. I've arranged everything as well as possible. Rose will tell you more at the station. Goodbye, Léa, and be strong for you and Rose."

She just barely managed to utter a goodbye before the German soldier escorted her down the stairs and outside to a waiting car. Only after she was in the back seat and the door closed did she think to ask what he meant by having arranged everything for the best. She pushed away her doubts. There was no turning back. She had signed the papers, committed herself, and—with a sudden clarity—she realized that this decision would define the rest of her life.

They arrived at the station in less than ten minutes. At the platform, she fumbled with the tickets inside the envelope—there were so many different trains to take—until she finally found the ticket for Paris and handed it to the police officer checking documents.

But where was Rose?

"Papers, mademoiselle," he said.

She passed him her identification card along with the letter from the German Employment Office. She glanced up, scanning the station, searching for her sister. The officer returned the documents and, with his hand, signaled to her to continue through the gate.

The sky was low and overcast. As Léa plunged her hands into her pockets to warm them, Rose came hurrying alongside her and the German soldier.

"Rose!" Léa felt almost heady with relief as they embraced. Léa pulled back first.

"I worried I wouldn't see you before I left," she said. "How did you get on the platform without a ticket?"

"Léa, I—"

A piercing screech stole Rose's words as the train arrived. People surged forth to board it.

"Why did the man at the German Employment Office say that my signing bonus was given to Virginie? I want it to go to you."

Rose took Léa by the arm and guided her quickly to the carriage matching the number on her ticket, the German escort still close behind. Rose carried their mother's brown suitcase, bumping it against her leg as they walked. Léa noticed for the first time that Rose had slung the leather satchel containing her pencils and sketchbooks across her shoulder.

"Go on," Rose said. "Up the stairs. I'll follow with the suitcase."

"I can carry it." Léa reached for the case, but Rose held it back waiting for her to board first.

When Rose joined her in the carriage, Léa imagined her sister was lingering because she found it difficult to say goodbye. She wanted to talk to her about serious matters and let her know it might be years before they saw one another again.

"Do you know that the contract is now for an indefinite period?" Léa said.

"Yes. It's all right." Rose gave her a small smile. "We're going to be fine."

"Promise me that you'll stay with Virginie and Paulette, no matter what happens."

"Here's the row," Rose said, checking Léa's ticket. "Your seat is next to the window. I'm on the aisle."

"Your— What are you talking about?"

Rose squared her shoulders. "I'm coming with you."

A whistle blew. Léa's heart knotted. What was happening? "Rose, get off the train."

"I won't. It's not fair that I should be free while you're not."

"Rose, you're wrong. I'll be fine. Please get off." Léa caught the German soldier's gaze on her and realized she was shouting.

"I've signed the contract. I'm as committed as you are." Rose said. "Nothing you can do now."

Léa could see it in front of her like the pieces of a puzzle coming together. Rose had been away these last days because she'd been completing the forms for the official at the German Employment Office, instructing him to allocate their signing bonuses to Virginie. That was why Maître Mallon wouldn't allow her to think it over for one more night, because Rose would have gone on to Germany on her own. Why hadn't he said anything?

The train jerked backward, then forward.

"Tell them you've changed your mind," Léa said. "Quickly, please. Just do it for me— go on, Rose. Please."

"You're all I have in this world. I couldn't face you leaving for Germany on your own. I helped you smuggle the wine. I should have been arrested with you. We're in this together." Despite the tears running down both their faces, Léa could see that Rose was adamant.

As the train picked up speed, Léa clutched the top of the seat to steady herself. Passengers waved from the platform, where Rose should be now, waving goodbye.

"We will look after each other, like always," Rose said.

Léa gritted her teeth, hands balled tight at her sides. How could her sister be so reckless? All she wanted was for Rose to be safe, and now she was accompanying her to Germany.

Léa turned away from her sister and sank into the seat, saying nothing. What had she done?

PART II

November 1942 – December 1944

Glashütte, Germany

14

Rose

Late November 1942

On the train, the knots in Rose's stomach tightened. Fiddling with the edge of her leather satchel, she wondered how long Léa would remain angry. In the crowded passenger carriage, men and women squeezed onto the seats, and the windows steamed up, so there was nothing to see outside. They sat next to one another, and every time Rose tried to start a conversation, Léa ignored her.

"What do you think Paris will be like?" Rose asked, trying again when she could no longer bear the silence.

Léa closed her eyes.

The morning after Léa's arrest, Rose had sought the help of Maître Mallon. She'd gone to the address written in Léa's notebook—on the top floor of an old building in the center of Orléans. Trudging up the rickety stairs, Rose recalled the *boiserie* paneling on the walls of his former office, where Léa had worked all those years, the tall windows that let in buckets of light. This building was nothing like that. The paint was peeling off the walls, the landing on the stairs wobbled, and no concierge checked visitors. Rose, panting by the time she reached the fifth floor, could hardly believe the state of the apartment inside—a single room with a sink in a corner and boxes stacked in every space. She wasn't sure where to sit because there were only boxes. He explained to her that the boxes held all his files and books.

"You must be here on account of Léa." He motioned to a box. "Has something happened?" His brow furrowed. "She was the best typist. Fast. Efficient. Diligent."

As Rose sat down, the cardboard caved inward. A light breeze drifted in through the dormer window, but the roof extended wide over the building, blocking the sun so it appeared to be dusk though it was morning. "Léa was caught smuggling wine and sent to an internment camp."

"Mon Dieu. Where?" His face was pinched.

"In Jargeau."

"When?"

"Last night." Rose should have insisted that Léa run back with her to the tunnel. They could have escaped together, but she'd only thought of herself, leaving Léa alone to face the consequences. She explained how they'd been kicked out of the boardinghouse, had gone to live with the LeBlanc family and, after Monsieur LeBlanc was arrested, smuggled wine for him, and that he'd been executed because of his Resistance work. Desperation rang in her voice as she told him everything, hoping there was a way to save Léa. "Is it possible to get her out?"

"Everything is possible in Occupied France," he said.

That was when he told her about the pressure the Vichy government was under to supply more workers to Germany for the war effort. Rose had seen the posters everywhere, initially encouraging people to sign up to work, then later, announcing that it was mandatory for certain age groups. And André had been sent. She leaned forward, listening intently.

"They go to the camps and prisons recruiting, promising to pay salaries and clear criminal records in return for working in Germany."

"Including women?" Rose was sure that Léa would never do anything to help the Germans win the war.

"Even if our leaders put us on the German side." He sighed. "I don't want to misrepresent what working in Germany would be like. It's an option but also a gamble."

As Rose listened, she traced a finger along the box's edge, trying to line up in her mind all that he was saying.

"There's no guarantee where she'll be sent—a munitions factory in Berlin, a farm in Saxony, a bakery in Hamburg." He rubbed his chin. "If I had some influence or leverage, I could try to persuade the officials at the German Employment Office in Orléans to give her office work away from a city, explain that she'd been an exceptional employee and is an excellent typist." He took a breath. "But I don't have anything to offer them in return for sending her to a small town."

"Why shouldn't she be in a city?"

"Bombing raids. Cities are industrial targets for Allied bombers."

Rose recalled the hours she and Léa had spent in the bunker under the vinegar factory, dust raining down on them as the building swayed from nearby detonations. She'd been sure they were going to die, but they'd survived. "How long would she go for?"

"The contracts provide a period of one year subject to renewal."

She didn't want Léa to go to Germany, but she thought it only right that Maître Mallon present the option to her. And if she agreed, then Rose was determined to go with her. It wasn't fair for Léa to go alone. And the money they earned could be sent back to Virginie, who would need it now that Édouard had been murdered. Whatever terrible things Léa would face over there, Rose wanted to be by her side, together, like they always were. Maybe that could make up for her not being with her on the night Léa was arrested. And alongside that thought, another sat buried deep inside, which—in quiet moments—her mind kept returning to, like an impossible dream—that maybe if she went to Germany, she'd find André.

She missed him. No matter how she tried not to think about André he kept finding his way back into her thoughts. He'd saved her from the wrath of the German soldier, told her she had talent and gave her and Léa a place to go after that awful Madame Martin threw them out. She couldn't forget him. As time passed, she knew she had to do everything in her power to find him. But it must be Léa's decision, and if she chose to go, then Rose wanted to do all she could to help.

"You said if you had more to offer. What do you need?"

"Money. That's all anyone in France cares about."

She thought for a moment. "What about me?"

He shot her a confused look.

"If I agree to go work in Germany, then you'd be offering two workers. Would that give you more leverage so Léa could be sent to a small town?"

"You don't want to do that." He stood. "Your sister's in a camp where the chances of survival are fifty percent. Your situation is different. And I believe she would want you to remain safely here."

Rose didn't want to be safe. Not if it meant being without Léa and André. She couldn't think only of herself like she'd done when Léa had slipped the key into her pocket and told her to run.

Maman had taught her to hold essential things close to her heart so that no one could steal them from her, which is why she made secret wishes to herself—that her mother wouldn't die, that she and Léa would always be together, that she would be reunited with André. She called them her little markers, holding them close. Of course, they didn't always come true, but they were something she could hope for. She wouldn't even tell Léa about them because her sister was too rational and solid, like the keys on the typewriter, to understand something like wishes.

"I don't want Léa to go alone. We've always been together. If she goes, I'm going with her."

"There's no guarantee you'd stay together."

"You said you could negotiate with the German Employment Office on Léa's behalf. Can't you tell them that in addition to Léa, her sister will volunteer to work in Germany?"

His gaze flicked toward the window.

"Two workers must be more valuable than one," she said. "Isn't that leverage?"

"I could make the argument," he said quietly.

"All I ask is that if Léa agrees to go, then keep us together, send us to the same place."

"I'll try." He gave her a tight smile.

"There's one other thing I must ask of you."

"Yes?"

"Once you've come to an agreement with the German Employment Office and know where we're going, I'd like you to write to someone on my behalf."

"Of course."

"He's from Orléans and was sent to Germany a few months ago." Rose handed Maître Mallon a small card with a name written on it. "Unfortunately, I don't have his address in Germany. Would it be possible for you to discover where he's been sent and write to inform him of where I am in Germany?" It was an impossible dream, but Rose had to try. "In case we aren't far from one another, or if there is any chance we could meet."

"André Simon," he read the name aloud. "The German Employment Office will have his file." He thought for a moment. "I can tell them he was a former client, and I have documentation to send to him. I don't see why they wouldn't provide me with the information."

"Thank you, it would mean a lot to me." Rose had done her best to make sure André would find her.

Now, arriving at Gare d'Austerlitz, the first time either sister had been to Paris, they stepped off the train. Rose looked around, her heart swelling with awe at all the platforms stretching like fingers on either side of them. A vast iron and glass dome extended overhead, casting shadows that danced across the hall. Rose's hand practically twitched, wanting to capture the narrow lines of light dotting the ground, the curls of smoke puffing from the trains as they lurched forward and backward, the elegant lamp posts. It was the most beautiful place she'd ever seen, and of course, she thought of the person who must have seen it just as she was seeing it now, for the first time, maybe even standing on the same platform—André. She could almost hear his voice whispering to her about the hallway's geometrical lines and the glass triangle at one end where the trains shunted out into the world.

The German escort who'd accompanied them from Orléans motioned with his hand that they should follow him to the end of the platform. The rush of people drove them forward, and Rose nearly dropped the suitcase. Léa grabbed her hand.

"Come on," she said, pulling her along.

Rose wanted to slow down. It was her first time in Paris, and she tried to take it all in, feel the place, remember the shape of the windows, the light coming through, so she could draw them in her sketchbook.

"Papers?" a police officer demanded at the end of the platform, where a phalanx of officers, checking papers, inquired where people were going.

Léa handed over their papers.

His eyes squinted at the letter she presented from the German Employment Office, confirming the two women would be traveling to Germany on the overnight train. Their German escort spoke to him in German and the officer nodded, saluted, folded the papers, and handed them back to Léa.

"Follow me," the German escort said. "Métro is straight ahead." He handed the sisters pale yellow tickets. "We're going to Gare de l'Est."

"What do I do with it?" Rose asked, staring at the ticket in her hand.

"You give it to the *poinçonneur*," he said, waving a hand at the stairs up ahead.

"What's a *poinçonneur*?" Rose asked.

"Ticket punchers at the entrance of every platform." He explained. "Have you never been on the Métro?"

Léa squeezed Rose's hand, as if warning not to ask too many questions. But Rose couldn't help it. Everything was new and different. Following him, they crossed the hall, footfalls and voices echoing off the glass overhead, hitting the stone walls with a cacophony like thunder. He guided them through the labyrinthine network of doors, passageways and stairs until he motioned to the one they would take to descend into the Métro.

Rose hesitated, unwilling to leave the train station—there was still so much she hadn't seen—but Léa grabbed her hand again and yanked her along.

"You're the one wanting to come to Germany, so keep up." Léa's voice was stern.

There were as many people mounting the stairs as going down and it was chaotic trying to make their way through the crowd. At one point, the guard stopped and grabbed a man who brushed Léa's shoulder, seemingly by accident. He shouted at the man to return whatever he'd taken. Léa's eyes went wide as the man reached into his pocket and pulled out Léa's small silk coin purse with the brass clips, dropping it into Léa's hand and dashing off up the stairs. Rose couldn't believe it.

"Pickpockets," their German escort warned. "Don't let anyone bump you. Understand?"

"Yes," Léa said, nodding. She pushed the coin purse into the front pocket of her dress.

They presented their tickets to the woman in the small metal cabinet at the bottom of the stairs, and she punched two holes in the middle of the yellow paper before returning them. The sisters moved down the tiled narrow platform. The wall, covered in white ceramic tiles, had a large enamel plate in the center that read *Gare d'Austerlitz*, and under it was a long wooden bench where people sat. A train drew into the station, and the passengers on the bench surged forward to the opening doors. Their escort pushed the sisters inside, following after. Then the doors closed, and the train was off.

"How many stops?" Rose asked, clinging to Léa's arm as she tried to steady herself inside the wobbly carriage.

"I don't know." There were no signs, only the train's direction. The windows were ajar, and the air carried the screeching of metal wheels as they sped through the tunnel. The sisters held on to each other. They watched until they saw the enamel sign for *Gare de l'Est*. Obeying a nudge from their escort, they stepped off the carriage onto the platform.

"Stay close," Léa whispered to Rose.

Rose gripped her sister's arm as they took the stairs out of the Métro. This was the central transit station from France to Germany, so German officers patrolled the hallways, checking papers and searching bags. The officers' rapid, deliberate movements, like gunfire, frightened Rose. She squeezed Léa's hand, wondering if her sister felt the same. Léa turned and nodded—the first positive sign Rose had got from her sister since telling her she was going to Germany. Rose wanted to hug her and leaned forward, but Léa shook her head.

"No," she said. "I haven't forgiven you—" she smiled "—yet."

As they made their way along a massive hall, Rose suddenly stopped and let go of Léa's hand, stunned by what was in front of her. A painting hung above the enormous entrance leading to the platforms. It depicted a train carriage full of soldiers in uniform, and on the platform, distraught family members saying goodbye. Rose had never seen anything like it. She was struck by the muted colors, especially the blues shifting between a river's darkness and the light of a summer sky. All the colors—green, pink, burgundy, brown, gray—shared a similar faintness as if the life had been washed out of every person and object.

But what drew her attention the most was the despondent expression on the faces of the women, children, and older men on the platform. Each bidding farewell as though they had no hope of seeing their loved ones again. Her gaze shifted to the far right corner of the painting, where a man held the tricolor French flag, partially obscured by his body.

She moved closer, squinting to read the painter's signature: *Albert Herter, 1926.*

Léa yanked her arm. "Come on."

In the distance, their German escort signaled impatiently with a wave of his hand, a severe look on his face. Glancing back at Herter's painting, Rose felt a sudden foreboding.

Tears pinched her eyes as she turned to Léa. But her sister was staring at their escort, tugging Rose's sleeve.

"Hurry up," Léa said. "Can't you see he's getting cross?"

Rose didn't want to leave without one more look so that she would remember the painting always. Letting go of her sister's hand, she took a few steps back. She let her gaze glide from the parents watching as their son said goodbye to his wife, holding their child in his arms, to an older man at the other end of the track, a bouquet in his hand, pointing to the ground. The painter must have been evoking the Great War and the fate of millions of men going east to fight the Germans. The irony of it all happening again.

"Rose," Léa shouted, "the train is going to leave."

Rose hurried over to Léa, her hand trembling as she gave her identity papers to a French police officer.

"Quickly," the officer said. "Your train is on platform twelve and departs in six minutes." He returned their tickets and papers. "If you miss it, you'll have to sleep on the platform until the next train in the morning." He waved them forward as more passengers pressed to board. Cupping his hands, he called, "Berlin train, platform twelve, five minutes to depart."

"Come on, Rose," Léa said, gently pulling her sister toward the train that would take them far from France.

Rose followed, though part of her was still with the painting in the hall. She remembered the book that Virginie had shown her, where she'd seen similar muted blues and browns in the paintings of the Old Masters. Had Herter chosen blue as a warning to dissuade those going to war against a neighbor again? She wrapped her arms around her waist, haunted by all those lives lost, sacrificed, families torn apart, futures shattered by war.

As she placed a foot on the train's metal stairs, she was sure she could hear the painter whispering a melancholy warning. Like the million-plus Frenchmen who didn't return from Germany after the Great War, would the same fate befall the sisters?

15

Léa

Léa put the contract on her lap and looked out the window as the train rattled to a stop. A sign on the platform said *Metz.*

The station's massive fortress-like façade loomed over the platform, casting sharp shadows that seemed to swallow the sunlight. Léa remembered the day all the typists in Maître Mallon's office gathered around a newspaper reading the headlines that announced Germany had annexed Metz and other cities on the eastern part of France. From all the German language signs and the red and black banners adorned with swastikas, Léa could see that the Germans had done their best to stamp out all forms of French life.

"Where are we?" Rose awakened, rubbing her eyes.

"We're in Germany," Léa said, glancing at the guard who'd accompanied them from Orléans. He sat at the far end of the carriage—uniform immaculate, posture rigid—he kept his eyes coldly on them. "I know where we're going," she said, pointing at the contract in her lap.

Rose sat upright. "Tell me."

"Our employment contract is with the Archimedes Company."

"Arc-chi-me-what?" Rose yawned.

Léa repeated the name. "They make calculating machines."

Rose's face went blank. "What's a calculating machine?"

"Maybe it's like a typewriter for numbers," Léa said.

Rose leaned forward, but Léa could see she was more interested in the scenery outside than in calculating machines or the terms of their contract.

"How can this be a train station?" she asked. "It feels like a church. Look at the clock tower." She pulled out her notepad and began sketching the outlines of the massive clock tower above the station. Léa noted a German soldier making his way along the aisle, checking tickets. She lifted theirs from her bag, ready to show him.

"Is this Archimedes Company in Berlin?" Rose asked, her hand moving swiftly over the paper. "Maître Mallon arranged that we shouldn't be in a big city. Where are we going?"

"Not Berlin. Let me check . . . it's in a town called Glashütte—"

"*Ausweispapiere und Zugtickets, bitte*," the German soldier said.

Léa presented their tickets and papers. He studied them, then looked at Rose.

"*Nein, nicht erlaubt*," he said, wagging a stout finger at her.

"What's wrong?" Léa asked. Then she remembered what had happened to Rose on the quai and told her to put down her pencil. "You're not allowed to draw."

"*Französisch sprechen ist hier verboten*," he said, turning back to Léa.

"*Ja*," Léa said, nodding her head in agreement.

The soldier's gaze fixed on Rose before he returned the documents to Léa and moved on.

"What else did he say?"

"Hush," Léa whispered to Rose. Léa then took Rose's pencil from her hand and, using the back of the sketchpad, wrote in small letters: *Speaking French is forbidden.*

"*Ja*," Rose said, turning to the window. The sisters sat in silence, staring at the strange, unfamiliar world outside.

Rose put a finger to the glass, drawing Léa's attention to a large poster fixed to the station wall. It depicted a German soldier in solid black, his steel helmet low over his forehead. Mouth closed, he held an index finger to his lips, a gesture that seemed to carry a silent threat. Below him, in bold, she saw three German words: *Spione, Verräter, Saboteure.* Though she could guess the first and third words, the one in the middle was utterly foreign. She looked at Léa, who wrote: Beware of Spies, Traitors, and Saboteurs.

As the train pulled out of the station, Léa wrote another message on the back of Rose's sketchbook. *Now we're the foreigners. Like we didn't trust them in Orléans, they don't trust us here.* Rose read it, nodded and pressed closer to the window in silent acknowledgment of this new world.

Both sisters, faces pressed close to the glass, watched with a mix of curiosity and apprehension as the train sped deeper into Germany.

* * *

Ten hours later, they heard the screeching and grinding of the train's wheels as it pulled into Berlin. The German escort hustled them between platforms, giving them no time to take in the station before boarding another train out of the capital. Léa read the name on the ticket: *Dresden.* Was Dresden north, east or south? The sisters sat in silence, their German escort at their side. After their reprimand in Metz, they didn't dare speak French aloud.

Disembarking at the massive Dresden-Neustadt station, Léa and Rose clung to one another as they followed their escort off the platform and entered the station's grand central foyer with large arched windows, columns and skylights. Rose, in awe, looked at the walls and ceilings adorned with coats of arms and decorative paintings. They passed many soldiers with bandages on their heads or arms, and some using crutches to help them walk. In corners of the grand hall, tents had been set up as sick bays.

The rumble of voices, the clacking of heels and the screeching wheels stormed up to the dome and echoed off the limestone walls. Disoriented, the sisters hurried after their escort to another platform, where a smaller local train waited.

They disembarked after a few stops and found themselves at a station called Heidenau. Another platform change, and they were on yet another train, this one crept along a river and through a valley with forests and small towns. When the train rattled to a stop, the doors opened onto a single-track station. Their escort guided them outside, where a bone-chilling wind greeted them. The sisters huddled together, trying to stay warm.

"Have we finally arrived?" Rose whispered.

"Yes," Léa said, recognizing the name printed on the platform sign—*Glashütte*—as the same one in their employment contract. A sense of relief washed over her. "We're here."

Their German escort raised his hands, indicating that the sisters should wait outside as he went into the station. It was very cold and damp. Léa put the suitcase down and blew on her hands to warm them. They were in a small valley with steep forested hills rising on either side. A fine mist clung to the conifers, black boulders breaking the orderly line as they rose out of the ground. She could hear water swirling, and guessed that the river the train had followed all the way from Dresden wasn't far off.

She had never seen a town built at the base of a valley. There was no opening through which the eyes could roam, just razor-edged hills blocking one's vision as if someone had come along and cut a knife down the middle of the mountain, trapping the town in the middle.

Their German escort emerged from the station, signaling for the sisters to follow. They walked on a street and entered a building across from the station where a crowd of men and women sat on benches, waiting. The guard instructed them to join these people while he deposited their papers at a desk manned by both uniformed officers and civilians. Then, he left.

Mostly they heard German, though some of the women sitting around them whispered in what Léa guessed might be Italian or Dutch, plus a swirling mix of unfamiliar languages, carrying both light, melodic and hard, guttural ones. The sisters didn't speak. They were so overwhelmed by the hundred or so people waiting with them, some asleep on the benches, others nervously looking around.

"*Schwestern* Cotillard," a stout woman called out from behind the desk.

The sisters stood, Rose clutching the suitcase, and approached the desk.

"I'm Lagerführer Klein, the overseer for your residence camp in Glashütte," she said in a hard, clipped French accent from Alsace. Like Metz, it had been annexed to Germany. "Your resident registration cards must be completed first." She raised her right hand, like a schoolteacher, extending thumb, first and second fingers, enumerating what this entailed. "Fingerprints. Photographs. Medical exams."

She led the sisters into a large room, divided into separate areas by three tables in front of which lines of women waited. At least it was warm inside.

"Join this line," she ordered.

As the sisters stood behind two other women, Léa glanced around and, with a gasp, elbowed Rose.

"What?" Rose whispered.

"Look at the table at the far end."

Rose turned. She raised her hand to cover her mouth. "Oh, please no."

Lagerführer Klein overheard her. "Body examinations are only for the *Untermenschen*."

Léa's knees wobbled, and she gripped Rose's arm to hold herself steady. Those poor naked women had been forced to line up before men, who shaved their heads and private parts, then lathered a cream on raw skin that visibly made the women wince with pain. It was an image seared in her mind, feeling their distress and humiliation as if the same was being done to her.

"*Untermenschen*?" Rose asked, confused.

"*Indésirables*," Lagerführer Klein said. "Poles and Russians. They're dirty, disease-ridden swine." She crossed her arms at her chest. "We keep them separate from the general population. It's forbidden for other workers to mix with them. Understand?"

"*Ja*." Rose swallowed, looking away.

All sorts of thoughts jangled inside Léa's head but it came down to one—hatred was the fuel running the engine of war—and she could see it here in operation, like some well-written play where everyone had a role to follow to reinforce the script.

Hatred wasn't natural. It had to be diffused, institutionalized, enforced: hatred for how people look, the language they speak, the country they come from, the religion they worship. Now that Léa saw the truth, with such clarity, she couldn't look away; it had lodged itself deep inside her.

And she knew that somehow she must fight this hatred with everything she had, and even if it only changed the life of one person, it would be worth it. It was what every person should do; it seemed so simple and clear, like a musical note ringing true. And yet, somehow it wasn't true here, where hatred was the hardest thing of all to conquer.

Lagerführer Klein motioned for her to move forward to the table.

Léa pressed her thumb on the ink pot and then on the empty square printed on the small gray card. She rolled it from left to right, as the man showed her, then did the same for her index finger. As she moved to the table for her photograph, her gaze fell once more on the women being shaved, and her resolve deepened. All the while, she sensed the watchful, persistent gaze of Lagerführer Klein on her.

Rose followed. As Léa watched her sister, she realized that this fight would take cunning and preparation, because her opponents were everywhere, waiting to take out anyone who spoke up. She would have to bide her time and come to know this new world before she could figure out how to fight it.

After they left the room and waited outside in the cold for their *Arbeitsbuch für Ausländer*—the foreigners' permit to reside and work in Germany—to be delivered, she vowed to help those poor women who had their dignity and rights stripped from them so that the men in power could run the engine of their war.

"Here," Lagerführer Klein said, handing them their *Arbeitsbuch* cards a short while later. "Carry them on you always. You'll need to show it to the guard for permission to enter the factory, or to use your meal coupons and purchase any items in shops with ration cards. Do not lose them."

The sisters nodded.

"I will now take you to the camp."

Léa breathed in the air, grateful to be away from what she'd seen inside. They walked along a stream, which must be a tributary from the river the train had followed because it was narrower and shallow enough that the pale brown stones under the water reflected the muted afternoon light. A gray sky and metallic smell hung in the air. Clouds rose from the factory furnaces, churning out rings of black smoke.

At last, they passed through a wrought-iron gate into a large compound, where a building was surrounded by tall evergreen trees. A man emerged from a guardhouse near the gate and conversed with Lagerführer Klein, who instructed the sisters to show him their work cards. He wrote their names down in a large book. Then, they proceeded to the building set back from the gate.

"Is this where we're going to live?" Rose whispered, pointing at the massive gray brick structure looming over the compound.

"Yes," Lagerführer Klein said. "Before the war, it was a factory. It's now been converted into a dormitory for foreign workers."

A group of women came down the stairs. Léa noticed they all seemed to be wearing a patch sewn onto the upper right side of their aprons—a yellow square with a purple border and in the middle of the square, a large purple P.

Lagerführer Klein stopped halfway up the stairs, her mouth pinching, as the three women descended. "Halt," she ordered, pointing a finger at one of the women, who seemed the youngest of the group. "*Komm*," she commanded in German.

The woman stepped forward slowly, knees bent low to the ground like a dog approaching a perceived threat.

"Look at the patch on your apron!" the Lagerführer said. "The stitching on it has come undone, and one corner is loose. How can anyone read it?" Then, like a flash of lightning, *smack*. She struck the woman across the face with a force that made her fall back.

Léa recoiled, bringing her hand to her face, as if she had also been struck and felt her skin burning. Lagerführer Klein straightened her dress, pulled her shoulders back and raised her chin as if to reassert her rightful control. "Fix that patch now before I dock your wages!"

The woman's cheek flamed red, and her gaze, for an instant, fell on Léa, before she turned and ran up the stairs.

"Go on, the rest of you Polish pigs, get back to work!" Lagerführer Klein said, continuing up the stairs.

The Lagerführer's actions and words felt like a blade in Léa's chest, tearing through bone and muscle, ripping her heart apart. She didn't understand why these women were treated so cruelly. Would the same be done to her and Rose?

"Will my sister and I be given patches to sew onto our aprons?" she asked.

The Lagerführer turned, her icy-blue eyes narrowing as she stared at Léa. "You're French. Those patches are for the *Untermenschen*." Her mouth tightened. "Those women must be set apart and isolated. The patches allow everyone, at a glance, to know who they are and how to treat them."

"Oh." Léa turned away, fighting off the nausea, helplessness and shock that her body struggled to absorb. How could she ease these women's pain and shame? She didn't know, but she had to find out.

"I'll show you to the bunk bed you will share on the second floor."

Léa looked at Rose, her face frozen in fear. And a voice inside her whispered, *Find a way to make up for it.* It was what Maître Mallon had told her to do. And then her mother's words came to her. *Keep a good heart.* With a new resolve, she lifted her skirt and followed the Lagerführer up the stairs.

16

Rose

December 1942

"*Aufstehen, funf*," the guard called out from the hallway.

Rose was sitting on the velvety red seat in the cinema in Orléans, her fingers intertwined with André's. The gentle caress of his thumb on her hand filled her with contentment and warmth. She longed for the dreamlike moment to continue and kept her eyes closed to prevent his hand from slipping out of hers.

"Wake up," Léa said. "It's five o'clock. The others are already moving." She felt Léa poke her shoulder. "It's the first day of December, too!"

Rose opened her eyes. It was still dark outside—surely not morning. She pulled the gray blanket over her head and turned to the wall.

"Our shift starts at six. We must wash, dress and eat." Léa yanked the blanket off her, and the icy air hit Rose. "Remember what Lagerführer Klein said: being late means the Meister will dock half our salary for the day."

The mention of the Lagerführer's name made Rose sit up. She'd never seen such brutality in a woman: willing to strike another over something as minor as the position of the patch on her apron.

Rose climbed down the ladder—Léa had the lower bunk—and her bare feet touched the freezing concrete floor. She quickly slid into the wooden shoes that were part of their uniform, feeling their discomfort as she clattered along the hall. They were too big, nearly impossible to keep on. The Lagerführer said they only came in one size. Rose found she could keep them on by gliding forward like a skater, sliding one foot after the other. Stairs were impossible. At least the sisters, arriving in Glashütte in winter, had worn their winter boots and could choose to use the wooden shoes only indoors to go to the washroom.

Rose and Léa squeezed between the women at the zinc trough. Though it extended nearly the length of the wall, there were only three faucets for forty women. Rose could feel the women's sharp elbows digging into her sides. Ignoring them, she inched closer and splashed cold water on her face. Bodies jostled from behind. She had to stand firm, bracing her hips against the trough long enough to rinse her face and brush her teeth.

After finishing at the wash trough, Rose queued for the next room, where toilets lined two sides of the walls with no doors or paneling for privacy. She was grateful that the single bulb from the ceiling flickered and dimmed, the light insufficient for the women to see one another.

Rose and Léa made their way to the canteen. Breakfast was a slice of bread with margarine and *muze*—a soup of fat-free milk sprinkled with dark bread flour. Yesterday, when Lagerführer Klein had given the sisters half their monthly salary upfront, she told them about the coffee they could buy in the canteen at the Archimedes factory for five *pfennigs*. Rose had carefully put the coins in the inner pouch of her apron in anticipation.

The smell of roasting coffee brought back happy memories of early mornings in the kitchen with her mother, smelling the nutty, caramel aroma as Maman turned the wooden handle, grinding the beans before setting the coffee on the stove. Her mother loved dipping a crisp croissant into the dark liquid; she had always said it was the simple pleasures we should never take for granted, like the flaky interior of a croissant drenched in coffee. Under the Occupation, buying coffee was nearly impossible, except on the black market, so it had been two years since she'd had any.

Outside, the sky was stone gray, though ripples of pink, orange and yellow edged the clouds. Something fragile and bright stirred inside her, a reminder of hope. Rose wished she had her sketchpad and pencil. Léa had told her not to bring them to the factory, but Rose felt incomplete without a sketchpad in her pocket.

"You'll be working in a factory with machines and must pay attention," Léa warned. "You can draw when you're back at the barracks."

Rose didn't want to draw at the barracks. She preferred being outside under the sky, among the stream, clouds, and trees. André would understand. Sometimes, she felt he was the only person in the world who *could* understand her desire to express herself through art. But to do that, she needed freedom—a distant memory now.

Lagerführer Klein blew the whistle, and the women marched in a line—Dutch, French and Italian at the front, followed by Poles and Russians bringing up the rear, guarded by an armed soldier. The line of women trickled away at each factory they passed, depending on where they were assigned to work. Across from the train station, a stone marker rose in the air on which the names of towns—Dresden and Berlin—and the distances to reach them were carved. The sky was no longer dark, and Rose would have liked to steal away from the women and find a quiet place where she could be left alone to sketch. When they reached the end of the town, they arrived at the Archimedes factory—a three-story building with large windows.

The Lagerführer pointed to a side door. "Show your pass and give the guard this card, indicating it is your first day. He will call the Meister, factory overseer, to come and collect you." She pulled out a card from a pile in her bag. "Your shift ends at four in the afternoon."

Rose's knees wobbled. Ten hours. She'd never cleaned that long. What would they have her do?

"Shall we wait for you to collect us to return to the barracks?" Léa asked.

The Lagerführer shook her head. "Return to the barracks as you wish. Town shops accept ration coupons. Be back by eight. Lights out at ten." She turned and walked away.

Rose nudged Léa. "You see, I could have brought my sketchpad."

"Then, bring it tomorrow. Come on, let's find out what we'll be doing."

The Meister was an older, burly man with a long gray mustache curled at the end. Rose wondered whether he applied wax to keep it in place because the gray hairs shimmered when the light hit them at a certain angle.

"*Bienvenue, mesdemoiselles,*" he said, startling the sisters with his ability to speak French.

"*Merci, monsieur.*" Léa smiled. "*Où avez-vous appris le français*?"

His beefy arms shot up, crossing like a railway sign as he switched to German. The sisters would soon learn he admired France and often dropped in French words, hoping it would help them understand.

Now, with his index finger, he motioned for Rose to follow and for Léa to stay. Leading Rose up one level, he brought her into a cavernous room lined with small windows, colossal machines clacking and wheezing to the ceiling. He indicated an empty stool in a row where women were settling for the shift. In front, a wooden table, and beyond it, a moving rubber belt with passing brass cylinders. The Meister tapped the woman who had just sat down on the shoulder and motioned to Rose with two fingers, pointing to his eyes: watch.

The woman's gloved hand lifted a cylinder off the rubber belt. Dipping her brush into a bowl of amber-tinted liquid, she coated the brass until it gleamed. Then, she placed it in a wire basket on the table.

"*Verstanden*?" the Meister asked, looking at Rose intently.

She nodded. He motioned to her to sit down and start.

The bench was hard, but she tried to forget it, hoping she would get used to it. Rose put on the glove, lifted the brass piece off the conveyor belt, and then painted it with the clear shellac. She hadn't realized how sticky the lacquer was until the woman beside her said, "*Nein*," and wagged a finger at Rose. She pointed at the uneven lumps on one side and made a circular motion with her hand, as if to say she should apply the layer evenly. Rose put the part in the wire basket and took the next one. This time, she was more careful, and the woman nodded and gave a thumbs-up.

A large white-faced clock hung on the wall. Rose kept glancing at it, wondering how long she'd be required to sit on the bench without a break. After an hour, the Meister counted thirty cylinders in the basket. The woman gave Rose a sour look. The Meister shook his head and said,

"*Hundert*." Rose nearly stumbled off the stool. He checked her neighbor's basket and counted one hundred and ten. Rose nodded. She would try harder. Maybe she'd been too careful with the lacquer, which slowed her down.

After three hours, the Meister tapped her shoulder to signal a stop. Rose's fingers were numb from gripping the brush. She put it down, removed her glove, stood, and stretched her legs. She rubbed her shoulders; her back felt as hard as rocks.

When the Meister turned away to answer a question, her neighbor winked, dropped two cylinders into Rose's basket, and shuffled downstairs to the canteen.

"*Danke schön*," Rose said.

The woman smiled and patted her on the back.

Léa stood waiting at the canteen entrance. As Rose approached with her new friend, she remembered the word the Lagerführer had used the day before. She gestured toward Léa and introduced her, saying, "*Schwester* Léa."

The woman smiled and put her hand on her chest. "Jana."

Then Jana's friends called to her, and she waved goodbye and rushed over to join them.

"Jana showed me how to coat the brass pieces with shellac. She added two of her finished ones to my wire basket to help me meet the quota." Rose sighed.

"She is a friend, then."

Rose nodded. "What do they have you doing?"

"I have to attach a lens to a metal mount."

"What's it for?"

"The lens goes in gunsights. My quota is ten an hour—one hundred a shift." She linked arms with Rose and led her to the canteen.

"We're not making calculating machines, then."

"No. We're building weapons."

Rose stopped. "Even the cylinders?"

"What did you expect? Germany is at war. They need us to build equipment so they can fight."

Rose felt sick. "Can we ask—"

"No. For the moment, we do as they say. Then, we'll figure out a way to make it up."

"How?"

"I don't know. But we will. Come on, let's get something to eat."

Inside the cafeteria, the tables had the flags of the nationalities of the workers—Italian, Dutch, Belgian, Danish, and French—so they would know where to sit.

Rose smelled the smoky coffee from the stove. They ordered coffees, soup and a piece of *kaffee kuchen*, paying with ration cards. They sat down at a French table, next to Frenchmen.

Two women stepped inside the canteen. Like the Polish women from yesterday, they wore headscarves and aprons with a patch bearing the letters OST for *Ostarbeiter* or Eastern workers. Immediately, one of the staff stood and shouted: "*Sovyetki! Raus!*"

Panic appeared in the women's eyes. One stumbled, clutching her apron, and both turned and ran out of the canteen.

"What happened?" Rose asked.

"They're from the Soviet Union," Léa said. Rose looked confused. "The Italian woman next to me speaks some French. She said Soviet citizens rank the lowest," Léa explained.

"Where do they eat if they can't come in here?"

"Maybe they have their own canteens?"

"They can't work ten-hour shifts without eating." Rose stabbed her fork into the cake. It didn't seem fair to eat it now.

"It goes to show, even when we think things are terrible for us, there's always someone worse off," Léa said.

Rose glanced at the two Frenchmen talking at the table next to them. "Do you think they're former prisoners of war?"

"Maybe. I met an Italian former prisoner of war this morning. He works at one of the watchmaking factories in town."

"Look, they're leaving." She sat up straight, watching as the men rose from their table. "I want to ask if they know André."

"Rose, don't get your hopes up. The chance of you finding—"

"*Bonjour, monsieur*," Rose said.

The men stopped, surprised to see Frenchwomen. "*Bonjour, mesdemoiselles*."

"How long have you been in Germany?" Rose asked.

"We were captured by the Wehrmacht in nineteen-forty, and held as POWs before being given the chance to change our status to workers. We have family to support in France, so we send our salaries back home. What are you doing here? Is it true that Laval insists on sending women to Germany, too?"

Rose barely registered Léa kicking her under the table. Hope fluttered in her chest—maybe these men would help her find André. She gripped the coffee cup with both hands.

"My sister and I volunteered." She watched their faces darken. "Do you know André—"

One of men leaned over and spat in Rose's coffee. "We don't talk to traitors." He turned to his friend. "Come on, let's go."

Rose's heart beat so fast she could feel her pulse vibrating in her wrist. She looked down at her coffee. Only two sips, and now it was ruined. Léa reached across the table, squeezing Rose's cold hand.

"You can't just blurt things out."

"But they're working here. Why do they blame us for doing the same?"

Léa shrugged. "They were prisoners of war. They hate the Nazis."

"I hate the Nazis." Rose hadn't considered the broader implications of coming to Germany. She just wanted to get Léa out, help Virginie and Paulette, and maybe find André. Now, she'd been called a traitor. "How are we traitors but they aren't?"

"Men hold us to a higher standard. Forget about it." Léa stood. "I'll get you another coffee."

"No, I don't want one." She pushed the cup away.

What if Léa was right and André held her to a higher standard? Would he call her a traitor, like the others? She shuddered—by coming here, she might not find him as she hoped, but instead drive him away.

17

Léa

February 1943

As the days barreled on, relentless snow one day, biting cold the next, the sisters toiled long hours on the factory floor. The dull winter sun shone through the factory window as Léa dipped a fine brush into the balsam and painted a thin line along the edge of the glass lens. With steady hands, she pressed the lens into the metal mount, ensuring it was centered. Her fingers, stiff and aching, and her neck sore, she took care not to touch the optical surface as any smudge would degrade the lens quality. Finished, she set the assembled piece on a rack for the warm oven.

The light bulbs overhead flickered. They'd experienced a blackout earlier in the day, but the Meister shouted at the workers to keep going. Léa, struggling to see, hesitated with the balsam, worried she might dab some on the lens. She picked up the next unfinished part from the assembly line, then glanced sideways at the woman sitting beside her. Her name was Maria, and she wore a purple P badge sewn on the front of her apron, marking her as Polish.

Unlike many of the women who bantered in German while working—Léa's German wasn't yet good enough to join in the conversation—Maria never spoke. Léa had the impression she wanted to be as small as possible, as if trying to become invisible. The Meister's frequent slurs directed at her—*filthy Polish pig*—made Léa's stomach churn with anger. Wanting to comfort her or at least show kindness, Léa would try to meet Maria's gaze, but she always lowered her eyes or turned away.

Today, Maria's right eye was swollen and red. As she worked, she paused, looked up at the ceiling and closed her eyes for relief. If the Meister saw, he berated her for taking a break.

"*Herr Meister*," Maria said softly. "*Apotheke*?" She swallowed and pointed at her eye.

"*Nein*," he hurled back, making Maria jump. He went on speaking in German, but what Léa understood was that he had no intention of letting Maria off to go to the pharmacy.

Maria nodded, wiped her eye with her sleeve and glanced at Léa before returning her attention to the assembly line.

Maria's eye reminded Léa of when Rose had been stung by a bee once and her eye swelled like a balloon. She glanced at the clock: nearly four. The Polish women had longer shifts and worked an extra two hours. The pharmacy would be closed by the time Maria got off work. Maybe Léa could go for her. She hated how Maria and the other Polish women were treated and didn't want the only words in Maria's mind to be the awful ones that the Meister and the Lagerführer constantly muttered at her. If she could bring the medicine, then maybe it would show that not everyone thought the same. The problem wasn't Maria; it was the others. Another injustice Léa couldn't bear.

At the end of her shift, Léa met Rose downstairs. They always walked back to the barracks together. Because it was winter and the town was set in a narrow valley, dusk fell early. The snow from the previous week hadn't melted, and its bluish-gray tint reflected the cold, fading light.

"Can you believe it's only been three months?" Rose said. "It feels longer. I wish we had something to look forward to other than work." She tucked her chin in the scarf wrapped around her neck.

"Did something happen today?" Léa asked, putting her arm in Rose's.

"The Meister increased my quota. Jana said that with the colder weather, many are off sick, so the rest of us must work more."

"We can't forget we're still the lucky ones." Léa was thinking of Maria and the other Polish women. She saw the sign "*Apotheke*" up ahead and pulled Rose a little closer. "I need to get something from the pharmacy. Did you bring your ration book?"

"Yes."

"Come on." Léa opened the door, and a bell inside rang. Before entering, she wiped her boots on the mat. Rose did the same, and the bell rang again as she closed the door behind them.

A mix of scents struck Léa—camphor, pine and something sharper, almost metallic. But it was the licorice root that stood above the others, reminding her of the winters when her mother had given them the root to suck on to soothe their sore throats. A man stood with his back to the sisters, speaking to the woman at the counter as a second woman emerged from behind a green velvet curtain at the sound of the bell. She addressed them in German.

Léa stepped forward, steadying her hands on the counter. She realized that she should have practiced her German because her words tangled, slipping between French and German. "I would like to buy medicine for an eye infection," she managed to say, her voice thin with embarrassment at her garbled pronunciation.

The woman puckered her lips as she examined Léa's eye. "For you?"

"No, someone else."

The woman wagged a finger at her. "*Nein*."

"But her eye is swollen." Léa made a round shape with her hand. "Like a bee sting. It's all red. Her shift won't end until after the pharmacy is closed, so I've come for her."

She felt the man at the counter turn and glance at her, then brush past her as he took his leave. She kept repeating the German words she knew—*medizin, rot, auge*—hoping that somehow she'd make herself understood. But the more she said, the more the woman's position hardened. Eventually, Léa gave up, and left with Rose.

Outside, the cold night air blew hard in her face and her eyes watered. The sky was solid black, as though someone had dipped a brush in ink and painted over the moon and stars.

"Mademoiselle, perhaps I can help?" a man said in perfect French.

Léa turned. He wore round glasses, but she could see beyond the lenses that his eyes were a soft, warm brown.

"I overheard you in the pharmacy. Is it conjunctivitis that your friend has?"

"I'm not sure."

"A poultice of Euphrasia can help heal an infection of the eye."

"Oh?"

"Yes, it's a compress made from wildflowers. The eye is quite good at healing itself. The herbs will relieve the pain and quicken the healing."

It was the first time since arriving in Germany that she'd heard someone speak of pain as if it was something to avoid. "Yes, it seems to be painful for her. How can I find this Euphrasia?"

"Come by the sick bay in the morning—it's on the ground floor of the barracks next to the train station—I'll have the poultice ready with some instructions in German." He tipped his hat. "If you arrive before your factory shift starts, I'll have more time to explain."

"I will. Thank you."

He crossed the street and disappeared into the darkness.

"Who was that?" Rose asked.

"A doctor, I think." Why hadn't she asked his name?

"Is he French?"

"He speaks it well. I'll find out tomorrow. Come, let's go." Despite the cold and bitter wind, she felt warmed by the gentleman's kindness. As they passed the river, she listened to the sound of rushing water echoing beneath the snow and realized it had been a pleasure to speak French again and even more to learn something that might help others. Their footsteps quickened as the wind picked up, and Léa glanced at the sky, noticing silver flakes twirling through the darkness.

Snow. The light flakes melted on contact with the ground. Léa had disliked the snow, especially how it turned to ice overnight, making the morning walk to the factory treacherous. But now it felt softer and she didn't mind so much. She even looked up, letting the flakes fall on her face before turning away from the river to the barracks.

* * *

The next morning, Léa got up extra early before the throng of women descended on the zinc trough. She combed her hair out, then wove the long brown strands into a single braid. She put on her uniform, apron and overcoat and set off early. She wanted enough time to stop by the sick bay before going to the factory.

It had snowed overnight, and the sidewalk was icy, so she took small steps to avoid slipping. The cold turned the sky crystal blue, and sunlight shimmered on the windows.

She found the barracks next to the train station, passing armed soldiers on the street who were supervising the loading of factory goods onto a train for shipment out. Smoothing the creases in her coat, she showed her work pass to the guard and explained that she was there to collect something from the sick bay. The guard motioned her to a door at the end of the hall on which a red cross had been painted on a white background.

Léa knocked. No answer. She tried again and heard footsteps as the door opened.

"Come in," a man said.

If not for his eyes, she wouldn't have recognized him as the man from last night. They were brighter than she remembered, maybe because he wasn't wearing glasses. He was taller and thinner, but she'd only seen him in a heavy wool coat. He signaled for her to follow him.

The sick bay had beds lined up in every available space. A corridor led to what she assumed were more rooms. As Léa followed him along a path between the beds, the sour smell of urine and sweat rose in the air. Some patients coughed and wheezed. She counted a dozen beds, maybe more, and wondered if he worked alone. It seemed too much for one person. He opened a door, stood aside, and waited for her to enter first.

It felt strange to stand alone in a room with a man since it had been months since she worked late with

Maître Mallon at the office. He had been her boss, while this man, well, she didn't even know his name. Léa tugged at the sleeve of her coat and glanced around the narrow space: a ceramic sink in a corner with a rickety wooden table next to it on which rested a stethoscope, thermometer and a handful of kidney-shaped basins; a cabinet with shelves and drawers stood against a wall; and farther along, she spotted a desk with a chair and lamp. To her delight, a typewriter sat on the desk. Her heart jumped a little because she was sure it was a Hermes, just like the one in Maître Mallon's office. She went to it, running her fingers along the round metal-rimmed keys and it suddenly brought her back to Orléans before the Occupation and happier times.

She looked a little closer at the keys and saw a German keyboard, with umlauted vowels on the right and the Eszett, or sharp S, where the question mark had been.

"That dreaded machine arrived a month ago," the man said. "I detest it!"

"How can you? It's a marvelous invention."

"Is that so?" He shook his head. "Pen and paper serve me just fine."

"Typing was my profession. I'm quite fast—eighty words a minute."

"Impressive. I write daily reports for all the patients in the sick bay, including their names, medical condition, and expected return-to-work dates. Every report must be typed. Unfortunately, my fingers fumble and get caught between the keys!" He held out his hands. "Maybe they're just too big."

"You'll get better with practice."

"My problem is time; there isn't enough of it," he said, rubbing his forehead. "And what would have taken one hour to write a report by hand now takes two or three because of that clunky machine. Never mind."

He bent down and opened a drawer, lifting a glass jar out of it before glancing back at her.

"Here you go. Euphrasia."

He unscrewed the jar and held it up for her to see. The gray paste inside had a mild grassy scent. He closed the jar and placed it in a paper bag with a square of cheesecloth, a ribbon and a piece of paper with German writing.

"Tell your friend to dampen the cheesecloth, take some of the paste and wrap it inside, then tie it and rest it on her eye. I've written down the instructions in German for her."

"Thank you. How much should I pay you?"

He waved a hand in the air. "Nothing."

"Please, allow me to compensate you for your time. You just said you don't have enough time and you've kindly given me some." Since the war started three years ago, she'd yet to meet a single person who did something without expecting payment in return.

"Euphrasia grows in the forests and grasses not far from here. We pick it for free in the spring and summer, then dry it for use over winter. It cost me nothing. Remind your friend to keep her eye closed for a few hours each day, and it will swiftly heal on its own."

With a relaxed motion, he leaned against the table and crossed his legs. "We haven't been properly introduced. I'm Josef. And you are?"

"Léa." Though he spoke fluently, she heard a foreign accent. "How did you learn to speak French like a native speaker?"

"I'm from the Protectorate of Bohemia and Moravia."

Léa frowned, her cheeks warming with embarrassment. She didn't know where that was, so she stayed silent, hoping her ignorance wasn't apparent.

"It was called Czechoslovakia before Hitler occupied it in 1938. My father worked with a pharmaceutical company in France, selling their products in Prague. I had a French nanny and learned the language from her."

She wondered what circumstances had brought him here and how long ago—but a knock on the door stopped her from asking.

"Herr Capek?" a man's voice came from the outer room.

Josef went to see what was needed, his expression turning serious, then he quickly returned.

"Another ill patient with fever. If you'll excuse me."

Since he seemed to be on his own at the sick bay and wouldn't accept payment, she considered how else she might help. Her gaze fell on the typewriter. "How about if I type your reports after my shift?"

He looked startled. "I can't ask you to do that."

"You're not asking. But I won't be as fast in German as I am in French, so you'll have to be patient. I'm a quick learner. I'll get better."

"It will still be faster than me." He laughed.

"I'll come by after four, if that's all right?"

"It's not necessary, and I don't think it's a fair exchange. But yes, thank you." He led her to the door. "I'll understand if you change your mind."

"I won't change my mind," she said.

Maybe this was how she'd make up for building weapons for the Nazi war machine. The gesture wouldn't make an enormous difference, but it would mean something to her. With this hope, Léa found herself smiling. For the first time since arriving in Glashütte, she didn't dread entering the factory to start her shift because she knew there was other, worthwhile work waiting for her after she finished.

18

Rose

April 1943

The sisters had been in this remote town on the border of Germany and Bohemia for nearly five months. Rose anticipated the arrival of spring. Every morning on the way to the factory, she looked out for the green shoots of tulips and hyacinths pushing up through the ground. But the mornings and evenings remained cold and damp. The days were too short and none had yet appeared.

Now that Léa went every day to the sick bay to type Josef's reports, she no longer met Rose at the end of their factory shifts. And Rose, seeking a warm place to sketch—the barracks had little heating—went to the church in the center of town, which was mostly empty in the evenings. The Gothic windows and the towering altar with gold figures reminded her of the times she'd gone to the cathedral in Orléans with her mother and sister to celebrate mass at Easter and Christmas. All week she'd been sketching the altar and was almost finished.

Tonight, she entered and sat on a pew at the back. After a day of back-breaking work lacquering all those brass cylinders on the assembly line—the rattling machines, their pistons breathing in and out like angry dragons she'd read about in fairy tales—sitting in the warmth and quiet was a gift. Even the sight of a few forsythia and pussy willow branches tucked in the stone vases on either side of the altar lifted her spirits.

Before taking out her sketchbook, she noticed, in the corner at the rear of the church, a stack of candles. They were likely for the altar. Rose hadn't seen any votive candle stands; she'd asked Léa about them, and she'd said that the Protestant church here didn't make offerings to saints like she was used to in France.

An idea came to Rose. Every night, the bulbs at the barracks flickered, signaling the start of another blackout. Maybe she could take one or two candles from the pile so she could continue drawing while Léa studied German, though her sister insisted she study to improve her German, too. With so many candles stacked in the box, she didn't think one or two would be missed.

She looked around. Rose was alone in the church. She stood, went to the corner and took two candles from the box. Suddenly, a creaking sound froze her. Had someone entered? *Thud*. Panic ripped through her chest—the door had opened and shut. Footsteps clacked on the tiled floor, coming closer. Should she put the candles back, or was it too late? She sensed a presence beside her.

"Excuse me, I thought no one would be here," a man's voice said.

Rose turned, throat tight. She'd been in Germany long enough to know what the black diamond "SD" insignia on the man's sleeve meant. A Security Service officer—Gestapo—in a field-gray uniform stood before her. Rose's heart pounded as she struggled to stay calm.

"Where are you from?" He glanced at her apron and the candles in her hand.

"France." Her voice shook with fear. She braced herself for a slap across the face or something worse, if he accused her of stealing as Madame Martin had.

"You are also here to make a prayer?"

Her thoughts scrambled. A prayer?

"It's not our tradition to light votive candles and place them before altars or shrines as in your country."

She looked down at the candles, trying to steady her trembling fingers. "I'm sorry." She looked up. His eyes pinned her. She wanted to run, but his gaze held her in a vise, and she had to wait for him to let her go.

"Since we're both in mourning—" he sighed "—you're forgiven." His voice took on a melancholy tone. "Perhaps I shall join you. Would you like that?"

"Yes," she stuttered.

"Don't be afraid. We're allies; our countries are on the same side." He removed one of the candles from her hand. "Isn't that why you're here, to help? No one forced you to come."

What he said was true, but also not true. She tried to hold these thoughts together, recalling the French soldier who'd spat in her coffee. He motioned to the pew, signaling her to sit. She stepped back and slid onto the wooden seat.

"Who are you mourning?" he asked.

"My mother." It was only half a lie. She hadn't come here to mourn anyone, but if she had, it would be Maman. He touched her arm in sympathy, and it took all Rose's strength not to flinch. His blue eyes locked on hers.

"Your mother died?" He tilted his head, and thick blond hair fell across his forehead.

Léa's warning not to tell anyone they were orphans came to her, but that was back in Orléans, under the harsh conditions of the Occupation. Rose couldn't see why it mattered here. "Both my parents are gone, my mother more recently."

"Then we share that in common. I, too, am an orphan, and until this morning . . ." He held back a sob. "It was only my brother Felix and me."

She relaxed slightly, knowing he had a sibling. She noticed the crease on his bottom lip. "What happened to your brother?"

"A letter came this morning. Felix died fighting in Stalingrad." His crystal blue eyes darted around the church, almost childlike in their confusion. "I sensed something was wrong when my letters came back unopened." His shoulders heaved; tears fell on his perfectly pressed uniform.

"My condolences," she said, trying to reconcile the man in the uniform with the innocent boy he must have once been, the one who had looked up at his mother with the same blue eyes full of love as Rose had looked at her mother.

"Should we light our candles?" she asked.

He nodded, removing a white handkerchief from his pocket to wipe his eyes. "Please forgive me, I shouldn't—"

He removed a brass lighter from his jacket pocket, flicked the top open and lit her candle. The swastika set in a red and white diamond in the center of the lighter called out like a warning, but she wanted to think of him as the eighteen-year-old he must have been when the war broke out. How could he have followed any other path than the one he was on now? Just like she had no other choice but to be here. The scent of tobacco and leather lingered between them. After he lit his candle, he returned the lighter to his pocket, closed his eyes and mumbled a prayer.

They sat side by side on the bench, both lost in their thoughts—his likely about his brother and Rose's about her mother. She sometimes couldn't recall Maman's face; it had been three years, and so many details had begun to fade. After she and Léa were gone, there would be no one else to remember her mother and all the moments of their life together—pitting cherries to make *clafoutis*, fishing on the banks of the Loire, sewing her first dress under her mother's watchful gaze—it would all vanish without a trace.

"Felix was my best friend," he said. "We used to fish together in the Müglitz." His hand drifted in the air. "He'd always catch the biggest brown trout, but he'd tell Papa I'd caught it."

"Maman taught me to fish on the Loire. The salmon and trout swam too fast for us, but we caught plenty of pike. We would make *quenelles*."

"Dumplings." He smiled. "How did you make them?"

"We mixed the pike with eggs and flour, rolled them into balls, poached them briefly and then poured a *béchamel* sauce over them before baking." Rose puckered her lips, touching her thumb and index finger to her mouth.

"Sounds delicious."

"It—"

The church bells rang out. When they ceased, an awkward silence fell. He leaned forward and blew out the candles, staring at the smoke entangled in the air.

"You and me," he said, in a strange tone.

"What?"

"Nothing." His voice shifted.

She stood to take her leave. "I must—"

"Show me your *Arbeitsbuch*." His voice sharpened into a command.

She inwardly balked at his mood change, but handed him her work pass.

"Rose Cotillard," he said, tapping the permit against the thick white knuckles on his other hand. "Which factory do you work at?"

"Archimedes."

"I am Kriminalinspektor Kurt Reinhardt, and I will speak with the Meister at Archimedes."

"Why?"

"So that you will receive special privileges."

"But I already do, compared to the Polish workers."

"The Poles are dirty swine. Of course you are at a higher level." Something dark passed across his face. "You will see what I have in mind."

Looking down, she tried to hide how his words made her recoil. "Thank you for the offer," she said, swallowing. "But it's not necessary."

"Are *you* telling me what to do?"

"Oh, no. It's only that I don't want to trouble you." She bit her lip, wondering what had happened to the man sitting with her on the bench from a moment ago, grieving for his brother. "I'd be very grateful for whatever you do on my behalf."

"That's the correct attitude." He handed the permit back to her.

"Thank you," she said, a chill running down her spine. Suddenly, it felt like the church walls had dissolved, and she was back outside on the cold, dark street.

"We shall certainly see one another again," he said, standing and knocking his leather boots against one another. He extended his right arm straight out from the shoulder. "Heil Hitler!"

Every part of Rose filled with disgust, but she knew what was expected and that if she failed to return the salute, he could cause trouble not only for her but possibly for Léa. It wouldn't take him long to know everything about her. She stood and raised her right arm straight out. "Heil Hitler."

He smiled, signaling his approval, then turned and left. The church door shut with a clanging sound.

Rose collapsed on the pew, the candle breaking in her hand.

19

Léa

June 1943

In the beginning, Léa had struggled to decipher Josef's handwriting. He wrote with an odd slant, and because he was left-handed, the ink frequently smudged as his hand swept over it. But after she became familiar with the curls, twists and lines of his script, as well as the German keyboard, her proficiency and speed increased.

What she liked best was the time that they spent together going over the reports. He checked her transcription and made corrections. She asked him questions on German grammar, which he kindly explained, helping to improve her fluency. And what made it all worthwhile was the extra time he was able to devote to his patients, since he was the only doctor for all three thousand foreign workers assigned to Glashütte by mid-1943.

That morning at the factory, Léa noticed Maria struggled to meet her quota. Her usually efficient assembly of the lenses on the gunsights seemed sluggish. Léa suspected that by the time the lunch hour rolled around, Maria would be behind and she knew from experience that once that happened, it would be nearly impossible to catch up.

"What's wrong?" Léa asked in German.

Either Maria couldn't hear over the clanging of the machines, or she lacked the energy to speak because she didn't answer. The poultice Léa had given her a few months back had visibly reduced the swelling and redness in her eye. And though at the time she'd been grateful, she warned Léa to be careful. "If Lagerführer Klein finds out you've given me medicine, you'll be in trouble."

"She won't find out." Léa had wanted to put her friend at ease. "And it's not medicine but herbs that grow wild."

"Someone could tell her. Don't trust anyone."

If someone had reported Léa to the Lagerführer, she'd explain that since Maria sat next to her on the assembly line, she would have been at risk if the infection had spread, and that she'd given the Polish woman medicine to prevent it from spreading to herself.

The Meister circled the assembly line on his midday rounds, inspecting the quota targets of each women. Léa's jaw tensed as he hovered near Maria. She could tell from the way he stroked his moustache that he was counting the lenses and already knew Maria was short.

When the bell rang for lunch, Léa stood and stretched her arms and back, delaying her departure. She listened as the Meister approached Maria, blocking her from joining the others.

"Sabotage will not be permitted here. You will work during the lunch break," he ordered. "And if you don't make up the quota, you'll stay after your shift until you do. Understand?"

"*Ja*," Maria whispered, her voice weak.

Léa bristled. Every time a worker from the East—either Poland or Russia—got behind in their daily quota, they were accused of engaging in sabotage. This was how workers were sent off to harsh labor camps where they were worked to death. Not wanting to draw the Meister's wrath, she removed her apron and arranged the items in her work area until he left. Once he was out of sight, she put her apron on and continued to work.

Maria exchanged a look with Léa. "Go. I'll be fine."

"All the lenses I assemble over lunch, I'll add to your pile."

Maria's bony shoulders drew together as she leaned forward to add the tacky balsam to the edge of the lens. "*Mein Schutzengel.*"

Léa smiled. Maria had called her a guardian angel.

"I'm not your *Schutzengel*, just a friend. And if the Meister insists you work tonight, I'll stay here too."

Maria turned to Léa. Her complexion suddenly whiter than the snow outside. "Thank you. I'm tired . . ." Her voice trailed off as she turned back to the machine.

"Have you not been sleeping well?" So many of the workers had become ill over the winter with insufficient rations to fight infections that lingered into the summer.

"No strength," she said.

"Take it slowly. I'm helping today."

The two women worked through lunch. Léa didn't mind skipping her meal. But she worried that with Maria's poor health, she needed to eat. Her face was already too thin, and her cheeks hollowed out. During the afternoon break, she went to the café and ordered a slice of coffee cake. Bringing it back in a brown paper bag to the factory floor, she intended on slipping it into Maria's bag for her to eat later. But when Léa arrived at her workstation, Maria's head was on the table, arms hanging at her sides.

"Maria," she whispered, shaking her shoulder. "Wake up."

"I can't . . ." she muttered.

The Meister saw and came over. "Get back to work," he commanded.

Léa put her hand on Maria's forehead; it was hot to the touch. "She has a fever. She should go to the sick bay."

"She's already behind on her production quota for the day." He put his hands on his hips. "Lazy Polish . . . I know her game and it—"

"Let me bring her to the sick bay."

"Now you want to go off and be absent too." He crossed his arms at his chest. "*Nein*."

Léa remembered all she'd seen that first day in Glashütte—how they'd humiliated the Polish women by shaving them, fearing they carried diseases that would spread through the town. If she could appeal to that irrational fear now, it might get Maria the care she deserved. "What if it's tuberculosis or typhoid?"

His eyes flicked toward Maria and then back at Léa. She hoped he was calculating the risk of missing production quotas versus exposing himself and the other women to disease. His stubby fingers tapped the sides of his arms. He was clearly getting sufficient food.

"Take her to the sick bay," he ordered, cursing them both under his breath. "But come back immediately."

Léa lifted Maria from the stool. She was light, too light. Léa tried to hold her gently so as not to squeeze her ribs.

"Where . . . we going?" Maria whispered.

"To the sick bay. It's not far." She turned to the Meister. "Please write a pass. If we're stopped, she'll be in trouble."

He grunted and went to his desk. Léa wasn't taking any chances. She knew the Polish and Russian workers weren't allowed to move around freely. Usually an armed soldier escorted them in groups back and forth from the barracks to the factory; all other times they required a special pass to be on the street on their own. It was part of the policy of keeping them strictly segregated from the German population.

The Meister returned with a pass. "Go on," he said, impatient for Maria to be gone now that she posed a potential threat to others.

Unsteady on her feet, Maria struggled to make her way down the stairs. Léa held her up, fearing she might faint. Outside, the sun shone bright on the sidewalk, blinding her eyes. A warm wind came off the hills, carrying the scent of pine in the air. The wind had an eerie howl like wolves in the night. A group of soldiers smoking outside a café eyed Léa suspiciously. She squared her shoulders, pulling Maria along, confident she had the pass in case they stopped and questioned her. She was grateful the sick bay wasn't far because by the time she reached it, her arms burned from Maria's weight.

Josef saw her at the door and immediately went to help. "What happened?"

"I don't know. Maria sits next to me on the assembly line. She's burning up with fever. The Meister eventually allowed me to bring her here."

Josef went to Maria's other side, releasing the pressure on Léa's arms. "I've got one empty bed," he said, lifting Maria gently in his arms and carrying her to the far corner. As Léa watched him place her on the bed, she was grateful that Josef treated Maria like he would anyone. There was a warmth to him that bathed the room in light.

He felt Maria's forehead and neck. "Let me get the thermometer."

While he went to his office, Maria turned restlessly in the bed. "Where is he?"

"Who?" Léa asked.

"Tomasz."

"Is he a friend?"

Maria's head swiveled left and right as she repeated, "Tomasz, Tomasz."

Josef returned and slipped the thermometer under Maria's tongue. "Hold her head steady until there's a temperature reading."

Léa nodded. "Hush, Maria, Tomasz is coming, be still." Placing her hands on either side of Maria's face, she felt the heat on her skin. Whispering Tomasz's name seemed to soothe her.

As they waited for the thermometer, Josef felt Maria's wrist for a pulse.

"I was worried that she hadn't eaten all day," Léa said. "Polish rations are less than ours."

"Only three hundred grams of bread a day. Watered-down soup. Meat only on Sundays." He shook his head. "They cannot be expected to work fourteen-hour shifts on starvation rations."

"That's why I went to the canteen to get some coffee cake that she could put in her bag and eat later. When I came back, she had her head on the desk."

He placed a stethoscope on Maria's chest and hunched over her, listening. In the windowless room, patients coughed and called out. Josef ignored them, giving all his attention to Maria.

"No fluid in the lungs. That's a good sign." He removed the thermometer. "Forty degrees. It's concerning but not yet dangerous. Would you mind going to my office and running one of the towels near the sink under cold water, rinsing it out, then bringing it back and putting it on her forehead to lower the temperature while I examine her further?"

Léa did as he asked, quickly returning. She placed the damp cloth on Maria's forehead.

"I want to examine her stomach, see if there's swelling." He undid the buttons on Maria's shirt dress. Despite the warm weather, she wore an extra layer, and he pulled it aside until he finally uncovered skin. Then he stopped.

"Léa?"

"Yes?"

"Come here," he said, pointing at the small swell of Maria's belly. Léa gave a slight gasp, raising a hand to her mouth. He quickly covered her stomach with her clothing, then his brown eyes locked on Léa's. "May we speak in private?"

She nodded and followed him to his office, sitting on the chair where she typed his patient reports at night. He gently closed the door behind her and leaned against the table, crossing his legs and placing his hands on his hips.

"Was Maria the one who had conjunctivitis?"

"Yes."

"Well, at least the Euphrasia worked." He lifted hands in front of his face, as in a gesture of prayer. "Did you understand what I showed you back there?"

"Maria is with child?"

"Yes. Do you know who the father is?"

"No."

"I heard you telling her that Tomasz would be coming. Is he the father?"

"I don't know. She never spoke about him with me. But she was calling his name out just now."

"I won't include the pregnancy in her patient report."

Léa didn't understand. Wouldn't he want to include her pregnancy in the report so that the Meister would give her shorter hours, time off, supplemental food coupons? "Shouldn't you include it so she'll be better treated?"

"It doesn't work like that. We keep the baby a secret, to protect it."

Léa's throat tightened. "From whom?"

"Tomasz is a Polish name. If he's the father . . ."

"What?"

"She'll be sent to a clinic for an abortion."

"Against her will?"

"Yes."

Léa grasped the edge of the chair to steady herself, a wave of horror sweeping through her. The idea that Maria's pregnancy might be forcibly ended was too terrible to imagine. He stepped closer and placed a hand on her shoulder, and she felt his warmth pass though her.

"All we can do is help her hide the pregnancy until the baby's born. Like you've done today by bringing her here. Keep a protective eye on her. After that, it's in God's hands."

She didn't know what to say. After all she'd experienced—the death of Édouard, the poor dead woman she'd seen in the camp in Jargeau, and the mistreatment of Polish laborers, she wasn't sure that she believed in God anymore. Maman would never forgive her for thinking such a thing, but if he was so powerful, why didn't he help the innocent who suffered because of this terrible war? She'd already lost hope in her country and now she was losing her faith.

She looked up at him. "Is there a positive outcome if the father isn't Polish?"

"If the father is German, the baby will live."

"Let us pray to God that he is German."

"It's not so simple."

"Why?"

"The baby will be taken away and raised by a German family."

"It's *her* child."

"As I said, we help her keep the baby a secret—that's all we can do. Anything else will require a miracle. Do you understand?"

No, she didn't understand. Not the hierarchy, the classifications, or why the beauty and sanctity of life had been cut and squeezed into artificial categories devoid of meaning. If she heard the Meister or Lagerführer utter *filthy Pole* one more time, she thought she would explode. They did it on repeat, like machines. That's what they were: automatons, an assembly line spewing out parts—the opposite of creative human beings who were different and unique and couldn't be placed into categories. They wanted to reduce people to numbers—ones and zeros. Numbers had no dignity and could be easily shuffled around and discarded. Léa was lost. None of it was real, and yet all of it was horribly real. She couldn't just watch it all unfold; she wanted to do more. She feared that not doing anything would make her a machine like them.

She looked up into his deep brown eyes. "Tell me how to help her. What can I do?"

"She needs more food, better nutrition. I'm guessing she's four months along. It's a critical stage for the baby."

How could she arrange for this? Léa's food ration coupons were hardly enough for her, but with her wages, she was able to buy food on the black market to supplement them. She knew that Maria and the other Polish women earned much less. She would find a way, even if it meant giving her rations to Maria, because a baby was innocent and needed protection. It was the least that Léa could do.

She glanced at the typewriter. He said he would keep the pregnancy out of the report. But who received the reports?

"The patient reports I type every night, where are they sent?" she asked.

"To Herr Reinhardt at the Gestapo office across from the church."

20

Rose

August 1943

Rose had been too ashamed and overwhelmed with guilt to tell Léa about meeting the Gestapo officer. She couldn't admit to her sister that she'd returned his Heil Hitler salute. In the four months that had passed since, she'd stayed away from the church, fearing he would go there looking for her.

And yet, since their meeting, boxes have arrived regularly for her—her name written on them and given either to the Meister at the factory or to the guard at the dormitory to pass on to her. Inside, she found oranges, socks, chocolate, tinned fish. There was never a note, but she suspected it was Reinhardt—who else could access such hard to get items? Every time a box arrived, shame and dread roiled in the pit of her stomach. She gave all the items to the sick bay, lying to Léa about how she'd come across them while trying to assuage her guilt about the gifts going to those in need. At least Reinhardt hadn't come to the factory or stopped her on the street—and because of that, she let herself believe that maybe he was losing interest in her and soon the gifts would stop.

Today, the Meister told her that she could have the afternoon off. When she asked why, he said something cryptic about her 'powerful friend,' and the other women on the assembly line stared at her, wide-eyed. A sour taste rose at the back of her throat. She refused and told the Meister she wanted to stay and work, but he insisted she go.

"If the Kriminalinspektor discovers I didn't follow his orders, he'll take it out on me."

It suddenly became clear to Rose that Reinhardt wasn't losing interest in her as she hoped. She could no longer keep what had happened in the church to herself. She had to tell Léa. If anyone could figure a way out of the mess she'd gotten herself into with the Gestapo officer, it was her sister.

Today, they'd agreed to meet at the vegetable garden the sisters had tended on the hill overlooking the town. All summer they'd grown green beans, onions, carrots and tomatoes. The latter were plentiful and Léa planned to bring some back to the sick bay for the patients.

Rose made her way along the winding path that led to the vegetable gardens perched on a slope that received abundant sun. She set about picking the tomatoes and placing them in a wicker basket.

The moment she heard Léa coming along the path, Rose stood and went to meet her. "I've got something to tell you—it's important."

Léa smiled. "Me first. I have a letter that arrived for you today and I think it's even more important." She handed her an envelope.

Who would write to her here? She flipped it over and read the return address: *André Simon, Richthofen-Gemeinschaftslager, Berlin.*

"André's in Berlin!" She felt her world tilt as if a miracle had occurred. He'd found her. It must have been through Maître Mallon. She clasped the envelope close to her heart.

"Aren't you going to open it?" Léa asked.

She needed a moment to take it all in. André had found her. It was almost too good to be true. Rose looked at her sister. "What if it's bad news? I don't think I could—"

"Don't be silly. Open it," Léa said.

Rose went to a large, flat rock near the basket of tomatoes and sat down. She read her name and address on the envelope again, recognizing André's light touch in his writing. Her hands quavered, knowing he had handled the paper before her.

Richthofen-Gemeinschaftslager
Barrack 6
Tempelhof Airport
Berlin-Tempelhof, SW 68

Rose Cotillard
Foreign Workers Barracks
Glashütte, Saxony, 17

14 May 1943

Ma Chère Rose,

When I received a letter from Maître Mallon informing me that you are in Germany with your sister, I could hardly believe it. To have read that you came to help Léa, but also you hoped to find me, makes me realize what a brave young woman you are, willing to endure hardship for others.

I can only imagine how difficult these last months have been. I hope your conditions are better than here in Berlin. I work for Weser Aircraft, where I assemble Stuka dive bombers. There are many barracks at the airport, but I live in one with eighty Frenchmen divided among ten rooms. We are a mix of STOs and former POWs, and you might imagine how well we have come to know one another over these last months. The hours are long and the work is hard, but still, we are the lucky ones, allowed to have beer and lemonade, which is much better than what others have. As I am sure you are aware.

Since I've been in Berlin, we've had a few air alerts warning of British bombers, but none of them serious. Though I'm not allowed to move around freely, I can apply for a day pass to visit the city, which should be granted since I have no marks on record. If you could come here, then we might spend an entire day together or more. There is so much that I'd like to tell you, but I can only share it with you in person.

I trust this letter reaches you safely. I don't know how many barracks are in the town of Glashütte, but I am confident that anyone who has met the beautiful and brave Rose Cotillard will not have forgotten her, and hence my letter will eventually wend its way to you.

Please don't delay in writing back after you receive this, confirming your correct address. I always want to know where you are, Rose.

With much love,

André

She read it one more time, savoring every word. *Berlin. Tempelhof Airport. French POWs. Beautiful and Brave.* And then her favorite part: *if you could come here*. All this time, she'd worried he would reject her like the French soldiers had done at the canteen, accusing her of being a collaborator. But he understood.

"What does he say?" Léa asked.

"He's in Berlin at the Tempelhof Airport with other French POWs assembling Stuka dive bombers," she said, realizing that he hadn't mentioned their love for one another and hoped that meant he was being careful not to let others know their secret.

"I'm happy you found him," said her sister, smiling. To be honest, I didn't think it was possible. You and he are meant to be together."

"He said he isn't allowed to move around freely the way we are but he can visit the city if he applies for a day pass. He wants me to come see him." She turned to Léa. "Can I travel to Berlin?"

"You'll have to apply, and if your record is clear, they will grant you permission. I don't see any reason why they wouldn't allow it."

"Come with me, please!"

"If you'd like me to, yes, I will." She squeezed Rose's hand. "A trip to Berlin to see André! Now you have something to look forward to." Léa squatted alongside her sister. "It's your turn—you said you have something important to tell me."

Rose lowered her eyes. "It's not something I'm proud of. I hope you won't hate me."

"Of course I won't hate you. What's happened?"

"I met someone a few months ago. After my shift ended, I went to the church to draw because it was quiet and warm inside. I noticed a pile of candles and decided to take a few—"

"You stole them? Were you caught?"

"No. But a man approached me and well, I talked to him. Anguish was etched all over his face. He'd just received news that his brother had died in battle."

"Who is this man?"

The name was seared in Rose's mind, the harsh K scratching like a saw at the back of her throat. "*Kriminalinspektor* Kurt Reinhardt."

Léa blinked. "I know that name. He's a Gestapo officer."

"How do you know that about him?"

"Josef told me that the sick bay reports I type, he then delivers to Reinhardt. He insists on knowing who is in the sick bay, for how long and when they will return to work. If a name stays on the report for more than a week, Reinhardt orders the person sent to a forced labor camp."

A bone-deep fear coursed through Rose. Léa had confirmed what she'd suspected—that he was a powerful man who could determine the fate of others. "I wished I'd never spoken to him. I only wanted to help, but then it was like something inside him snapped and he changed. I hated making that awful Heil Hitler salute. I didn't want to, but I feared if I didn't— "

"Slow down. Start at the beginning. Tell me every detail, don't leave anything out." Worry flickered in Léa's eyes. "Do you think he was following you, trying to make you betray others?"

"Oh no, I'm sure it was all by chance. He was grieving his brother's death. He even cried. His pain was real. He felt so alone, almost desperate. He confided in me—a stranger—as if I was the only person he could talk to. Isn't that sad?"

"Too many enemies. Not enough friends," Léa said. "What did you tell him?"

"I did my best to console him, telling him about Maman and that I'm an orphan too . . ." She stopped. "You told me not to, but I thought here it wouldn't matter so much."

"Herr Reinhardt is an orphan?"

"That's what he said. It was just him and his brother, Felix, like you and me. That's why after he received the letter that Felix had been killed at the Battle of Stalingrad it tore him up."

Rose went on to tell her about how he asked to see her work pass and told her he'd speak with the Meister at Archimedes so that she could have extra privileges. She pressed the heels of her hands against her eyes. "I told him I didn't want him to do that, and that's when he snapped, raising his voice, questioning if I was telling him what to do. When he made the Hitler salute, I felt I had to do the same."

"It's all right," Léa said. "It would only have angered him more if you hadn't done it."

"But oh, how I regret it. He thinks I'm like him, believing in the same things as he does. It's awful."

"Have you seen him since?"

"No. But he's been sending me gifts." Rose looked down. "The oranges—"

"That was all from Reinhardt? Oh, Rose, you should have told me earlier. We could have sent it back to him."

"But wouldn't that only anger him more?"

"Maybe. But now that you've accepted his gifts—"

"I'm tied to him?" It was what she feared. "Today the Meister insisted I take the afternoon shift off. When I declined, he said it was on the orders of 'my powerful friend.'" She took a breath. "What should I do?"

Léa looked at her with an even gaze. "What do you want to do?"

"I want him out of my life."

"After all that's happened, is that possible?"

"I don't know." Rose looked down at the letter in her hand. "I love André. I want to see him."

"Josef said Reinhardt approves all travel requests for foreign workers."

"Then he could refuse my demand to go to Berlin?"

Léa nodded. "He could do much worse than that."

Rose stood and paced. How could this have happened after one meeting? Heart thumping, she walked around the vegetable garden, kicking the weeds and tall grass. And the answer came—because she'd been kind and given him the salute. It was a mistake. She never should have spoken to him. The realization that it was her fault knotted in her stomach. She turned to Léa. "What can I do now?"

"Only you can decide."

"What would you do if you were me?"

Léa thought for a moment. "From what you've told me, I don't think he's going to stop . . . maybe he expects that the gifts will eventually bring you to him."

Léa was making it worse rather than better. "I'll never go to him." It made her sick to think of it. Again, Rose glanced at André's letter. This should have been the happiest day of her life, being reunited with him, but it was the worst and all because she showed kindness to a Gestapo officer. "It's not fair. Why me?"

"Do you remember Juliette?" said Léa. "The woman I met at the camp in Jargeau? I told you about her."

"The prostitute with a three-year-old boy?"

"Yes. She sold herself to men to protect and feed her child. Then she came to Germany, thinking it was better to work in a factory for the enemy than as a prostitute."

"Why are you speaking about her?"

"When Juliette told me her story—" Léa glanced at the sky "—it changed everything for me. If she could sell her body to protect her child, then I could come to Germany to protect you. Don't you see that we're the lucky ones? Our choices are terrible but we still have the luxury of choice. We can choose to take the difficult path, the one we don't want but which can help others."

Rose couldn't believe what Léa was suggesting. "Are you saying I should pretend to have a relationship with Reinhardt, a man I detest, and somehow it will help others. Who will it help?"

"No, Rose. I am not saying that." Léa pointed to the tomatoes in the basket. "But in a way, it's what you've been doing already, giving the privileges he offers you to others." She took a breath. "Now you could do it with more intention. The Polish women need food, clothes and medicine. You've seen how they struggle, how they're treated. It's almost winter. We won't have much more to supplement their rations." She touched Rose's shoulders with both her hands. "Imagine how much more we could do for these women with *his* help. We can't feel afraid when we're thinking of others."

Rose stepped back and buried her head in her hands. "You know he'll want something from me in return." Her voice quavered. "What will I do then?"

Léa winced. "The thought of him— It's terrible. So you must think of all the people that you'll be helping. Reinhardt would never want a Polish or Russian woman. You have power, Rose. And if you use it to do good, then you have nothing to fear."

A terrible sinking feeling overcame Rose. As much as she hated to admit it, deep in her heart, she knew Léa was right.

21

Léa

September 1943

A bitter cold air seeped through the cement walls in the sick bay's office. Leaves had already begun to scatter on the ground; winter felt around the corner. Josef sat beside Léa with his glasses perched on the crown of his head, pinching the ridge of his nose with his thumb and forefinger.

"What did you just say?" he said, distracted.

Léa had urged him to change his bloodstained clothes—the red had deepened to a wine color. Earlier, he'd spent the afternoon trying to save an Italian worker whose hand had been caught in a milling machine, severing an artery. Josef couldn't stem the bleeding in time. The man died. Later, he'd lamented to Léa about the lack of medical equipment that prevented him from doing his job.

"Should I send Rose with the death certificate to bring with the other reports to the Gestapo office?"

"Yes." He tilted his head to one side. "Why is your sister doing this?"

As if summoned, Rose pushed the office door open. She'd been so quiet that neither Léa nor Josef had heard her open the sick bay's front door. Josef stood.

Rose stared at his clothes, wide-eyed. "What happened?"

"Factory accident," Josef said, sliding his chair to Rose so she could sit. "Léa has told me so much about you. It's an honor to meet you."

"She has told me about you, too. *Énchanté.*"

He closed the door, looking uncomfortable, and fixed his eyes on her sister. "Rose. Forgive the lack of preamble. But if I may be frank, I worry about your plan to go to the Gestapo office tonight." He cleared his throat. "How did you meet Herr Reinhardt?"

"By chance. I was alone in the church." Glancing at Léa, Rose shifted her weight in the chair. "He came in, sat with me, we talked, and he took a liking to me, said he would speak to the Meister to grant me privileges. I haven't seen him again."

"Maybe it's a godsend. Why go to him now?"

"I want to help the Polish women who need more food. Léa told me about Maria."

"We must find another way that won't put you in danger." He leaned back against the counter. "Privileges come with strings attached."

"You mean to report on others?"

"Not only that."

Rose sat very still. "I'm prepared to do what I must. If he presses me for information on others, I'll say I don't know anything or give him false information."

"Herr Reinhardt's job is to sniff out false information." Josef shot a worrying look at Léa. "He's not a stable man. Nor is he someone you can control, despite what you might believe. I don't think either of you should be involved with him."

"But, Josef, you don't have the medical equipment to save lives," Léa said. "If we can manage—"

"He's got a temper," he cut in. "It doesn't take much to set him off."

Léa had never met Reinhardt. She could only go on what Rose had told her. Now that Josef had raised such concerns, she felt less confident. But Rose was in a bind. Reinhardt had been sending her gifts for months; it was clear he desired a relationship. Should she risk upsetting him now by returning any future gifts only to find she might not be able to see André? Or should she try to speak with him to understand his intentions better and possibly find a way to help those in need? She looked at Rose. "Maybe Josef's correct. We can always find another way to help the Polish women."

"You know I don't have a choice. He said we would meet again." She exhaled. "I can't make him disappear. And I want to see André."

"He's Gestapo," Josef cut in. "I don't think you know what that means."

Rose bit her bottom lip. "Everyone has a weakness. He showed his to me. I *can* do this."

Léa heard the determination in Rose's voice. She had something to prove. And what harm could there be in her delivering the report for one night? If she felt unsure, then she could stop. "Assess him tonight. If you feel too uncomfortable, you don't have to continue," Léa said.

The church bell rang six times. Rose needed to go so that she would have enough time to return to the barracks before dinner. After gathering up the pages of the report, Léa put them in a gray folder and handed them to her sister.

"The Gestapo office is on the other side of the church," Josef said. "The white building with a saddle roof. Third floor. Say as little as possible. The more you speak, the greater the chance he has of catching you in a lie."

Rose nodded. "OK."

"Good luck and be careful," Léa said.

After Rose left, Josef sat down. "I never liked Reinhardt. He used to come here, asking questions about the patients as if he didn't believe they were ill. And he threatened the sick with accusations of sabotage if they didn't return to work. After he sent a few back to the factory and they died, he left me alone." He rubbed his hands, chapped from the dry air and constant washing. "He's a wolf."

"We're living in the time of the wolves."

"That's why Rose should keep her head down, wait for this horrible war to end."

If everyone did that, then where would they be? She'd already seen that behavior in France. "I don't think she has that option," she said, as Josef approached her. "Rose may have some power when she meets him again. He hasn't seen her for four months but he's been sending her gifts, trying to draw her to him." She looked away. "And Rose has other reasons for doing this. We're not like you."

"What does that mean?" he asked gently.

She sucked in air. "France is an ally of Germany. We weren't rounded up, we came here willingly."

"I don't believe that."

"It's true."

"I mean, no one ends up in this old mining town on the edge of Germany working ten-hour days because they *want* to be here. War is a massive uncontrollable wave, sweeping up all life in its wake. Don't blame yourself." He took a breath. "In Prague, when the Germans first annexed Bohemia and Moravia, the economy was in such a spiral, with no work or food, the Germans easily convinced many to come and work in Germany so they could send money back home."

"But you didn't do that, did you?"

"I was rounded up later."

"What happened?"

There was a long, strained silence before he spoke. "A group of Resistance fighters attacked a German convoy outside Prague. I didn't know anything about it but happened to be on duty at the hospital in Prague when one of the fighters was carried in through the back door, a bullet lodged in the chest."

"Did he survive?"

He closed his eyes for a moment. "I should have reported him . . . the Gestapo arrived, found him and put an end to his life. Then they rounded up all the staff in the hospital who had interacted with the patient and sent us off to work in Germany."

"I'm sorry. What a price we pay for trying to do the right thing?"

He looked at her. "It's why I'm a doctor, to save lives." He shrugged. "I don't know how else to function."

"If you were given a choice, would you have come here to help the enemy?"

"It depends on the context." He smiled. "In the end, how you ended up here isn't as important as what you do while you're here." He slid the chair closer to her.

"Not all would agree. At the canteen, French soldiers spat at Rose, calling her a traitor. Her beau is in Berlin. She plans to visit him. She wants him to be proud of her. Mostly, she wants to be proud of herself, to hold her head high without shame, knowing that she didn't ignore suffering but made a difference."

He smiled. "I admire that. How big is the age gap between you?"

"Three years. But we've been on our own for the last three years after our mother died."

"Then I'd say you've been a good role model for her. Will you go with her to Berlin?"

"Yes, we've put in a request for a leave of absence."

"Berlin has everything. I could have saved that man today if—"

"Tell me?"

"I had basic items like a tourniquet, gauze, bandages, antiseptics, even gloves." He shook his head. "I don't have any money to buy them."

"If Rose develops a relationship with Reinhardt, he—"

"No. I could never forgive myself if she got in trouble with him because of me. You mustn't allow her to do this."

"Let's see what happens tonight. Rose says he's lonely and seems to need her."

He tilted his head. "What if that's a ruse, to draw her to him?"

"How could he have known she would be in the church?"

"I don't know. Perhaps I'm paranoid, overreacting. Rose is terribly brave and good like . . ." He stared at her.

For a moment, Léa wondered if he might kiss her. Did she want him to? Yes. But he didn't move, so she stepped away, flustered. Foolish, she told herself. Josef, a doctor, was refined and educated. He would never be attracted to a simple typist like her.

"I haven't thanked you properly for all the time you spend typing the reports," he said.

"It's nothing."

"Can I ask you something?"

"Yes."

"Do you— Who is this French beau waiting for Rose?"

She'd expected a question about herself. Wrong again. Feeling a burning rise in her cheeks from embarrassment, she grabbed her bag. "A man named André from Orléans," she said, a little too quickly. "I'm going to the barracks. I want to be there when Rose returns."

"Léa?"

"I have to go." She nearly ran for the door. "See you tomorrow." She was being childish and didn't want to make a fool of herself in front of him. She couldn't let him see that she was imagining him having feelings for her that he didn't have. She liked typing his reports and didn't want her presence in the sick bay to make him uncomfortable. Ever since Léa had seen André and Rose together, she'd yearned for the same sort of love. It was silly. She didn't need romantic love to have an enjoyable, fulfilling life. There was nothing wrong with being alone. She must stop dreaming about things that weren't meant for her.

22

Rose

At the church square, Rose hesitated. Nagging doubts buzzed in her mind. Was Josef right that she couldn't handle the Gestapo officer? Should she reconsider and play it safe? Maybe he would forget her and she could just wait out the war. Yet fortune had put her in this unique position—to help others and possibly see André in Berlin—and she would never forgive herself if she didn't seize this chance. She had to try.

It began to rain. Thick, heavy drops signaled a larger storm on its way. Tucking the file inside her coat, she ran across the street to the building with the saddle roof. She opened the door, expecting someone might appear and demand her work card. But the corridor was empty and quiet. The door clicked shut behind her. She removed the file from her coat and reached for the wooden banister.

The treads creaked and the boards bent under her weight. With each step, she felt fear and unease rising within her. It was one thing to meet a Gestapo officer by chance, another thing entirely to seek him out. *You can do this.* Reaching the barren first floor, she guessed everyone had left for the day. She continued until she arrived on the second floor. A door to the left of the stairs stood ajar. She heard the crackling and popping of a fire in a hearth, along with the pungent scent of ash and smoke, drifting into the corridor.

"Herr Kriminalinspektor Reinhardt?" Rose called out, not wishing to startle him.

Clomp, *thud*. She stiffened at the sound of his jackboots on the wooden floor.

A foreboding figure appeared at the door. "Is that Fräulein Cotillard? Why are you here?"

"I've brought the sick bay report." On the way over, she'd worked out what she'd say.

"Where's Herr Capek?"

"He's completing the paperwork on the death of an Italian worker this afternoon and couldn't get away." She held out the gray folder, doing her best to keep her arm steady.

Taking it, he motioned with his hand that she should step inside. The warmth of the fire enveloped her, melting her resolve a little, reminding her of all he had, which she lacked. *It's only on the surface.* She had an inner strength and she'd seen his weakness. Squaring her shoulders, she pushed the shaky moment aside and took in the room. In the center stood a large desk with papers stacked on it and a lamp with a green shade.

"Remove your wet coat and sit down," he commanded, pressing a brass bell on the table. "I'll call for tea."

She hung the musky, wet wool coat on a wooden stand near the door before settling into the chair across from his desk. An older woman opened a side door. He gave her curt instructions to bring two teas. Rose felt the burn of the woman's gaze before she retreated.

"What is your connection to Herr Capek?"

"My sister types his medical reports. She asked me to come tonight to deliver them."

"I see. Have you liked my gifts?" He smiled.

"You're very generous."

"How long has it been since we met in the church?"

"Four months, about. You came to say a prayer for Felix."

He turned to the window. The rain fell hard outside, knocking against the glass. "You were kind to sit with me that night."

Hope stole through Rose that she might reestablish the personal connection they'd had in the church. "We were both mourning family."

"At the time . . . I had no idea the scale of the loss." He rubbed his hands together. "It's only recently come to light."

She wasn't sure what he meant. A side door opened, and the woman entered carrying a tray with tea to the table. "Anything else, Herr Reinhardt?"

"No, that will be all. You're dismissed."

The woman bowed and left.

"Sugar or milk?" he asked.

Rose would have liked a spoonful of sugar to sweeten the tea, but it was already a privilege to be out of the cold on a stormy night, and she wouldn't allow herself more. Every comfort might weaken her resolve. That was why he sent her all those gifts. "No, thank you."

"I've just been reading that you and your sister have put in a travel request for Berlin."

She started, nearly spilling the tea on her dress. She hadn't expected him to know about Berlin so soon. *Say as little as possible so he can't catch you in a lie.*

"May I ask, what is the purpose of the Berlin trip?"

She put the cup down, wrapping one hand around the porcelain, giving herself time to think through what else he might know or could find out. Maman had always warned that on the few occasions where a lie was merited, keep it as truthful as possible.

"To visit my cousin."

"His name?" He lifted the pen from his desk.

"André Simon, my aunt's son. He works at Tempelhof Airport in Berlin."

"Ah, yes. The letter."

She swallowed. She'd memorized every word in André's letter by heart. He hadn't said anything about love, just that he wanted her to come to Berlin. She was safe.

"He's quite sentimental for the summers we played together on the quai in Orléans. I told him I will do my best to visit." André had been discreet. He must have known the Gestapo would read his letters and wanted to protect her.

"I think my office could easily grant permission for such an outing." He put the pen down. "However, I would require some cooperation on your part."

She withdrew her hand from the cup; the tea had now turned cold. "What could—"

"It's about Herr Capek." He leaned back in the chair, placing his elbows on the armrests. "He has been tasked to provide minimal medical care."

"Isn't that what he does?" She could see from the hardening of his jaw that she was not meant to speak without him asking her to.

"Where is the list?"

"What list?"

"Of the patients who cannot return to work quickly. I need the names to arrange their transport."

"Transport?"

"To other camps, of course. They cannot stay here if they're unable to work."

Rose had heard rumors about death and concentration camps that circulated among the foreign laborers. That threat kept the production line going, the quotas met, because there was always the fear that something worse awaited them if they stepped out of line. Of course, Josef wouldn't put a single name on that list. No good caring man would. "I don't know."

He leaned back in the chair. "Isn't it fortunate that destiny placed you and your sister in close contact with him? Now, I'll have two pairs of eyes and ears in the sick bay, reporting to me on what's going on."

Rose's leg began to shake as it always did when she felt a wave of fear like blackness descending. Curling her right foot around the chair leg, she let her panic coil tight against the wood, all the while holding his gaze. "I haven't spoken with Herr Capek much. It's my sister who works with him on the patient reports."

"Léa?" He read her name from the file on his desk.

"Yes."

"Well, perhaps she can provide you with what I'm after. Please ask her to observe Herr Capek. To facilitate communication, I expect you to bring the patient reports at night from now on. I will inform Herr Capek by letter of my decision." He gulped down the rest of the tea, emptying his cup. "These nightly visits will allow you to share with me what you've learned and, I hope, provide the names I require for my list." He looked down at his desk.

Rose nodded, sensing their meeting was drawing to a close, but she still hadn't procured vouchers or money to support the other women. "There is one thing I wondered—"

He raised his head and stared at her.

"Is it possible to obtain more food vouchers?"

He gave her a puzzled look. "Aren't enough provisions provided for the French workers?"

"They're easily stolen."

"Give me names. The thieves will be severely punished."

"I don't know who steals them. It happens at night; people go through my things, and in the morning, the vouchers are gone." She took a breath. "It could be women from another barracks."

"I can't say I'm surprised. The Slavs have a natural predilection toward crime. Of course, I can arrange . . ." He thought for a moment. "Rather than going through the administrative burden of requesting more vouchers." He opened a desk drawer. "Why don't I give you a small amount of cash every night when you come with the reports?" He pulled out a five-Reichsmark note from his wallet and handed it to her.

She could hardly believe her eyes. Five Reichsmarks every day. She'd earn the equivalent of a second salary in a week. "Thank you."

"I'll give instructions that the train tickets for you and Léa should be issued for next month. Autumn in Berlin. Save some of those Reichsmarks so that you two can enjoy yourselves in our esteemed capital with your cousin." He smirked. "Did I get that right?"

She nodded, noticing a sharpness in his tone, like the blade of a dagger. Had she missed something?

"I think we've concluded a satisfactory agreement?"

"Yes." Maybe she was overthinking. She'd accomplished what she came here to do.

He stood. "Goodnight, Fräulein Cotillard."

"Goodnight, Herr Reinhardt."

Rose took her coat and dashed down the stairs. The unease she'd felt on the way up had worn off. She would help Josef to protect the sick and do what she could to keep any name off the list by distracting the Kriminalinspektor with her nightly visits. Léa would be proud, and she would go to Berlin to see André. Tucking the five-Reichsmark note inside her pocket, Rose reached the last tread in no time, her step lighter than before.

23

Léa

October 1943

Léa, sitting next to Rose in the third-class passenger carriage, stiffened at the throng of soldiers and police at Berlin's Anhalter station. When the sisters stepped down from the train, it was as if the midday sun had disappeared behind a cloud. The platform was as dark as a bruise. Léa pointed at the camouflage net covering the roof and stretching over the many tracks. On the opposite platform, a train with a red cross painted on a white background was parked. Bandaged soldiers stepped off it while medical workers unloaded endless numbers of wounded soldiers on stretchers.

News of the Wehrmacht's defeat at Stalingrad, then at Kursk had cast a different light on the seemingly invincible power of the German army. Josef believed both losses marked a turning point in the war. *They won't recover from this; now it's just a matter of how long and how bloody until they're crushed.* It was the bloody part that worried everyone. As the army retreated, it rounded up Polish and Russian citizens forcing them to come with them. It almost seemed like the Wehrmacht were taunting their enemies to chase after them and collect the booty they'd stolen on their retreat.

On the bright side, though Léa hesitated to think about it that way, was Rose's connection to Herr Reinhardt. The Reichsmarks he provided augmented the sick bay's resources, allowing them to purchase equipment, medicine, and food from farmers who sold their milk, cheese and meat on the black market. Supplementing Maria's rations had made a huge difference in her and her baby's health. Now, the malnourished Polish women arrived at the sick bay, receiving both food and medicine. Josef believed it was the former that saved more lives.

"Rose, stay close," Léa said, taking her sister's hand as they exited the station. At the back of her mind, she couldn't shake Josef's warning that Reinhardt was a wolf. He continued to try and persuade Rose to stop taking the money. *Nothing is free—he'll demand more from you.* But Rose was already in too deep. She'd been trapped in a web of her own making, unable to stop delivering the reports without arousing suspicion. All she could do was continue bluffing her way through, trying to convince Reinhardt that all the rules were being followed at the sick bay and hoping he would lose interest in all of them.

They walked along Stresemannstrasse, weaving between the workers and deliverymen to avoid being knocked over. A cold wind blew, whipping around the buildings and cutting through their thin coats like a sharp knife.

"Have you ever seen such tall buildings?" Rose asked. "Does Paris looks like this?"

Léa, too, was overwhelmed. Even though Josef had warned her that four million people lived in Berlin, she couldn't imagine what that looked or sounded like until she saw and heard it for herself.

They were on their way to the Kaffee Post, located off a side street from the famous Unter den Linden. André had written to Rose asking her to meet him there today at one o'clock.

"Are you excited to see him?" Léa asked as they passed a wooden shack on a strip of sidewalk. Men loitered outside speaking a foreign language—Léa figured it was a makeshift barracks for foreign workers.

"A little nervous. What if it isn't like before and we don't have anything to talk about or . . ."

Léa squeezed her hand. She suspected Rose was apprehensive about the change in her physical appearance over the last year. It was true that the long hours at the factory had taken a toll. Dark circles under her eyes, her complexion pale, her cheeks hollow. Her clothes had patches at the elbows, and the sisters still wore the same boots they'd worn on the day they left France. Léa wanted to put Rose at ease by telling her that none of these things mattered.

"André cares about who you are inside. He knows what you're going through because he's experiencing the same. It will be fine."

"I hope so." Rose smoothed out her hair. "Are we going the right way?"

Léa stopped to glance at the map Josef had given her. For a year before the war, he'd studied medicine at the Friedrich Wilhelm University, so he knew Berlin well and had helped the sisters plan the best route to walk from Anhalter Station to Unter den Linden, advising them to take the main roads to avoid getting lost on the side streets. "Yes, we need to cross Potsdamer Platz up ahead. Look how busy it is!"

The sisters made their way around the massive square teeming with trams, buses, cars and pedestrians. The noise was deafening—horns honking, bells ringing, and men leaning out their windows barking, *Aus dem Weg Idioten*—as Rose and Léa headed east to Leipziger Street.

"Look at the rooftops," Rose said, pointing at more camouflage nets. "Is that to confuse the bombers?"

"I think so." Léa now understood how much Maître Mallon had protected them by requesting they be sent to a small town. Some buildings looked as if they'd recently suffered damage from a bombing raid, while every street corner had a sign pointing to the nearest bomb shelter.

"Do you think they're expecting a large bombing attack on Berlin?" Rose asked.

"It seems that way."

"I hope André will be safe."

"He'll know what to do." Léa wanted to reassure Rose, but she was worried about how the war would come to an end. It was hard to fathom if people like the Meister, Lagerführer or Kriminalinspektor would one day stop believing in their racial superiority. They'd spent all these years treating men and women as if they were no better than rats. How could a switch be flipped in their brains and they'd suddenly become human again? She couldn't see it happening other than by force. And the more she walked through the streets of Berlin, the more it felt like a veil of death hung over the city—adults wore black crepe bands on their sleeves, women dressed in all black—the city was in mourning for its lost sons, husbands and brothers who had died fighting for the Third Reich. And yet there was no sense that it had been enough. If anything, the will to fight seemed as strong as ever like the country was gripped in a senseless death wish.

Just before reaching Friedrich Street, where they would turn north to join Unter den Linden, the sisters passed a massive building with an imposing stone façade. Two eagle sculptures, gripping a swastika in their claws, perched on top of columns at the building's entrance. Léa read the sign: *Ministry of Aviation*. She thought of all the lives that had been lost and all the lives that still had to be sacrificed before this dammed war would be over.

She feared for the people who would be trapped inside the city as the worst came. What about her, Rose, André and Josef? Would they all be swept up in it, too? How would they survive the violence that was surely headed to Germany? Berliners glanced nervously over both shoulders as though they knew something terrible was coming, and now Léa knew it too.

Kaffee Post was at the end of a quiet street behind the elegant shops on Unter den Linden. There were no tables outside, only a large window where customers could line up for pastries. Léa overheard the Italian, Dutch and French accents of the foreign laborers milling around outside, taking advantage of their lunch break to be in the fresh air.

The sisters went in and took the last table in the corner. It was round and small with only two chairs. "Shall we wait for a bigger table?" Rose asked.

"No. I'll leave you two to get reacquainted and return to Potsdamer Platz to find the medical supply shop."

Léa had no intention of intruding on their reunion. In her pocket was a long list of supplies to bring back for Josef.

She imagined Josef in his office typing the reports. Though it was silly—since they were just friends—she missed him. The best time of the day, what she looked forward to, was being by his side. She liked his warmth, the kindness and respect he had for others, and all he taught her about caring for the sick. She'd begun to do more than typing the reports, helping with other, smaller tasks.

They ordered two coffees. "Will you tell André about Reinhardt?" Léa asked.

"Do you think I should?"

"Yes." Maybe men understood other men in ways women couldn't. If André backed up Josef's warnings about Reinhardt, it might give Rose the push she needed to stop meeting with the Gestapo officer, if that was even possible. The sick bay had built up enough resources to get through a few months without the extra money and who knew how much longer the war would go on. "Tell him."

After the coffee came, Rose leaned forward and asked about Josef. "Could you ever love him?"

"What?" She laughed. "There's nothing between us. Why would you think that?"

Rose shrugged. "Just curious. You spend a lot of time together."

"We're working together."

"Right." Rose sipped her coffee. "Has he ever tried to kiss you?"

"I said there's nothing between us."

"I still dream about the night I kissed André in the cinema."

It seemed somehow wrong to think about love surrounded by the haunting images on Berlin's streets—black crepe bands, camouflage nets, bomb shelter signs—all pointing to the violent end awaiting them. "Have you ever wondered how we will get back home?" She asked.

"The French army will come and get us." Rose sipped her coffee.

"Most of that army is over here in prison camps."

"You mean we will have to find our way home?"

"Maybe." Léa sighed. "I don't know."

"What about all the POWs? They won't just leave them here."

"Remember how the French POWs at Glashütte dismissed us. One of them spat at you, as if we didn't deserve to be French. Do you think they will change their opinion after the war? Will anyone care what happens to us or welcome our return?" She breathed in deeply. So much hatred had been ginned up in people, turning them against one another, that she suspected not even the war ending would stop it.

24

Rose

The entire time Rose was in the café, her gaze switched between Léa sitting across from her and the door, with the possibility that André might appear. She worried he might not come—maybe he wouldn't get a day pass—but she kept looking for him, waiting, her leg moving up and down, knocking the table. And then, she saw him standing there—and her heart somersaulted. She stood, the blood rushing through her legs carrying her to him. He reached out and pulled her into his arms as if they were two lovers alone and not in a crowded café. He held her close and for the longest time neither spoke. They didn't need to. She could feel his heart pounding against her own. Twelve long months they'd been apart, but now she felt as though he'd never left her side.

"Welcome to Berlin," he said, pulling back and removing his hat. His black curls had been shorn and thin blue veins like tributaries were visible on his skull. "Let me get a good look at you." He smiled. "Just as beautiful as ever. How are you?"

"Good," she said, holding his hand as they'd done in the cinema a year ago. "It's lovely to see you again."

"It's wonderful to see you."

"Come, Léa's here too."

He followed Rose to the table. Léa stood.

"Why don't we all go outside?" André glanced over his shoulder, crushing his hat in his hand. Rose could see how thin and pale he'd become. His movements were no longer light and carefree but heavy like weights were tied to his limbs.

Outside, he put his hat on. The wind had quieted, but the sun struggled to lift above the clouds. While Léa and André talked, Rose—disoriented—felt as if she'd arrived at a house where she'd once lived, but there was no longer a front door and she wasn't sure how to get inside. Then, Léa left, and it was only the two of them.

"Let's walk," he said, steering her toward Unter den Linden. "Was it hard to get permission to come to Berlin?"

"Not too hard. It's in the contract that they give us time off."

"That's good," he said. "Tell me about where you work."

"In a factory manufacturing rangefinders. I lacquer tiny cylinders. There's a daily quota."

He nodded. She looked at his hollow cheeks and bony shoulders. "And you?"

"I'd like to tell you something else." He turned to her. "My father's dead." His expression hardened. "He died in the Moosburg Camp in Bavaria. I don't even know where that is."

"Oh, I'm so sorry." She stopped and took his hand. It was cold. "When did you find out?"

"Last week. He's been dead since Christmas—that's nearly a year ago. Maman wrote to me after receiving his personal items." He squeezed his eyes tight. "You're the first person I've been able to tell."

Her heart twisted as she watched him holding back tears. "What happened?"

"The letter said he was shot trying to escape." André choked up. "I feel terrible. I should have done something. He had to have known—"

"There was nothing you could do." The front door reappeared, she'd found the handle, opened it and was back inside. She touched his gaunt face and he leaned into her hand.

"Thank God you're here," he said, kissing the palm of her hand. "I've missed you."

"Me too."

They stood on the busy Unter den Linden, cars and people swirling all around, but they didn't notice—they were just two lovers with all the time in the world. Rose wished there was something she could say to ease his grief, but she couldn't find the words. She wondered if simply being present, giving him her hand to hold, was enough.

"Come," he said, after a while. "Let's go to the island. It's calmer there."

They walked to a bridge, stopping to look at the water reflecting the buildings on both banks. As Rose gazed at the reflections, she thought about Léa—with a sister, she never really felt alone. She imagined how hard it must be for André, whose siblings were all much younger, and he had learned of his father's death by himself, so far from home. Crossing the bridge, they entered a park and settled on a stone bench bordered by boxwood hedges. It was a beautiful, peaceful place, and for a moment, the war seemed far away.

"Are you still drawing?" He looked at her with what appeared to be hope flickering in his eyes.

"A little. I've been sketching portraits of Polish and Russian female workers."

"That's wonderful, Rose," he said. "I still remember your stunning portrait of Léa. I'd like to see more." He took her hand. "It's mostly Russians at Tempelhof—three barracks for men and eight for women."

"How are they treated?" She could guess the answer, but she held out hope that maybe in Berlin, people would be more open and accepting.

"I hardly see them. Their barracks sit behind ours, but they keep them separate in a subcamp with a guardhouse and trenches to prevent them from escaping." He sighed. "I'd do anything to get out of Berlin before the bombing raids get worse, but I can't see how." He took a breath. "I fear I'll end up buried under the rubble."

"Don't say that." She touched his face, letting her hand linger on his cheek.

"How else will the war end?"

"There are signs for bomb shelters everywhere. You'll be safe in one." The memory of that horrible night in Orléans, when she and Léa huddled together while the Luftwaffe bombed the city, flashed through her mind. She squeezed his hand, trying to ease his fear.

"They don't let foreign workers into the shelters. When the planes come—sometimes once a week, other times nightly—it's endless. RAF bombers buzz overhead, hundreds at a time, and the sky flashes with fire. The roar swallows everything. Compared to here, Orléans was just sparks. This is a nightmare. We watch it happen, rooted in fear, daring to cheer as each blast pounds in our chests. We pray we won't be hit next."

"They don't let you in the shelters?" she said, alarmed.

"The things I've seen are inhumane."

"Can you ask for a transfer?" she asked gently.

"It doesn't work like that." He shook his head.

But he couldn't stay here helpless, a sitting duck for the bombers. Léa was convinced Berlin would continue to be hit, maybe levelled, and all the preparations seemed to indicate that was what they expected. Rose's thoughts jumped to André's poor mother—she imagined losing first a husband and the possibility of then losing a son in Germany would shatter her. Then her own feelings surfaced. André was the only man she'd ever kissed and the ache of possibly losing him was overwhelming. She couldn't abandon him. Her mind raced for some way to get him out of here.

"Has any foreign worker been transferred out of Tempelhof?"

"There was a fellow from Lyon. He had some special skill, and they sent him to a factory in Hamburg."

"So, it's possible."

"Forget it. I'm glad you came. Maybe we won't see each other again," he said, his voice raw.

"No," she said. "You'll make it through this war—I know you will."

He waved a hand in the air, trying to look unconcerned, but his jaw tightened. Rose leaned forward, refusing to let it drop. Her mind spun to the one person who had the influence to help André. "There's someone in Glashütte who might be able to help."

"He'd have to be powerful to arrange for the transfer of a foreign worker."

"He's the Gestapo officer overseeing security for the foreign workers."

André's eyes went wide. "How do you know him?"

"We met by chance on a day when he was grieving the death of his brother. We've developed a relationship of sorts." She told him about the sick bay, Léa typing Josef's reports and how she delivered them to the Gestapo office every night. "I try to use my contact with him to get extra items like food vouchers or cash. The Eastern and Russian women's rations are nearly at starvation levels."

He looked at her for several seconds. "Does Léa know about this?"

"She encouraged me to engage with him."

"You're putting yourself in danger."

"I'm a woman—he doesn't see me as a threat or suspect me at all."

"He's a Gestapo officer." André frowned. "Everyone is a suspect."

"He's human. He needs someone to listen. That's all."

"Does he know about me?"

"Yes. He approved my travel request to come here. He also reads your letters. He sees all our correspondence before we do and sometimes crosses things out."

"So he knows about *us*?"

She shook her head. "I told him you were my cousin."

"Your cousin, eh?"

"I could ask him to have you transferred to Glashütte."

"You'd do that for me?" His eyes brightened.

"Didn't you save me from that angry German soldier who wanted to arrest me for spying? Now, it's my chance to return the favor."

"This is different. You're dealing with a Gestapo officer."

"What can I tell him? To see if there's a match in one of the factories in Glashütte?"

"At Tempelhof, I work on the timing mechanisms for fuses so that when they release the bombs from the Junkers, they explode at the correct altitude. I hate thinking that I'm hurting innocent people. Sometimes . . ."

Rose leaned forward. "What?"

"I alternate the switches, so they won't work the way they should."

"Sabotage?"

"If I can. There are a lot of eyes on the assembly line. If I do it too much, they'll trace it back to me."

Suddenly, she was seized with the uneasy feeling that even if she could arrange for André to be transferred, what would happen if he sabotaged production in Glashütte, and would she be implicated? Asking him to promise not to do it felt selfish. She didn't want to be like everyone in Orléans—desperate for safety and comfort and unwilling to take risks.

A light rain began to fall. "Are you ever worried you might be caught?" she asked.

"I used to, but after what they did to Papa . . ." he began, but she brought her finger to his lips.

"I understand," she said. "Be careful. I don't want anything to happen to you."

"With you by my side, nothing bad can happen. You're my good luck—"

"Shh," she whispered, pressing her lips to his. The rain fell harder.

"Let's go under the stairs," André said.

They ran across the walkway and stood under the elegant stairs attached to the grand building overlooking the gardens. The rain came down in heavy sheets. Rose's dress was drenched. She shivered. He brought her close, enveloping her in his warmth.

"It's beautiful here," she said. "What's this place called?"

"*Museumsinsel*—Museum Island. Behind us is the Altes Museum, built in the neoclassical style and overlooking the Lustgarten where we were just sitting." He kissed her forehead. "Have you heard of it?"

"No, tell me about it." She wanted to spend every day like this, in his arms, talking.

"Altes was designed by Friedrich Schinkel. Inside is a rotunda modelled on the Pantheon in Rome. We studied it at L'Ecole des Beaux-Arts." He pointed in the direction of the bridge. "Farther along, there's a stunning building designed by his student, Stüler. And on the other side of the river, a building by Alfred Messel that took twenty years to construct. All famous men in the world of architecture." He sighed. "I fear none of these buildings will survive what's coming."

"The air raids?"

"They'll blow Berlin to bits."

"Must they?" she asked. It seemed such a terrible waste.

"The Allies can defeat the Wehrmacht on the battlefield. But to conquer the nation and its people, yes."

"By destroying buildings?" Rose didn't understand. "They're only stone and glass."

"But they hold a connection to Germany's great past. Buildings are mirrors for people to look into and see their culture and identity reflected back. That's why the French kings built Versailles and all the châteaux along the Loire River. People are fragile and die, but what a great nation builds lives on, passing from one generation to another." He hugged her close. "If Berlin is destroyed, the Nazi ideology that triumphed here will end."

Rose shuddered. How many people in Berlin and other German cities would have to die, even after the Wehrmacht was defeated, before this horrible war would draw to a close? Maybe it was what they deserved. The problem was that someone she loved was here and he might not survive the bombing.

Léa and André believed it was only a matter of time before the Allies attacked Berlin on a scale never seen before. Rose could almost feel the danger in the air like the pulse of an approaching electrical storm. She had to get André out of Berlin before it arrived.

* * *

Later, on the train as the sisters made the journey back to Glashütte, Rose told Léa about her idea to get André transferred.

"You will ask Reinhardt?" Léa said, incredulous.

"It can't hurt to try."

"Do you not worry that this will bind you even more to him?"

Rose looked out the window.

"Remember how we talked about—"

"And you said we have to make choices." She turned back. "Sometimes terrible ones, for the greater good. If it comes to that, I'm ready. But so far it's not like that. He's lonely, and since he's in a position where he can't talk to anyone, he wants me there to listen."

Léa leaned back on the wooden seat. Rose could see by her raised eyebrows that she worried about where this latest twist in her relationship with Reinhardt would lead.

"Do you remember when it was only about getting food vouchers to save Maria's baby and help the Polish women?" She leaned forward, lowering her voice. "Maybe you think all he wants is for you to listen. But what if you're wrong?" She pressed her lips together. "Are you prepared to deal with the consequences?"

"If it saves André's life, yes."

"You're still madly in love with him after a year apart?"

Rose smiled. "Yes. And I'm worried. He told me that the foreign workers aren't allowed in the bomb shelters. How will he survive the bombing campaigns the Allies will carry out? André said they will destroy Berlin and everything in it."

Léa sighed and looked out the window. "Even if he has access to the shelters, it will be an experience like no other." She watched the river running alongside the tracks. "Maybe those who do survive will wish they hadn't."

"If I can save him, I must try. What's the worst that will happen? Reinhardt will say no."

Léa reached over and touched Rose's knee. "I'm proud of you. It takes a lot of courage to face a Gestapo officer and ask him to do things to help others." Her respect for Rose beamed bright in her eyes. "Maman would be proud, too, if she were here now."

Rose wanted to say it had nothing to do with courage. Every time she stood alone in the room with Reinhardt, dread and fear coursed through her veins, but what terrified her more was letting those feelings render her helpless, so she did nothing. She'd lived like that for too long, and she wasn't going back.

25

Léa

November 1943

At the assembly line, while Léa was heating the balsam, she heard Maria exhale in short bursts. She looked up. Maria sat on the edge of the stool, doubled over, clutching her stomach.

"Are you all right?" Léa whispered.

"It's time," Maria said, gulping for air.

"Let me finish—"

"Can't wait." She stood and pointed to her soaked skirt.

Her water had broken. Léa needed to move her to the sick bay before anyone noticed. Maria, already underweight, had hidden her bump well with layers of clothing under her apron. Though it wouldn't be possible to keep the baby a secret after the birth, by hiding it this long, at least the authorities couldn't force her to abort it.

Now, it would be up to the Meister to determine the number of days off work Maria would be granted after the birth, so she could rest and recover. Josef said the range was between three and eight days. It would likely be the only chance Maria would have to bond with her child, because after she went back to work, Lagerführer Klein would order the baby placed in the Foreign Worker's Children's Home.

Léa stood, leaving her station.

"Where do you think you're going?" the Meister asked.

He must have eyes at the back of his head, Léa thought, because he always knows the minute I move from my station.

"I'm taking her to the sick bay," she said, standing in front of Maria to hide her damp skirt.

"Again?" He huffed. "What's wrong with her now?"

"Dr. Capek will send you a copy of his report."

"Who will make up the quotas for you both?" He flung his arms up in frustration, but fortunately didn't order them back to their workstations.

Since Rose began delivering the sick bay reports to the Gestapo office, Léa had noticed a change in the Meisters' attitude toward the sisters. Though she felt uneasy about Rose's deepening interaction with Reinhardt—Rose said he kept her in his office every night for half an hour, sometimes more, talking about Felix, his parents and German and Prussian history because that was the subject he'd studied in school before the war—she also valued the broader freedom it granted her.

Outside, Maria stopped on the street. Sunlight hit her shoulders as she doubled over, holding against another wave of pain. Léa rubbed her back. Coal smoke and street dust swirled in the air. She could feel the throbbing in Maria's body. The short intervals between contractions alarmed her because she didn't want her to have this baby anywhere but in the sick bay.

After the pain subsided and Maria stood upright, they continued walking, Léa counted the seconds until the next contraction hit.

"Come on, just a little farther," she said, encouraging her.

Léa helped her up the stairs into the sick bay. Maria's eyes widened, and Léa understood the pain was escalating fast. She guided Maria onto the bed while Josef washed his hands before coming over to examine her.

"The contractions are seventy seconds apart," Léa said. "I timed them on our way here."

He nodded and examined her. "She's fully dilated." He turned to Léa. "You were right to get her here so quickly."

She was spending more time at the sick bay, taking on an increasingly supportive role. Josef had too much to do—in addition to typing reports for the Gestapo, he kept an inventory of the medical supplies, tracked financial accounts and disinfected all items used during the day to prevent the spread of disease. This was all on top of his day job of looking after the patients. Léa had seen that he needed help, and once she was proficient with the German keyboard and could finish the patient reports in no time, she began to disinfect the medical equipment by soaking them in chlorine tablets mixed with water.

"Maria, I need you to push," Josef said, gently.

Léa went to Maria's side, lifting her back so she could sit up and use her upper body to give her more power.

"*Arhhh*," Maria shouted. Léa pulled her hair back away from her face.

"The baby's crowning," Josef said, leaning forward. "Push, Maria, push."

A few pushes later, and a dark-haired girl slid out. Josef cut the umbilical cord, placed her on the scale, then wrapped her in a blanket before putting her in Maria's arms.

"Thank you," Maria said, guiding the baby to her breast.

"You did all the hard work." Josef smiled. "Get her to feed well tonight so she can put on weight."

Léa noted how tiny the baby appeared. "What's her name?"

"*Ewa*," Maria said, "it means Eve."

"That's beautiful." Léa leaned down and kissed Ewa on the crown. "For a beautiful girl."

Léa cleaned up the towels and mopped the floor. Two women were scheduled to come later tonight to clean the sick bay, but she didn't want to leave the afterbirth mess on the floor or bed, and Josef had too much to do to tend to it. When she finished, she found him in the office, writing notes for the reports.

"It all happened so quickly," she said. "Her labor couldn't have taken more than two hours. I thought labor was a twelve- or eighteen-hour event."

"Maria had a compressed labor."

"What's that?"

"It can happen when a baby has a low birth weight. Small babies move through the birth canal more quickly. When I weighed the baby, she was at just under two kilos."

"What would a baby normally weigh?"

"Three kilos." He wiped his forehead. "Can you give Maria an ampoule of Betabion, please? She's going to need to pass the Vitamin D on to the baby in her milk." He sighed. "I hate seeing them so vulnerable."

Léa nodded and made her way to the medicine cabinet. Betabion was one of the items she'd brought back from Berlin. After returning from the capital, she'd helped Josef arrange everything he'd requested, asking him about each one in the process. He required four boxes of Betabion. "It's vitamin B or thiamine," he explained. "Those suffering from malnutrition lack vitamin B."

"What is the outcome of a vitamin B deficiency?" she asked, returning to the office.

"It can make the blood too acidic and cause nerve problems. If mothers don't have enough vitamin D in their milk, their babies will have trouble feeding."

He turned away to concentrate on his notes, rubbing his neck with his hand. As Léa watched, she felt a sudden urge to reach over and do that for him. She could sense the tension like knots under his skin from everything he took on. Outside, the situation weighed on both of them: the retreating German army was bringing back many Polish and Russian forced laborers, a few of whom were arriving in Glashütte. All were in poor health, and it was already winter, straining the sick bay's limited resources.

"You're doing the best you can," she said, gently, hoping her words would ease his stress.

"Am I?" He drew a breath as if to refocus. "I need to rearrange things, find a more efficient process. I've got people standing outside the sick bay waiting to get in, and if I can't see them within a few hours, they have to return to the factories and won't be able to get the time off to come back."

Léa, too, was worried about running out of supplies. She knew she wouldn't get permission to return to Berlin for many months, if at all. But she had an idea and wanted to share it with Josef to see if it might help.

"I spoke to a Norwegian worker who regularly receives a certain tonic from her family."

"Which one?"

"Cod liver oil."

"It's an excellent source of iodine and vitamins A and D." He put his pen down. "Can she get more?"

"No, but she suggested we write to the Red Cross, telling them our situation and requesting regular supplies of cod liver oil. Norway is the main source for Europe."

"We have nothing to lose by trying. All they can do is say no."

"Was Ewa your first delivery?"

"Oh no, I've brought quite a few babies into the world?"

"How many?"

He thought for a moment. "A dozen." He looked down. "Not all of them lived, unfortunately."

"What does it feel like to be the first human contact for a baby?"

"I'm not, it's the mother. She's the one who provides everything the child needs through the umbilical cord. I'm just a helper."

"So you don't feel anything?"

"I feel honored and awed. It's magical. But I'm always vigilant. If something goes wrong, then I'm ready." He went quiet. "Sometimes there are seconds in which everything is on the line and making one wrong move will end that new life before it has a chance to take its first breaths. I couldn't live with that on my conscience. So, mostly I'm on guard, expecting the worst so that I'm ready to counter it and save a life."

"I think you're amazing." Léa felt that Josef unlocked the best in her.

"You do?"

"I wish I could help you more."

"You're doing so much. I'm grateful."

"Do you ever worry about how the war will end?"

He half-turned away. "Why worry about what I can't control?"

"To be ready, have a plan, know what you're going to do."

"I'm too busy living in the present." He returned to his notes. "I don't have time to think of the future."

Kiss me, she whispered inside her head. It was a moment of desire so intense and sudden that it nearly overwhelmed her. What was she thinking? Clearly, he wasn't interested. She'd been coming to the sick bay to work with him for nine months and he hadn't tried to kiss her once. Maybe it was seeing Rose and André together in Berlin that made Léa, after denying it to herself for so long, crave love, too. She had to stop. If Josef hadn't kissed her by now, he never would.

She stood. "Let me type a letter for the International Red Cross, requesting deliveries of cod liver oil. The sooner we get them, the better."

26

Rose

December 1943

After returning from Berlin, Rose discovered that Reinhardt was out of town. The first night she delivered the sick bay reports to the Gestapo office, it was Frau Birks—the one who always made tea on Reinhardt's orders—who opened the door.

"Herr Reinhardt is away," she said, lifting her shoulders and extending her arm. "You may leave the report with me."

For the entire week, Frau Birks again opened the door.

Rose wanted to know how long he would be away. She worried about André and his safety. A transfer would take months, and from what she could read of the headlines in the German papers, the Allies had intensified their bombing campaign.

The second week, Rose finally mustered the resolve to speak to Frau Birks. "When will Herr Reinhardt return?"

She snapped the file from Rose's hand. "Missing your lover?"

Rose bristled. "I don't understand."

"I know why he sends me home after you arrive." Her voice was husky and rough like a smoker's. "The whole town is talking about it."

"If that is the case, and I don't believe it is, they're only repeating the malicious gossip you spread about the man you work for, showing a great disrespect for him!"

"Fräulein Cotillard, let me give you some advice," she said sharply. "Herr Reinhardt is a good man. Too trusting for the position he's in. If you abuse the trust he has placed in you, then you will pay a very high price." She pointed a finger at Rose. "I will see to that myself."

Rose colored. Why was she spreading untrue rumors? Could she be jealous, or had she learned something about Rose that made her suspicious? She would speak with Reinhardt about his secretary upon his return.

It wasn't until Christmas Eve that she saw him.

"You've been away so long," she said, handing him the report.

"Did you miss me?" His tone was sharp.

"I missed our talks."

"As did I." He motioned to the chair across from the desk and then rang the bell.

Rose stiffened at the familiar creak from the side door opening. She expected a glare from Frau Birks' small, dark eyes, but the woman kept her head down, carrying the tray and setting it on the desk.

"That will be all. Goodnight, Frau Birks."

She left without a glance in Rose's direction.

"Did you travel far?" Rose asked.

"Dippoldiswalde, the district headquarters for Glashütte. Important meetings and other matters to attend to." He motioned to the tea.

Rose reached for the cup and blew on the liquid to cool it. Sensing he was a little on edge, she wondered if something had happened while he was away, something that weighed on him. She wanted to speak of André but she needed to find a way to bring him up. "Still, you must be tired with so many reports to catch up on."

"Frau Birks brought the reports by car every morning," he said in a businesslike tone. "It's a twenty-minute drive. So to answer your question, I am all caught up on the reports."

Should she mention her exchange with his secretary? Rose hesitated, unable to gauge the direction their conversation was heading.

"Frau Birks' brother resides in Dippoldiswalde." His forefinger circled the cup's rim. "He directs the Gestapo office there, which supervises the regional offices, including Glashütte. I report to him."

Her hand, still holding the cup, froze in midair. "I see."

"Do you?" His eyes, sharp as blades, locked on her. "I'm aware of what Frau Birks is saying." He cleared his throat. "Am I right that she mentioned it to you while I was away?"

Rose put the cup on the desk, forcing herself to look at him. "Yes."

"I cannot dismiss her." His mouth twitched. "I've warned her brother."

"What did he say?"

"He trusts her."

"It's my fault. I've caused you trouble." Her eyes dropped.

"You have nothing to be sorry for," he said, trying to reassure her. "Your behavior has always been exemplary."

"But my presence has led your secretary to talk about us in a way that is not . . ." Rose, searching for the right word, leaned back in the chair and crossed her legs. "I should have anticipated that she would have such a reaction."

"How could you have?"

"I don't know, but I shouldn't have let it get out of control." She kept her voice even, looking for an opening to guide their conversation around to André. If she appeared too desperate, it might make him suspicious. "Shall I stop coming? I can tell Herr Capek to deliver the reports as before."

"No." He squeezed the pencil, knuckles cracking. "Enough discussion of Frau Birks. How was your trip to Berlin, and your cousin?"

"It was . . ." She shook her head. "I've taken enough of your time." She started to rise.

"There's no rush. Stay a while and tell me about your cousin."

She took a deep breath, readying herself to touch his vulnerable nerve. "He finds the situation at Tempelhof challenging."

"In what way?"

"It's not the work. He's quite skilled. It's the workers. There is only one barracks of French workers, the rest are . . ." She paused.

"Go on." He lifted his eyes with renewed interest.

"Russian. Ten barracks of Russians. Men and women." Her lips pinched as if she'd tasted a lemon. "They work on the assembly line together."

"I sympathize with your cousin's predicament. The Russians are barbaric." He exhaled. "They killed Felix." He gazed out the window and thought for a moment. "What does your cousin do?"

"Something about timed fuses for the bombs loaded onto the Junker." She could see his mind turning. Recrossing her legs, she waited.

"There are companies here that perform similar work. Would your cousin want to come and work here? We have fewer Eastern workers than in Berlin, and he would also be close to you."

Her heart hammered at the prospect that he'd taken the bait, but she kept her excitement hidden. "Is that possible?"

"Yes." He smiled. "I could request that your cousin be transferred to Glashütte for similar work, but in a more conventional environment than in Berlin."

"I don't know what to say. I would be so grateful."

"Consider it my Christmas gift to you." He took a piece of paper. "I will see to it right away, if you agree. What is his full name?"

"André Simon." She stood. The room was dimly lit, owing to another blackout, and the only source of light came from the flickering candles on the table. "Thank you, Herr Reinhardt. I think truly it was not a coincidence that we met all those months ago."

"Eight months ago, to be precise." He stood and came to her. "I consider us friends, please call me Kurt." He reached into his pocket and pulled out a five-denomination Reichsmark note, holding it out for her.

The moment she touched the bill, she saw a predatory glint in his eyes. A warning told her to put an end to this, stop it now, don't take his money, turn around and leave, but André's life depended on what she did next, as did the well-being of the patients in the sick bay, so she pushed her unease to the back of her mind. "How long will it take to transfer him from Berlin to Glashütte?" she asked.

"The paperwork will take some time. It is December now, but if I move quickly, submitting all the necessary documentation by the end of the month, your cousin should be in Glashütte sometime in January, if everything goes smoothly."

Rose's heart skipped a beat.

"There is one thing I would like from you."

"Yes?"

"Since we're both orphans, you understand what it is to be without parents. Now, after losing Felix, I am completely alone and as you see from your interaction with Frau Birks, I feel as though others don't understand me." He stepped closer.

Rose stiffened. A ball of fear lodged in her throat. What would he ask of her? And if she refused, might she risk upsetting him and ruining André's chance of escaping Berlin?

"I would like a private moment between us." He held out his arms. "An embrace of friendship." He hesitated, seemingly waiting for Rose to agree. But agree to what? Her mouth went dry. Delay. Find an excuse. He stepped closer. "All I ask is for you to hold me."

"Hold you?" Her voice trembled.

"Yes."

She had to stop herself from backing away as a beat of fear drummed in her mind. Maybe he would pin her down, and with no one in the office or the building, he could do as he pleased. Then his arms circled her shoulders, pulling her close. He was rigid, stiff. She had no choice but to crush down the fear and return his embrace. As she did, she felt a lightening, as if he was again the man she'd first met in the church eight months ago. Maybe human touch, denied to him for so long, had now revived him. When had he last been embraced or even touched by someone? Holding him, she listened to his steady heartbeat. Eventually, he let go.

"Thank you. It must be our secret," he warned. "Frau Birks would not understand. She's a bitter woman."

"Yes. I won't utter a word of it to anyone, I promise. Goodnight."

Despite the darkness, Rose skipped down the stairs. She knew the steps by heart, had taken them nightly for months, just as she was sure she knew Reinhardt. He wasn't a threat. He'd agreed to transfer André to Glashütte in return for a hug. It seemed ridiculous, even too easy. She stopped halfway, wondering if she'd missed something.

A chill along her spine. What if it was too easy and he and Frau Birks were working together to set her up, and she couldn't see it? Why had he stopped asking her about Josef, and what was happening at the sick bay? At the back of her mind, a faint voice warned that something was off, but she couldn't pinpoint what and further she didn't want to believe it because all that mattered was getting André out of Berlin.

She was searching for problems that didn't exist. Reinhardt was still a human being, despite the evil things he believed or did, and that gave her hope. She'd spent a year in Germany and survived. André would soon be by her side. With him, Rose had the courage to face whatever awaited in the coming year.

27

Léa

January 1944

Léa's fingers were as stiff as ice. There was no longer enough coal to heat the factory—all of it went to running the machines. Tucking her hands under her armpits to warm them, she then lifted the polished lens to attach it to the rangefinder's metal casing.

Her shoulders throbbed after hours of leaning over the worktable, the coal-fired pump's hum and the conveyor belt's rumble echoed in her head. She checked the white-faced clock, grateful her shift would soon end.

Léa hoped that Maria would be allowed to see Ewa at the Foreign Children's Home tonight. After each shift, Maria tried for a quick hug or kiss, or to bring food, but the home limited contact, offering excuses to keep her from Ewa. When refused, Maria spent sleepless nights worrying about her baby daughter.

Léa and Josef were concerned about Ewa's deteriorating health. Ewa was severely underweight. At first, Maria had breastfed her twice daily, but her milk supply had recently dried up. Maria heard the children ate only potato flour and thin milk. Léa remembered Josef's warning: the home was meant to isolate the children from their mothers so they wouldn't survive.

As the bell rang, ending the shift, Léa discreetly slipped a Betabion ampoule into Maria's apron pocket. She tried to give her one every week, knowing thiamine would help her baby's poor diet. Maria smiled, but the fear and despair showed in her eyes. Léa longed to comfort her with a reassuring touch, but the Meister's watchful gaze stopped her.

On her way out, she passed Lagerführer Klein and the Meister talking. From the way the Lagerführer's shoulders were set forward and rigid, and the Meister's arms were crossed at his chest, and he was shaking his head, she guessed they were arguing. Maybe they, too, were on edge the way everyone was after the increase in Allied bombings all over the country. Rumors circulated that many cities had been destroyed, with tens of thousands dead. The women in the barracks were frightened by what they'd heard. *If they want to close down the factories by bombing the workers, then might they bomb Glashütte too?* Léa tried to reassure the women that Glashütte was too small. The Allies targeted large cities like Berlin and Hamburg. Rose remained anxious for André, who had yet to arrive.

"Fräulein Cotillard, may I have a word with you?" the Lagerführer called her over.

Léa stiffened. Had the Meister seen her slip the ampoule into Maria's apron? She wasn't allowed to take medicine outside of the sick bay. In fact, she shouldn't be doing most of what she did at the sick bay. Over the last few months, Josef had taught her how to monitor a patient's vital signs, such as pulse and respiratory rate, clean wounds, apply dressings, and administer simple injections.

"Yes?" Léa braced for the worst.

"Come, let's walk together. I've noticed that you spend a lot of your time at the sick bay."

She didn't want to get Josef in trouble. "I only try to help."

"Indeed, well, that's why I want to talk with you."

She swallowed, hoping none of the patients had reported her.

Stepping outside, she felt the last of the sunlight on her face. The winter months' short days were the hardest to get through, especially as coal and gas shortages meant there was no place to go to escape the cold—all supplies had been diverted to the Wehrmacht. Every day was a constant battle to stay warm.

"With Herr Reinhardt's approval, I'm reassigning you to the sick bay."

Léa stopped. "I won't be working at the factory anymore?"

"Not for the foreseeable future."

There had to be some catch or trick. "I don't understand."

"Dr. Capek needs the support. I received a telegram today about a group of Eastern workers arriving by train at week's end." Reaching into her dress pocket, she removed a linen cloth and dabbed her nose with it. "I've been warned that they may not be in good condition. You will support Dr. Capek to establish a registration and clearance center for these women. I don't want them released into the wider population until every woman has been checked for disease and Dr. Capek issues a full report to Herr Reinhardt."

"They're all women?" Léa found it odd.

"That's what the telegram said. It will be the first of many passenger trains to arrive, which is why he needs additional support. Are you willing to do this?"

"Yes, of course."

"I've arranged for one of the storage rooms at the back of the train station to be cleared out and bunk beds installed. Because of the risk of disease, we'll place a tent at the far end of the platform for screening and to serve as a reception area. Between the tent and the storage room, it should provide sufficient space for the women to be housed until Dr. Capek confirms they are healthy enough to be sent on to farms and cities to work." She clicked her tongue. "They won't be staying here; we don't have the room to house them, and their labor is in demand elsewhere. But as the first entry point into *das Reich*, our responsibility is to ensure that they are ready to work." She cleared her throat. "Questions?"

"Where is the train coming from?"

"From the East—Ukraine, Russia—why does it matter, they're all *Untermenschen*." She grew impatient. "I'll leave you to inform Dr. Capek."

Léa went directly to the sick bay to tell Josef.

"She didn't say where from the East?" he asked.

"Russia and Ukraine. She said it's the first of many convoys. We need to clear them medically so they can be sent to farms and factories all over Germany. Why are they sending Russian women here?"

"It might be a sign that the Wehrmacht is in retreat, and with few men left to bring back as they've all been killed in the fighting, they're sending the women to work." He breathed deeply, like someone coming up for air. "Another turning point. This war can't go on forever."

"The Lagerführer seemed worried that the women would be—"

"Yes, we must plan for the worst."

"Our medical supplies are so low."

"We'll find a way," he said, stepping closer. For a moment, she let her mind imagine, like before, that he would take her hand. She wanted him to—despite his never having shown her any sign that he would, the desire he stirred in her had only grown with time, but his arm hung at his side, unmoving. "You will work here every day?" He smiled. "How can I be so fortunate?"

"Josef, can I ask you . . ."

He leaned forward, his weight shifting onto the balls of his feet.

What could she say? The woman who'd never gone on a date, never felt the warmth of a man's hand in hers, never been kissed. *It's like looking at the sky at dawn.* She wanted to know if Rose was right—that a kiss stirs the soul. *Just ask him.* Summoning all her courage, she said, "Would you like to kiss me?"

"Would *you* like me to kiss you?" He was so close she could feel his breath warming her face. "I tried once before, and you ran away like you'd seen a ghost."

She stared. "You did?" How had she not seen that?

He took her hand and lifted it to his lips. His knuckles, chafed and white, the skin cracked from the harsh soap, yet the tenderness of his touch didn't surprise her. A doctor's hands, intent on healing. She sensed that, if he could, he would never let her hand go. He was close enough that she could smell him—sharp soap and musky sweat—and something beneath it all. She thought of a sun-soaked meadow, a dress drying on a line, the shallow part of a stream where the light touched the bottom. It was silly but blindingly honest—Josef smelled of sunshine. She laughed.

"What's funny?" he asked.

"You and me. This. How could . . ." She gripped her hands together, not daring to utter the word that was on the tip of her tongue. "The world is driven by so much hate."

"Only love can conquer hate." His mouth grazed hers, his breath warm on her lips. And finally, the kiss she'd waited for so long and with it, a wild, untamed feeling surged in her chest.

Léa's heart, usually steady, beat with a new rhythm. She had always held her hands tight in her lap, trying to keep everything together, but now they loosened and reached up to touch his face. His kiss filled her with wild wonder. He was leading her somewhere, and with all her heart, she would follow.

28

Rose

February 1944

Rose watched the sun break over the steep hills. She hadn't been able to sleep. She nodded off for an hour, then woke with a start, opening her eyes to see if it was daylight. The previous evening's visit to Reinhardt had set off a ticking time bomb inside her after he announced that *her cousin* would be arriving the following day.

Four months had passed since she'd seen André. During that time, the war had undergone a fundamental shift that she was just beginning to grasp. It was impossible to know what was really going on when she received such sparse information.

The headlines in the German papers announced that the *relentless bombing campaigns were terrorist acts inflicted by Britain and the United States on the citizens of Germany.* Hamburg had been targeted because the celebrated U-boats were manufactured there. Rose shuddered to think what fires the Allies planned to unleash on Berlin. At least, André would soon be here and safe.

A copper light fell over the spruces dotting the slopes. Rose wondered what life would now be like with André by her side. It was almost too good to believe. She imagined all the places they could go together to be alone—the forest, where they would walk along the birch and linden. It would be their refuge, the place they could meet and be themselves. Glashütte was too small. Their movements would be noticed and reported back to the Gestapo office. They couldn't stroll hand in hand as they had in Berlin. Here, they'd play the role of cousins. She'd have to carefully stick to that because she'd seen Reinhardt's temper flare in short bursts and feared what he'd do if he discovered that she'd lied to him about André.

She felt a stab of guilt at the lie. It had come so quickly from her mouth that she hadn't had time to think it through. Why *had* she lied? If Reinhardt knew André was the man she loved, then Rose would lose all power over him. And it felt good to finally have some control, to direct what happened to her and those she loved rather than being helpless and letting others determine her fate. She needed to be strong. How else could she stand in his office, listening to him, and when he asked, wrapping her arms around him, if she had no power? She needed to believe that her meetings with Reinhardt were some sort of buoy, like a lifeline—a way for her to protect Léa, André and Josef.

But doubts stirred at the back of her mind. She tried to quiet them. If Reinhardt had any intention of pushing himself on her, as Léa intimated when she talked about consequences, then he would have done it already.

Rose had no regrets. Now that she'd set off on this path, she had to continue; the only way forward was through. She couldn't turn around and go back. She believed there was a purpose behind everything, something like a secret hand steering her, though she didn't understand how to explain it. She'd never shared this with Léa, lacking the words to articulate it. But she felt it when she drew, a sense of purpose and direction that guided her hand, creating something out of nothing.

Later, as she walked to the factory, she noticed the sky was the color of the blue dress her mother had made and she'd worn on her date to the cinema with André. A ripple of reassurance passed through Rose. It had to be a sign sent from Maman, telling her she was on the right path.

The morning shift stretched by slowly. Rose checked the wall clock, willing the minutes to pass quicker. At lunch, she went to the canteen, hoping she'd find André sitting at the table with the French flag among the former prisoners of war, whom she did her best to avoid because they were so quick to judge her, and remembering their anger made her shudder to think what would happen after she returned to France. But André wasn't there. And it was silly to think that he would be assigned to her factory. There were many factories in town. It was the not knowing that made her crazy. Rose went outside and walked along the road up to the station. Near a parked train, soldiers escorted women from the carriages to the white tent at the far end of the platform. She glimpsed Léa and wished she could go and speak with her, but under the Lagerführer's strict orders, no one was allowed near the women from the East until they passed their health checks.

She returned to the factory, cleaning the rangefinders as they came across the assembly line. The windows were all open and when the machines grew quiet she listened for the blow of a whistle or the screech of wheels on metal rails—but all she heard was the rush of the river outside.

Jana gave her a curious look and pointed to the rangefinders passing her on the assembly line. Rose had fallen behind on the day's quota. It was impossible to concentrate. She'd spent so much effort arranging for André's transfer that she couldn't settle her mind and focus until she knew he was here. At least now she didn't have to worry about the Meister shouting or docking her pay—because of Reinhardt, he wouldn't dare to.

Finally, the shift ended. Rose went outside. It had begun to rain, so she hurried to the train station. The platform was empty. Even the soldiers guarding the tent were gone. Now the rain was falling hard. And as the drops drenched her clothing, a realization suddenly hit her: had Reinhardt played a trick on her?

She paused, her stomach churning with a mix of emotions. All this time, she'd thought she had some kind of agency with him. But maybe it was the other way around. Perhaps he enjoyed misleading her? If this was true, and he had no intention of transferring André to Glashütte, then André was still in danger. She thought of the newspaper headlines—the photographs of destroyed buildings, flames and tracer lights spinning through the sky following all the bombings. She needed to talk with Léa. Her sister would know.

Rose, drenched from the rain, entered the sick bay. Léa was talking with Josef, and as her rubber soles squeaked across the floor, they both turned to her.

"What happened?" Léa asked.

"André's still in Berlin." Rose tried to hold back tears. "Maybe—"

Léa shook her head and put an arm around Rose, steering her toward the back of the sick bay.

"Come to the office," she said.

Josef opened the door and Léa guided Rose inside. She heard the door close and then a voice.

"Rose. I'm here."

Regret gave way to relief. Joy. With a cry, she rushed into his arms. "I thought—"

André held her. "Didn't it rain the last time we were together?"

"Yes." She laughed. "I was waiting at the station looking for you."

He held her tight. Reinhardt dropped into her mind, but she pushed him out. Not today. She wouldn't allow him to impede on this part of her life. Today was for André. The two of them together at last. She no longer had to check the newspaper headlines at the end of the factory shift to see if there had been Allied bombing raids on Berlin. She exhaled, grateful for this moment. He pulled back, cupping his hands on either side of her face.

"You look more beautiful than ever," he said. "I don't know how to thank you for getting me out of Berlin. You've saved my life."

She smiled and ran her fingers through his thin hair. "I'm so happy."

"Now, it's my turn to look after you."

She wanted to tell him that she didn't need looking after, that she could take care of herself and him and Léa too. "You don't need to."

"This war isn't over yet." He looked at her and her heart quickened.

"But the end is getting closer, isn't it?"

"Yes." She heard him inhale sharply. "It's also getting closer to us."

"We're together," she said. "That's all that matters."

* * *

February had given way to March, then April, and now it was spring. Every day, at the end of her factory shift, André waited for Rose. He usually stood across the street, leaning against the wall, pretending to be reading the paper, and after she appeared, he'd follow her through the town, keeping a safe distance so no one observing would think they were together. They'd walk until they reached a narrow path that led into the woods. He'd come up from behind, whispering, *Rose*, in her ear.

It was the only time during the week they could be together—ninety minutes sandwiched between the end of her factory shift and the moment she went to the sick bay to collect the typed report for Reinhardt.

Today, Rose didn't see him and she wondered if he might already be waiting for her at the place they'd agreed to meet. There were three spots they rotated—the forest, the old washhouse by the river, and today, the vegetable garden on the hill, overlooking the village. She turned left, crossed the main street, and made her way through the narrow alleys that led past the cemetery and along a slope of houses nestled in the hills at the edge of town. A path led up to the allotments, where people who lived in the center of town, without gardens, grew vegetables and fruits.

On the weekends, the allotments were busy. Midweek, people tended the crops only in the mornings. At this hour, there was no one, so they had the place to themselves.

She climbed up the stone steps leading to the top of the hill. All over the hills wild apple trees grew and a single large walnut tree. She and Léa had been coming here in the summer to collect fruits and nuts from the trees that didn't seem to belong to anyone. Rose never could have thought that one day this would be the place where she and André would meet regularly to talk.

A few weeks back, they'd discovered an old battered hut that had probably once been a garden shed. The red paint outside peeled and curled, faded from the sun. When they first entered, the door was broken and all sorts of bricks, pots and garden tools littered the small interior. They cleaned it out, stacking the bricks outside. André had fixed the door, and brought two stools from the factory and repaired them and a rickety table that they found inside. Rose had swept it clean and put flowers in a small vase that they set on the table. They'd taken to calling it their house.

Now, that she'd reached the house, she suspected he was inside, waiting. She glanced through the tiny window near the door. André sat at the table, concentrating on a drawing. A warm feeling enveloped her, like she'd sunk into a hot bath, as she anticipated wrapping her arms around him.

"I missed you," she said softly, sneaking up behind him, grazing his ears with her lips.

He turned, and put his arm around her waist, bringing her close. "Hello, my love."

"Have you been waiting long?" she asked.

"I got out of the factory a little early, so I came up here first. How was your day?"

"Long. But I was able to miss the quota by five cylinders!"

André clapped. "Bravo, that's five less gunsights made today."

"The Meister wasn't pleased." She settled opposite him. "Jana, who sits next to me on the production line, was two under the quota today."

"Did you tell her your plan?" His eyebrows lifted.

"No, but since we've been working together for so long, we're in a certain rhythm. I think she noticed I've slowed down."

Rose didn't tell him she'd made a secret wish that everyone on the factory floor wouldn't meet their quota—anything to try and reduce the number of gunsights and rangefinders to be placed on German tanks and airplanes. "I think she understands what I'm doing and is trying to do the same."

"Excellent." André pumped a fist in the air. "If everyone in the factory slows down, then the overall production suffers without the Meister being able to blame one person." He smiled. "I call it sly sabotage."

"He's been observing us more closely. I think if he could, he'd crack the whip over our shoulders like we're horses, forcing us to move faster."

André shook his head. "He can't risk damaging the cylinders. Those items are expensive to produce. That's why you've got more power than you think."

She glanced at the sketch on the table. "What are you drawing?" She pointed to the image on the paper—a building with massive windows, a flat roof and a tree in the center of a courtyard.

"Show me first your sketchbook. I want to see the portraits you've done this week."

Rose handed him the book. He thumbed through the pages. "These are excellent."

"Now, you tell me, what are you drawing?"

"Our house. One day I will build it for you and we will live there together."

She laughed. "Must it be so big?"

"Depends." He rested a hand on hers—a craftsman's hands. She loved their heft and how they could turn what was in his head into something concrete that she could step inside. "Tell me how many rooms you want."

"Just one for us."

He reached over and swept a strand of loose hair from her face. "What I'm asking is how many children should we have?"

Rose had never thought about having children. She'd seen her mother struggle to raise two daughters after their father died, and then Léa scrambled to earn enough money to take care of them both following their mother's passing. Children seemed to be a burden, an anchor weighing one down. André came from a large family, so naturally, he would want children. She turned her head toward the window. "I don't know."

"You have plenty of time to figure it out." He paused, glanced at his sketchpad, pencil moving as he continued drawing. "A modern house should be simple and flexible. Inside, let's keep it all open with as few walls as possible. How does that sound?"

"No walls?"

"I want to see you every moment."

"What about the bathroom?"

He nodded. "You're right, we'll need a wall there." He turned to her. "And the bedrooms, too." He made quick flourishes with his hands. "But the rest—kitchen, living, dining—will all be one large space. And here, in the courtyard, windows will fold back like doors extending the space outside."

"Oh, that sounds lovely. But what sort of tree would you propose in the courtyard?"

"Olive."

"A symbol of peace?" she asked softly, liking the idea.

He nodded. "Their form is robust like a sculpture."

"I think the silvery foliage is beautiful, and they keep their leaves all winter."

He smiled. "I can see us happy living there—children running, you drawing, me designing. We have a shared vision, Rose. We will build our future together."

She let this settle within her, then she leaned forward and kissed him. Breathless, she pulled back, slightly in awe at her boldness. "If we get hungry, we can eat the olives!"

He laughed. "Or make oil." His knee brushed hers. "Maybe we'd never have to leave—our sanctuary."

"A sanctuary of peace," Rose said happily.

He put the pencil down, folded the paper into a small square, then handed it to her. "Hold on to it, Rose, and never let it go. It's our dream," he said. "If we can see it in our mind's eye, then we can bring it to life. The most important thing is never to give up hope on a dream."

The church bell rang the half hour. At the next clanging of the bells, she would have to go. But for now, they had thirty marvelous minutes together. She stood, walked over to him, and perched on his lap. He took her hand.

"Promise me you'll keep drawing, Rose, no matter what happens." His voice trembled slightly. She wondered if there was an unspoken fear of losing the Rose he knew. He placed his palm flat against hers, his fingers curling around hers like a lifeline.

"I promise." With her other hand, she reached up and touched the scar on his forehead. She never could have imagined on that day in Place du Martroi when she first noticed this pale, ragged spot above his eye that a year and a half later they'd end up together in a small town in the far eastern part of Germany. She wanted to believe that if they'd made it through all this and were still together, then nothing could ever come between them.

But then Reinhardt popped into her mind, unsettling her. Their conversations—she couldn't really call them that because he was the one who did all the talking—were increasingly him ranting about ancient Germanic warriors and knights and the end of time. He seemed to live in another world of his own making, which he wanted to bring her into, while all she wanted was to extract herself from him. She'd hoped that after André arrived, she could stop delivering the reports to the sick bay. She tried to tell Josef, but she knew how much he relied on the five Reichsmarks to buy extra food and medicine, especially with the women laborers arriving a few times a week from the East and hadn't yet found the right moment.

He reached into his coat pocket and pulled out a small sketchpad. "Another one for you. Always remember you're an artist," he said, handing it to her.

They kissed, and as she pulled away, she realized that the best thing she'd ever done was to bring André to Glashütte. He supported her during the long shifts at the factory, often finding clever ways to obstruct the quotas. And, with his help, she managed to forget, at least for a while, her strange evening sessions with Herr Reinhardt.

29

Léa

June 1944

It was the last week of June, and Léa and Josef waited on the platform under a blindingly white sky. Two soldiers stood nearby, as always, in case any of the women tried to escape while leaving the train.

The stationmaster held up a red flag as the train approached.

"It looks like a cargo transport," Léa said, shaking her head. "The women have always arrived by passenger train. I don't understand."

"They must be prioritizing passenger trains for the troops," Josef said, glancing at the manifest. "Twenty women are listed—ten in each of the last two wagons. You take the first one, and I'll check the second."

Léa took a deep breath, fearing the worst. She would need to quickly prioritize which women to treat first, based on the severity of their conditions. With Olga, a Russian worker they'd brought to translate, she and Josef followed the stationmaster, flanked by the soldiers, to the end of the platform. He lifted the metal bar off the brackets on the penultimate wagon's door—no windows, only a thin opening running along the top. He turned the latch and slid the wooden door open.

Léa gasped, burying her nose in her elbow to mask the stench. A few women groaned. Others stared silently. Their sunken eyes and jutting cheekbones showed how thin they were. She stepped forward, avoiding the waste bucket near the door. Darkness filled the wagon with despair. Frustration and anger surged in her—how could these women be transported like animals? But Josef's words came back to her: he'd warned that after the successful Allied landings in Normandy at the month's start and Soviet victories in the East, the Wehrmacht knew they couldn't win and, in their retreat, they would seek revenge on the defenseless.

It was hard to see in the murky light, so she would need to bring the women out one by one to assess them.

"Olga, ask them who needs help first. They've been traveling together; they will know."

Léa listened to Olga addressing the women, and she heard them answer back—their voices crackling with fear.

"They say help Anna, then Nadiya. Anna has a deep cut on her hand. Nadiya is with child." Olga made the sign of the cross. "There's a woman—no one knows her name—who they fear is dead but they've been too afraid to check."

"Where is she?"

"At the back of the wagon on the left."

Léa used the wall as a guide. Her eyes burned and watered. She found the woman, her hand cold and stiff. She didn't need to take a pulse. "Olga, hand me a blanket from the platform." She covered the woman and whispered a little prayer that she would now find peace.

She turned back to the rest of the women. "Anna, Anna?"

"*Da*," came a deep voice. A strip of light crossed an older woman's face, helping Léa find her in the darkness as she stumbled past the others.

A sharp, ammonia-like odor pierced the air. The wound on Anna's hand had likely not been cleaned. Her body was warm to the touch, which meant an infection had set in. Anna was the priority. The sooner Josef could deal with her hand, the lower the risk of complications. "Come, let me help you outside."

On the platform, she got a clearer look at Anna's mangled hand: the digits were swollen and red, and pus gathered like drops of thick honey on the skin.

"Josef?" Léa smiled at Anna, trying to mask her worry so as not to send the woman into a panic. She turned to Olga. "Ask her if she's in pain."

"She says it throbs and burns. She's afraid she'll lose her hand."

"Tell her not to be afraid. Josef, I need—"

"I'm here. Let me have a look." Josef turned the woman's hand over, examining the skin and pressing his fingers against the swollen, red palm. "Infection for sure. What's her name?"

"Anna." Léa rubbed her back, trying to reassure her.

"I'll bring her to the tent to clean it now, see how deep the cut is and whether I'll need to operate. Can you and Olga bring the others from the wagon?"

Léa wanted to ask the soldiers to help, but they'd already retreated to the tent, distancing themselves from the sick women. "Yes." Léa turned back to the wagon. "Nadiya," she called.

"*Da*?" A young woman's voice rose up, and she waved her arm in the air.

Léa went to her. "Can you stand?" She bent down, circling an arm around Nadiya's shoulders. "I'll help you." Léa lifted her up, supporting her to the door and out onto the platform.

Nadiya blinked in the stark daylight, her hand on the small bump under her coat. "Olga, ask if she has any bleeding."

"She says she bled, but it stopped a few days ago. She's afraid for the baby."

"Tell her it's a good sign that the bleeding stopped. I will give her some medicine to help." Léa thought of the two boxes of Betabion back at the sick bay. She turned to Olga. "Help her to the tent, give her some water. Then come back to assist with the others."

Léa returned to the wagon. "Who's next?"

The women responded, each pointing to the person they thought was the most needy. All were unsteady on their feet. She'd seen that they'd been given some food, as eggshells littered the ground and she guessed the women had had just enough to survive. She made her way to each one, offering reassurance until the wagon was empty, except for the woman who had died during the journey. Then she began to unload the other wagon.

It was late afternoon by the time all the women were in the tent, and Josef had made a preliminary assessment. Léa counted nineteen women, and had Olga deliver a note to Lagerführer Klein to request someone take care of the dead woman on the train. Though the women were bony, dehydrated, malnourished and still in shock, Josef was confident that after a few weeks in the sick bay, with good care, food and rest, they would all recover.

"But will they be given a few weeks?" Léa asked.

"Probably not. But we will suggest it in my report."

"How is Anna's hand?"

"I should operate. The injury hasn't gone as deep as the bone, but I need to ensure the infection is all cleared out." He wiped his face. "Dirt likely got into the wound. Olga said the women were forced by the Wehrmacht to dig tank traps against the Soviet army."

Léa looked at the women: grandmothers, mothers, daughters, sisters, aunts. A week ago, they'd been digging trenches on a battlefield. Now, they were helping one another survive and not giving up hope.

She wondered if Lagerführer Klein had intended the opposite—expecting the women would look out for themselves and arrive near death. Is that why she'd enlisted Léa, because saving Russian civilians was beneath her? Without the money Rose received from Reinhardt, they wouldn't be able to buy medical supplies. Maybe Rose was right; he hadn't wanted more from her than friendship. With André here, Léa wanted to believe everything might work out. She, Rose, and Josef would do what needed to be done to save lives, proving that *fraternité* could be nurtured even during war.

"I'll need your help with the operation," he said quietly.

"Of course." It was just the two of them, along with the women in the tent.

He touched her arm, clearly restraining the urge to pull her close. "You were extraordinary today. Thank you."

Over Josef's shoulder, Léa saw Nadiya watching.

"You must be exhausted," he said heavily. "I'm sorry to ask you to do more."

"Don't be. I want to be here. You can't do this on your own."

"What would I do without you?" His finger touched her nose.

"You don't have to worry about that because I'm not planning on going anywhere," Léa said, grinning. "Except to the sick bay to get the Betabion for Nadiya. Can I bring anything else?"

Josef listed off a few items in response.

"We still have to write the report for Reinhardt. I will request that these women remain in Glashütte to work because they will require medical care over the next months. Go on and get what you need from the sick bay. We've still a long night ahead."

She left the tent and took the steps down the platform to the street. The sun was beginning to sink behind the hills, the sky a honeycomb of gray and blue. Her legs were watery and sapped of strength from a full day on her feet. But working with Josef was so much more fulfilling than assembly line work. Together, they were saving lives. And one day of hard work was nothing compared to what those nineteen women had gone through digging trenches for the Wehrmacht.

The world was a dark place but people could change that by bringing light. Josef had showed her how. Léa even had the notion that one day, after the war was over and she returned to France, she'd like to go to nursing school. She didn't mind the blood, syringes and waste pans—it was an incredible feeling to alleviate someone's pain and help them through a difficult situation.

Up ahead on the steps leading to the sick bay, she saw Maria, pacing frantically.

"Are you OK? Josef is—"

Maria opened her mouth, but only a small sob escaped her throat.

Léa could see from her red and swollen eyes that something terrible had happened. "What is it?"

"Ewa is dead."

"Oh no, Maria." She took her in her arms and held her close. "I'm sorry," Léa whispered. She stroked her back, a wave of despair hitting her. She wished she could have done more to protect Ewa, but the baby had been taken away. A few times she'd expressed her concern to Josef. He'd said it was out of their hands and it was impossible to save everyone.

"Come inside," Léa said, "tell me what happened."

"My baby starved to death," Maria said, backing away, eyes wild with panic.

"Is that what they told you?"

"They wouldn't tell me anything. They won't even allow me to see her." Her face crumpled, shattering like broken glass.

"I'm sorry."

"I should have—"

"Don't blame yourself. It's not your fault."

"It's all my fault. She was innocent. It was my duty to protect her." She looked away. "Maybe it was wrong to have brought her into the world."

"Don't say that."

"She suffered. Her life was all pain. It makes no sense."

"No, it doesn't. But if you didn't carry her full term, she would have never had a chance. At least you gave her that. It was all you had to give. What happened to her isn't your fault. If the war had ended earlier, she'd be alive."

Maria leaned into Léa's chest. "I want her back. Please. Why did she have to die?" Her body shook with silent sobs.

Holding Maria tight, Léa shut her eyes. If only she could take this pain from her. But she couldn't, not ever. It would be a pain she'd bear for the rest of their lives.

Léa wondered whether Maria was right, and it would have been less cruel not to have intervened. Yet Josef had told her of the many babies who never had a chance to live, and at least Ewa had her chance. She wished she could have protected her from the dangers after she entered the world, but that wasn't in her power. Was it in anybody's?

Léa and Josef had tried to save a life. In the end, they'd failed. Was it wrong to try? Maybe. As the war dragged on, the lines between right and wrong grew increasingly blurred, and Léa wondered if one day she would be unable to tell them apart.

30

Rose

That night, Rose rushed to bring the report to Reinhardt. In the office at the sick bay, she'd waited for Josef to finish dictating the last pages to Léa. Every time Léa pressed the typewriter's carriage return lever, a loud *thunk* reverberated in the room, reminding Rose of the sound of the clock in Reinhardt's office, and his penchant for punctuality.

The longer she waited, the more the unease that had been gnawing at the back of her mind grew. For the last weeks, she'd felt a change in Reinhardt, not so much what he said, but how. His rants had taken on a sharper tone as he railed against the Boshelvik forces of chaos and unreason. *The greatest virtue isn't goodness but courage*, he'd said, slamming his fist on the desk. She no longer had the sense that he was speaking to her, or even enjoyed her company. She wasn't sure why he kept insisting that she deliver the reports to his office. Léa said his behavior was likely due to the uncertainty and stress brought about by Germany's retreating position in the war. Everyone could see they were losing, and it was only a matter of time with the non-stop Allied bombings of all major cities until the country collapsed. Whatever the reason, Rose had grown weary of the Gestapo officer, and she feared that being late tonight could upset him.

"Good evening, Herr Reinhardt," she said, slightly out of breath, having climbed the stairs two at a time. "Please excuse my tardiness."

He looked up from the desk, a cold glint in his eyes. "A busy day at the sick bay?"

"Yes." She put the report on his desk and took a seat. She didn't think he would keep her long; she would need to return to the barracks before eight. Usually, he rang the bell on his desk, signaling to Frau Birks to bring tea. But tonight, he started reading, his slender finger tracing down the center of the page as Rose waited.

"Nineteen Russian women," he said, leaning back in his chair. "One dead." He reached for the small glass on his desk and downed the liquid inside, wincing as it hit the back of his throat.

She smelled alcohol and a hint of anise—schnapps. "It's curious, isn't it, Rose?"

"Curious?"

"Yes. Russians arriving now when the war is nearly over?" His glassy blue eyes stared at her.

He seemed particularly cold tonight. Rose wondered if her lateness annoyed him or if he'd been drinking schnapps for some time before she'd arrived. He usually liked it when she gave him her undivided attention, so she leaned forward, hoping to encourage him to talk and let her leave early.

"Do you think we would have been friends if we'd met in other circumstances?" he asked.

"I don't know. Perhaps."

"We're so similar, both orphans with siblings. We're destined to be together."

The air in the room was still and hot. The windows closed, yet somewhere outside, a door opened and shut.

She gazed at the window, wishing she could be out there and not in here.

"I need your help, Rose."

"With?"

"Tell me the value of a Russian."

The clock ticked on. It would soon be eight. Now he was rambling about Russians again. Previously, he'd blamed them for Felix's death and promised retribution. Rose decided he'd drunk too much, and she should leave. She stood. "Please forgive me, I must—"

"Sit down," he ordered, gesturing with his index finger to the chair.

Beads of sweat gathered on her back. She glanced at the closed window, debating whether to cross the room and open it for relief, but she forced herself to remain seated, knowing disobedience could provoke him.

"How many Russian lives equal a German one?"

"I don't know." Her mind raced—what was he talking about?

"Guess."

What terrible game was he playing? She felt that he was a cat and she the mouse. Perhaps if she gave him a number, he would stop. "Two," she said.

He shook his head. "Much more."

"Three."

"You know better than that." He wiped his mouth with the back of his hand. "You're an intelligent woman, why are you playing dumb?"

"I honestly don't know."

"Are Slavs inferior?"

He *was* toying with her. She would give him the answer he wanted, and then surely, he would let her go. "Yes."

"Then tell me how many Russian women for one German soldier?" He stared hard at her, his eyes unreadable.

The atmosphere turned thick with tension.

"I'm waiting," he insisted.

"Four."

"You want me to give you the correct answer, Rose?"

A trickle of air escaped her mouth like a warning whistle. Over the last months, she'd felt something had been building inside him; she hadn't known or understood what it was, only the sense that it was terrible and dark and he was obsessed with it. Tonight, she grasped that it had to do with Felix's death.

"A single German soldier is equal to fifteen worthless Russian women. That sounds about right, doesn't it?"

She didn't speak.

"This is where I need your help, Rose." He kept repeating her name, as though he was entitled to. "It's up to you to decide."

"What's up to me?"

"You like saving lives, don't you?" His eyes locked on hers. "Isn't that why you lied to me about André?"

She shrank at the mention of André. How had he found out? Suddenly, she felt unbalanced. He was leading her somewhere that she didn't want to go. Wet patches gathered on the cotton dress under her arms.

"I know about your secret meetings, that you're in love with him." He emptied his glass and refilled it. "But tonight, we must discuss something important. There are nineteen Russian women, but only four can live." He sneered. "You see—fifteen women must die to avenge my brother's death." He stood. A vein pulsed on his forehead. "You choose." He lifted the report in his hand and hurled it at her. The metal ring holding the papers struck her chest and then fell to the floor.

She started, knocking her elbow on the back of the chair. She tried to stand but he'd moved first, reaching her side of the desk, blocking her way. Her pulse pounded as he placed his hands on either side of the armrests and bent close.

"Go on, choose which four will live," he said quietly.

Rose's body froze. She wanted to run—return to Léa and André. But he stood over her. A tear ran down her cheek.

"What about the pregnant one?" He smiled. "Will you order her killed?"

"None of them," she said, her voice trembling. "I don't want any of them killed."

"I didn't want Felix killed, but they murdered him, and now they must pay," he said, wiping away the tear on her face with his finger. She winced at his touch. "Rose, Rose, are you afraid of me?"

"No."

"Good. I don't want you to fear me. All I want is for you to look at the names and choose."

She glanced at the pages splayed on the floor—the report Léa had painstakingly typed with the nineteen Russian names all in a row. Her mind flashed to Léa's warning on the train about getting too involved with Reinhardt. Now she understood the consequences. Trapped by his demand to choose who would live or die, Rose's realization jolted her: she'd underestimated his madness. Steeling herself, she slid her chair back to stand, but he blocked her. "I can't choose."

"Oh, I think you can. If you don't, I'll kill all the women—is that what you want?"

She shook her head. "No."

"Then listen to me carefully." He stared hard at her.

Rose didn't flinch or look away. He was so close that for the first time she saw the narrow, ragged lines of the scar on his left cheek, the black rims framing his blue eyes, the juddering Adam's apple in his throat. And it was as if she was seeing him for the first time.

He turned and walked to his desk, then sat down. "You don't want anyone to die, do you, Rose?" he said, kindly.

"No."

He smiled, and a small flicker of hope bloomed inside her.

"You see, I understand you better than you understand yourself." He pushed a small box toward her. "I have a proposition for you."

She swallowed, her eyes on the box.

"Open it," he said.

"A proposition?"

"You no longer have to decide who will live and die. Open the box; then you'll understand." His tone was firmer now.

She took the box and opened it. Inside was a ring—two small diamonds set in a simple gold band. "Whose ring is it?"

"It's yours. You take it and all the women will live. You don't take it—all nineteen women will be dead at dawn."

Throat tight, her heart pitched like a barge in roiling waves. "I don't understand. What happens if I take it?"

"Then you will be my wife."

"Marry you?"

"Marry me."

A rushing in her head followed by a surge of darkness. Overwhelmed by shock, she closed her eyes and sank back against the chair. She could feel herself plummeting down into deep, cold water. She was back in Orléans, diving into the Loire like when she'd been a child, and she wouldn't come up for air. Holding her breath, she would try to stay under for as long as she could, watching the bubbles escape her mouth and nose. There was nothing on the surface of the water for her to return to—go deep and hide where it's safe. And then, she felt a buoy slip under her arms, and a force dragging her to the surface. The stench of wet wool mixed with sweat on his uniform. She opened her eyes: he was again standing in front of her.

"I will not repeat my offer."

"Marry you . . . properly?"

"I want you to remain here with me after the war."

"But I must return to France, that is my home."

"That will be your choice."

But what choice did she have? No matter what she said to him, her life would never be the same. She'd heard of men who court and charm. Men who force themselves, taking what they want. But she hadn't known there was another type—a hunter who treats women like prey. She had not known that such men existed until she met Reinhardt. He'd been hunting her since that first day in the church, slowly drawing her in with gifts, then money, realizing she would give it to Josef and Léa for the sick bay, and finally bringing André here, all the while taking his time, setting the trap for her to walk into. Now, all he had to do was slam the door shut, and she would belong to him.

"I will make you a home here," he said.

She tried to reason with him. "Felix was important to you, as is Léa to me. She will return to France and I must go with her."

"No. You will stay here with me."

She was sweating heavily, her dress sticking to the skin between her shoulder blades.

"As man and wife?"

"Let me be clear: I will never touch you, I promise, if you don't want me to. I do not believe in forcing myself on a woman. If, over time, you develop feelings for me . . ." His voice trailed off. He leaned forward, placing a tentative hand on her shoulder, but when she winced, he removed it quickly. "Only if it came about from your own free will."

"Free will?" Her voice was weary. "If I understand, I will marry you, and all nineteen women are saved. I don't marry you, they die."

"I'm offering you a bargain," he said. "Marriage in exchange for nineteen lives."

He had lost his mind. But he was standing before her like he always had. She knew he he hated the Russians enough to kill all the women tomorrow if she said no. To give up André and her life for him, she would demand more, the most she could get. She would ask him to protect those she loved. "You must do more."

His face twitched.

"You will help Léa, André and Josef escape Glashütte before the Soviet army arrives."

"I'm the one with terms," he shouted. "Not you!" Returning to his desk, he fumbled to fill his pipe with tobacco.

Now she was watching him, and he didn't seem to like it because he kept his back to her. He thought he knew her better than she knew herself, but she would prove him wrong. She stepped forward, the first step of many in this new life, and touched his shoulder.

"I will be a good wife to you in exchange for the nineteen Russian women and my sister, André and Josef."

He turned around, his face red and eyes big. "Round it up to twenty since there's an unborn child," he said sharply.

"I will marry you," she repeated, lifting the ring out of the box. "I will carry this in my pocket and then put it on my finger after the war, staying here and being the good wife you want. In exchange, you will save all the Russian women, my sister, André and Josef." She held out her hand. "Do you agree?"

He threw the pipe on the wooden desk. It rolled off the edge and fell to the ground. Why did he hesitate? Did he not have the power to help Léa and the others escape?

No, his skill was tracking people—where they went, whom they spoke to, what they said. He knew things she could never know. His contacts were extensive. The only way for Léa and the others to get out before the Soviet army arrived—everyone said they were months away and the fact that he had made her this offer tonight meant the rumors could be true—was if Reinhardt arranged it. The question was whether he wanted her enough to do it. She would make him. He was wrong about her. She knew herself better than he did. She stepped closer, placing her other hand on his face, waiting. A few moments passed, then she felt his grip firm and solid against her hand.

"Agreed," he said.

She dropped the ring in her apron pocket and left.

31

Léa

October 1944

Tonight, Josef would journey to Dippoldiswalde to purchase medical supplies, returning in the morning. Lagerführer Klein had allowed Léa and Rose to stay together in the sick bay to care for the patients while he was away.

"Will you be all right for a night?" Josef asked.

"I'll be fine," said Léa.

"Is Rose on her way?"

She nodded. "She's coming back after delivering the report to Reinhardt."

"We're not expecting any more convoys this week, so it should be quiet." He bent down to kiss her. "Maybe we can figure out a way for you to get permission to spend the night in the sick bay while I'm here."

She laughed. "I would love that, but I don't think Lagerführer Klein would approve."

It was true that they had so little time together during the day, stealing moments to be alone, closing the door to his office and holding one another or kissing until a knock drew Josef away. As the sole doctor for all the foreign workers, he faced constant demands on his time.

A honk outside. The car was here, a black sedan parked in the dimly lit street, its headlights casting long shadows. Josef turned to Léa. "I'll be back before you know it," he said, trying to reassure her.

"Have a safe trip." Léa saw him to the door. *One day,* she thought, *after the war is over, we'll have all the time in the world to be together.*

She had a long list of things to do. First, she would change the bandage and disinfect the wound on the patient's foot. In the ten months since she'd been working at the sick bay, Josef had taught her how to do many things, allowing her to operate independently and giving him more time to tend to severe cases. After Léa finished changing the bandage, she would tidy up and stack all the items that needed to be cleaned and disinfected on the counter next to the sink.

She looked forward to spending time alone with Rose. They hardly saw one another anymore except for early in the morning while preparing for their shifts, and at night before bed. But they were always in a rush and rarely had time to sit and talk freely. When Léa had worked at the factory, they always had lunch together. But since moving to the sick bay, she didn't have time to meet Rose for lunch. They were both so busy, and any free time that Rose had, she naturally spent with André.

Léa had noticed a change in her sister. Her eyes no longer sparkled like they used to. It had started in the summer, not long after the Russian women arrived in cargo trains. Léa mentioned it to Josef, but he couldn't see anything different about Rose. Perhaps it was something only a sister would catch.

"I'm back," Rose said, entering the sick bay.

"All good with Reinhardt?" Léa was at the sink washing the medical equipment to prepare it for disinfection.

"Same as always." Rose put the five-Reichsmark note in the tin can on Josef's desk, then joined her sister at the sink. "I'll help you disinfect the equipment."

"What you're doing with Reinhardt—"

A kidney-shaped pan slipped out of Rose's hand and fell on the floor.

"We appreciate it."

Rose picked it up and put it in the sink.

"I don't want you to think—"

"Can we not talk about Reinhardt, please?" Rose said.

"Has anything happened?"

"Why on earth would you think that?"

"Because you haven't looked at me once since you entered—it's almost like you've got something to hide."

"You're being ridiculous."

"Am I?"

"I'm washing the pans." Rose shook her head.

"Look at me, Rose."

Her sister turned and Léa saw something fixed and hard in Rose's eyes. "What is it? Tell me, I will—"

Thud. The door opened. Léa turned to see Nadiya gripping the doorframe.

"What's happened?" Léa asked.

Nadiya's skirt was damp. An image of Maria flashed in Léa's mind.

"Has your water broken?" Léa called out.

"Yes," she said. "The baby's coming."

Léa turned to Rose. "The baby's early. Josef won't be back until tomorrow. Can you assist with the delivery?"

"Of course," Rose said. "But have you delivered a baby before?"

"I watched Josef deliver Maria—"

"*Ahhhh*, I can't," Nadiya cried out. "It hurts."

"Oh, yes, you can," Léa said, hurrying to Nadiya. "Rose, wash your hands, then bring her to bed in the back room. I'll get everything we will need and meet you there." She stroked Nadiya's back, gentle and steady. "Don't worry. You'll be fine."

"Promise me something?" Nadiya looked straight at Léa's eyes.

"What?"

"Don't leave my baby here." She winced against the pain. "In case I—"

"You aren't going anywhere. You and the baby will be fine."

Nadiya squeezed Léa's hand. "My child was conceived in love." She exhaled in quick puffs. "If she's orphaned—"

"Don't think like that," Léa said. "Nothing will happen to you."

"Take her out of here!" Nadiya's eyes were misty, and her face shone with sweat. She held Léa's gaze. "Promise?"

All that mattered was quelling the fear in Nadiya, who had somehow talked herself into a panic. "I promise," she said, in a soothing tone, directing her to Rose, who had just returned. "She'll bring you to the back room. I'll join you shortly."

"I know I can trust you. You and Josef will care for my child. You'll keep a promise."

Rose glanced at Léa, arching her eyebrows as if to ask what promise.

"I'll tell you later," she whispered, dismissing Nadiya's ominous tone. "Count the seconds between contractions."

Now, Léa needed to silence the hammering in her head because Rose was right—she'd never done this before. Léa's pulse pounded, making it hard to concentrate. She closed her eyes and took a few quiet breaths, allowing her time to slow her pulse and clear her head. She'd seen Josef do that when situations came at him from all directions and he needed to ground himself. Opening her eyes, she felt better. Nadiya's alarm was natural for a first-time mother. What she didn't need was for Léa to panic, too. Though she wished Josef could be here, she was confident she would handle the labor, until he returned in the morning.

Focus! Towels, water, and something to wrap the baby in. She moved swiftly, collecting all she needed and putting water on the stove heat. Then she found the knife Josef had used to cut the umbilical cord and sterilized it by holding it over the flame on the stove.

She went to the back room, where Nadiya walked and leaned on Rose for support. She sang in Russian, filling the room with a beautiful, melancholy song. "Ohhhh," Nadiya cried out. "Another one."

"A minute between contractions," Rose said.

Could she be ready so soon? Maybe she'd had the contractions for a while before coming to the sick bay. "Let's settle her on the bed."

"Get behind her back, so that she's upright and will have more strength to push," Léa told Rose.

Léa placed her hand on Nadiya's swollen midsection, as she'd seen Josef do with Maria. She felt the baby low in the womb. Nadiya's abdomen tightened sharply as another contraction seized her.

"I think you're ready to push," Léa instructed.

Nadiya gave a weak push.

"Try harder, with more force. Your baby wants to see the world," Léa said.

Rose stroked Nadiya's back and wiped the sweat from her forehead with a cloth.

Nadiya cried out, gripping Rose's hand tightly. "I can't," she sobbed.

"Yes, you can," Rose urged. "Do it for your baby. Sing to her the way you were singing just now."

She hummed a slow melody, interspersed with cries of pain.

"That's right, push Nadiya," Rose said, encouraging her.

Léa worried Nadiya was too weak; her face had gone pale, which was the opposite of Maria's bright red cheeks when she'd been in labor. A flutter of dread ran through Léa as she sensed something was wrong. But then, the baby's crown emerged, just like with Maria, and for a moment, relief washed over her. She glanced up at Nadiya, whose lifeless pallor filled her with new fear.

"I can see the baby's head. One more push and your child will soon be in your arms."

Nadiya's toes dug into the mattress as she pushed. The baby slid out fast, and Léa caught the tiny body, wrapping the infant in a cloth.

"Bravo, Nadiya," Rose said. "It's a girl. Now, you can sing to your daughter."

Nadiya smiled and closed her eyes, humming lightly.

"Rose, come hold her while I deal with the placenta."

Rose guided Nadiya back gently down to the bed before joining her sister. As she bent over to take the baby from Léa's arms, *clink*—something slipped from her pocket, rolling across the floor to Léa's feet. It was a ring. And even from here, she could see the glint of a precious stone.

"Is that yours? Where did you get it?" Léa asked.

Rose didn't answer as she bent down, took it and tucked it back inside her pocket.

"I found it," she said.

"It's got diamonds on it. Where would you find a ring like that?" Léa asked, carefully handing the baby to her, the umbilical cord still attached.

"In the canteen," Rose said.

Léa frowned. She would ask her more about the ring later. Now, she needed to focus on Nadiya. *Get the placenta out to cut the cord.* That's what she'd seen Josef do. She massaged Nadiya's belly and after a few minutes, the placenta slipped out, and along with it, a rush of blood.

"I think Nadiya's fainted," Rose said. "Look how pale she is."

The blood kept flowing, gushing, and pooling around Léa's feet. She didn't know what to do. Josef had once told her that undernourished mothers in labor risked having a weak uterus that could fail to contract after birth. Is that why Nadiya was bleeding so much? If the uterus didn't contract, she would hemorrhage. Léa's throat went dry. She didn't know how to save her. The room went still and quiet.

"Nadiya, wake up." Rose's voice cut through the silence. She turned to her sister. "Check her pulse."

Léa felt for a beat on Nadiya's wrist. She found a faint one. She reached for the knife and cut the umbilical cord, thinking that might help. But the blood continued to flow, pooling on the floor. She got up and touched Nadiya's face, her skin clammy and cold.

"Hold on. Breathe. You're going to be fine. Open your eyes." She checked the pulse at her wrist. Nothing. She checked the other wrist and the world slowed to a halt. "Please, Nadiya," Léa whispered. "Please open your eyes." But Nadiya was perfectly still, all color gone from her flesh.

"Oh, Léa." Rose swallowed. "How did—?"

"She lost too much blood." Léa's breath was ragged. A death and a birth in a single moment. She closed her eyes as the baby's first cry pierced the stillness, breaking her heart.

"It's not your fault," Rose said, reaching out to comfort her sister.

Léa began to cry. It was her fault. Nadiya should be singing to her baby, rocking her in her arms. If only Josef had been here, he would have saved her.

"It's all right, Léa," said Rose. "The baby is safe. You did the best you could."

Léa wiped her eyes. Nadiya's death felt like a portent of what was to come. All the hope she'd carried for the future dissolved. "We're destined for the same fate, aren't we?" she whispered.

"No. We're going back to France," Rose insisted.

Léa turned to her sister. "No one is coming to save us. We'll never get out of here. The train lines have been bombed to bits, and any still functioning will soon be destroyed. There's no way for us to get to France. We're going to die here like Nadiya."

"We will save ourselves," Rose said, her voice strong. "We'll find a way out. I have a plan."

Léa's heart ached to hear her sister speak like that. She wished she could be the one consoling Rose. For two and a half years, she'd hoped for the war's end, but now its approach filled her with dread.

The baby cried.

"Hush, little one," Rose whispered. "You're safe." She looked at Léa. "What will we call her?"

"Let's give her a Russian name, to honor her mother."

"Back in Orléans, there was a girl in school I sometimes played with; her father was Russian."

"What was her name?"

"Katya."

"That's a beautiful name." Léa smiled sadly. "I promised Nadiya to keep her child, and I will honor that. If I don't adopt her, she'll be sent to the Children's Home for Foreign Workers." Léa sighed. "Nadiya once told me that in her language, her name means hope. Now, we have to offer Katya the hope her mother isn't here to give."

Rose stepped closer, and Léa took Katya, cradling her in her arms. Katya cried. Léa tried to console this new life, even though the future felt more uncertain than ever.

PART III

1945

Glashütte, Germany

32

Rose

February 1945

Four months later, Rose awoke to darkness. In the past weeks, sleep came only in broken, restless fragments. The war was twisting toward its violent end, but for her, a new battle was about to begin.

In a woven basket on the floor, Katya stirred gently. Leaning over, Rose saw the baby's bright eyes shining in the gloom. She kissed her on the forehead, the skin cool against her lips, then cradled her on her chest and covered her with the blanket.

Katya was smaller than expected for five months, but Josef assured the sisters she was doing fine. To Rose, she was perfect. Katya hardly cried. Since they carried her everywhere in a sling at the front or back, she smiled at everyone. André claimed he'd never seen such a happy baby, and said it was the love of two mothers—Léa, who cared for her during the day in the sick bay, and Rose, who watched her at night and in the mornings.

She thought back to the night Nadiya had died. She and Léa had stayed up talking about how they would care for the newborn—with Reinhardt's money, they could pay a local wet nurse to feed Katya—and then about how they should keep Nadiya's memory alive for her daughter. "Imagine, one day the child might want to know who her real mother was, what she looked like, if there's a family photo or a name of a hometown," Léa had said. "All we have is her *Arbeitsbuch*."

The day after Nadiya's death, Rose walked up the stairs to the barracks where the Russian women lived, determined to find something among Nadiya's belongings that they could save for Katya. It was late afternoon, and the barracks were empty. Rose knew the Russian women worked longer hours, so she assumed they were still at the factories.

The guard checked her pass, and then she climbed the concrete stairs to the third floor, where she knew Nadiya had been living with the other women since arriving by cargo train months earlier. She reached the top floor and found an eerie silence in the corridor. She passed the bathrooms on her left, and farther along on her right, the door opened to a large room with bunk beds. She stepped inside.

Something was wrong. Not a single picture on the wall, no curtains on the windows, no pillows or sheets on the iron bunk beds. Her footsteps echoed off the empty walls. Where were the eighteen women who'd been living here? And what had happened to Nadiya's things? A small knot of panic began to form in Rose's chest. She looked out the window. The sun outside was blinding, filling her with a sharp fear. Perhaps there was a reason, she told herself, trembling. In desperation, she hurried to find the guard.

"The top floor is empty. What happened to the women living there?"

"They were sent away this morning," the guard said.

"Sent where?"

He shrugged. "I don't know. I was only told to clear everything out so there would be no trace of them."

No trace. She swallowed. "Were they sent by train?"

He shook his head. "Two trucks pulled up before dawn. They loaded the women and all the items they were allowed to carry in the back of those trucks."

"But you don't know where they went?"

"I don't make it my business to ask questions, especially when Kriminalinspektor Reinhardt gives the orders."

She went still. "Herr Reinhardt sent them away?"

"He came here to oversee the loading of the trucks."

A crushing weight pressed on Rose's chest, stealing her breath. Had Reinhardt betrayed her, shattering their fragile pact before it had begun?

"Thank you."

She turned away from the guard and the barracks. How had she not anticipated his betrayal? He was a Gestapo officer—what did honor mean to him? She felt the ring in her pocket where she'd carried it ever since his proposal. Rose had done what he'd asked, lying to her sister and André. Was it all for nothing? He had promised that the Russian women would survive if they remained here under Josef's care. She had to confront him and learn the truth. She would not uphold her end of the agreement if he had broken his.

Her blood thumped in her ears as she trudged through the town. With each step she took, she heard the guard's words repeating in her head—they were sent away—and with it the shuddering possibility that they had been sent to death camps. She reached the building across from the church, pulled the door open and took the steps up to the Gestapo office. She'd never been here in the middle of the day, but she'd already decided that if he wasn't here, she'd wait, refusing to leave until he returned.

She heard the crackling of the fire as she approached the open door. How was it fair that Nadiya had died and the other women were in a truck being transported to a camp. Yet he sat in his warm office. She stepped inside. He looked up.

"Rose." He lifted one eyebrow. "What are you doing here at this hour?"

"Where are the Russian women?" Her voice trembled. "We had a deal. You've—"

"I've kept them safe."

"Tell me where they are."

"Trust me."

Feeling bolder, she lowered her voice. "Bring them back." She reached for the ring in her pocket and held it in the air. "Or our deal is off."

"You don't know what you're talking about." A faint tic in his jaw. "If they're here when the Soviet troops arrive, which will be very soon, then they won't survive."

He peddled lies; his words were a slap in the face, a cruel reminder of the twisted reality he lived in. "Why would they kill their people?"

"Russia is an old military power. It understands the true nature of war."

"What does that mean?"

He dropped the pen and leaned back in his chair. "The Soviet army doesn't care about its own people. They fight with blind rage, destroying all in their path. Do you think it matters how many of their own die?" He wiped his mouth with the back of his hand. "That's how they took Poland, Yugoslavia and now East Prussia and Silesia from us."

Rose looked at the window. Long shadows fell across the floor as the sun made its way down the valley. Reinhardt spoke of vengeance. For weeks now, she'd felt something in the air, a faint trembling of the ground and now she knew what it was—the rage of the Soviet army marching closer.

"I have very good information, from a source I trust, that any Russian civilian—male or female—found on German territory will be considered a traitor to the motherland and sent to the Gulag." He frowned. "Those women won't survive the Gulag."

"It's not their fault that they were dragged from their homes and brought to Germany."

"You speak of logic and rationality." He took a beat. "The Soviet command believes in brute force. They will have expected that those women should have fought to the death. Now, they'll see them as traitors." Strain showed around his eyes and jaw. "I sent them out of Germany to Prague. If they're found on Czech soil, it's better." He sighed.

"If it's not safe for them, what about me?" she asked.

"I will protect you. I'm making many arrangements to secure your safety. You can trust me." His eyes narrowed on her. "Have you spoken to André?"

"Of course not."

"Perhaps you should."

"You mean, tell him I'm marrying you?" She almost laughed.

"Do you want him looking for you, wondering, doubting whether you're still out there needing him to come rescue you? Or do you want to let him go so he can be free to love someone else?"

She had never considered how André would endure after this, or what he would do. The thought that he might come searching, refusing to abandon her, filled her with a fierce, aching love—and with dread. Reinhardt's gaze burned her. "André will move on," she said, holding her hands tight at her sides.

"Only if you let him go."

“How?”

“Tell him it’s over.”

“I don’t think that’s necessary.” She didn’t want to hurt him.

Reinhardt leaned forward, resting his elbows on the table. “You don’t understand men,” he said quietly. “After the war, André will poke around, asking questions, looking for you. It could cause problems. And don’t you want André to live free of guilt? Or do you want him haunted by the belief that he left you behind?”

She hesitated. There was a ring of truth to what he said. André would not give her up easily, especially after she’d saved his life by arranging for him to leave Berlin. “But how will we ensure he joins Léa and me and Josef when we flee?” Her voice tightened a little. “If he thinks I no longer love him, maybe he won’t come.”

“Leave that to me.” He reached into the desk and pulled out a paper. “I’d like you to sign this.” He handed it to her, along with a pen.

She read the word at the top: *Heiratsurkunde*, Marriage Certificate. And then her name at the bottom pressed next to his. The pit of her stomach dropped. She looked up—he watched her.

“What are you waiting for?” he asked, an edge in his voice. “You still don’t trust me?”

She had agreed to marry him and carried his ring in her pocket like an anchor weighing her down. But to sign the paper that gave her life away was final. Last night, talking with Léa reminded her of the times in the boardinghouse when they’d shared everything. Léa had been probing her about the ring intermittently, ever since she’d set eyes on it. Rose had stuck to her story that she’d found it, but yesterday she had almost told Léa the truth. If she did, maybe her sister would help her find a way out.

Had Reinhardt sensed her hesitation? She held the paper in her hand. One signature, and then he owned her. She wouldn't be able to change her mind. He flexed his fingers and she noticed the individual veins on his hands, the way his white cuffs rimmed the gray wool uniform.

"Go on. Time is running short. There's much I need to prepare for your sister and us. Show me that I can trust you." His voice held a warning.

Rose had come this far; how could she turn back? There was Katya, Nadiya's baby, to bring to safety. *Be strong.* It was the right thing to do. If anyone could protect them against the Soviet army heading their way, it was Reinhardt. She lifted the pen and signed.

Now in the barracks, Rose heard voices outside. Katya had fallen asleep on her chest, and she returned her to the basket and got up and went to the window. A sliver of light appeared at the edge of the sky. On the road that ran in front of the barracks, she could make out three people huddling together.

"What is it?" Léa asked, slipping down from the bunk bed and joining Rose at the window.

"There are people outside. I think something's happened."

"Let's get dressed," Léa said.

Rose strapped Katya to her chest in the sling, then put on her coat and boots. Halfway down the stairs, they met the night guard, an anxious look on his face.

"Fräulein Cotillard, there are injured people on the street—" his voice trembled "—they've walked all night."

"From where?" Léa asked.

"Dresden," his eyes went wide. "What they've said . . ."

Rose felt a chill along her spine. "Did something happen in Dresden?"

"Come quickly. I've given them water."

They followed him outside. The air was bitterly cold; frost covered the ground. As Rose approached the gate, she could see a man hunched over two women sitting on the ground. The sharp smell of ash and smoke hung on their clothing. The man had a stiff blanket wrapped around his shoulders as if he'd dunked it in water, then draped it over himself and it froze in that position. He turned to Léa, streaks of blood on his face and shards of glass on his skin, his eyes bloodshot and swollen.

"What's happened?" Léa asked.

"They bombed Dresden," he said, coughing.

The younger of the two women whimpered, holding up her arm; the skin on her hand was bloodied and black. "Flames everywhere, the sky on fire," she said, breathless. "A wind carried the flames like waves devouring all . . ."

The third woman looked up. She had cuts all over her face, and a black eye with a bruise that swelled down to her cheek. "Windows blown out, glass hit us from all directions."

"We tried to seek shelter in the train station, but it was a ball of fire, completely destroyed."

Léa glanced at Rose, who wanted to tell her not to worry, Reinhardt had a plan. She squeezed her sister's hand instead.

"We need to get them to the sick bay," Léa said. "Josef will clean their eyes with drops, then tend to the cuts on their faces and hands."

Rose nodded. "Are you strong enough to walk a little more?"

"Yes, we can. We came with others," the man with the blanket said, pointing in the direction of the road out of town. "They need a doctor."

"Others?" Léa didn't see anyone behind them.

"A few kilometers back. They couldn't walk anymore. One is badly injured. We went ahead to get a doctor."

"How many?" Léa asked.

"Ten. We were all camping on the banks of the Elbe River. We'd already lost our homes when the Russians came into Silesia. We thought we'd be safe in Dresden." He shook his head.

"You're safe now," Léa said. "The doctor is at the sick bay, just up the road." She turned to Rose. "Take them there and I'll go look for the others."

The guard stepped forward. "I'll come with you, Fräulein Cotillard, to help bring the others. Let's take the mule with the cart."

Rose could see that the scales had been lifted from the guard's eyes. Was it the first time he'd seen his own people become refugees? If the lack of food, coal and medicine hadn't been enough to show him that the end of the war was coming, and Germany would lose, then the bombing of Dresden would.

The injured man and Rose, with the younger women, made their way along the street. The sun was now up. People opened their curtains. When they reached the sick bay, Rose turned back and saw in the distance a massive plume of smoke gathered in the sky. She gasped. "Could that be from the fires at Dresden?"

"Yes." The man crossed himself.

Rose drew in a breath, saying a little prayer, as her mother would have, for all those souls struggling to stay alive in a burning city.

A grave look crossed Josef's face as he saw Rose enter with the three patients.

"What happened?" he asked, helping to bring the patients over to the empty beds.

"Dresden was bombed. These people walked here."

"We came in a group," the man said as Josef examined his face.

Rose told him that Léa and the night guard had gone with the donkey cart to find the others in the forest who couldn't walk any farther. "I'll find André, tell him, then I'll come back to help."

It was still early enough that she might have a chance to see André before he entered the factory for the morning shift. She passed a crowd gathered around a large red poster in the town square. Rose shuffled to the front to read the poster: *The Führer will avenge the people's suffering. Do not give up! In a few days, retaliation will come! Glorious victory to the Third Reich!*

She turned away from the crowd, her body ice cold. She needed André, to feel his warm hand in hers. He was lining up outside the factory. She signaled to him, and he followed her behind a building where they were out of sight.

"Have you heard?" she asked, breathless.

"About Dresden? Yes, it's horrible," he said, stroking Rose's cheek. "Don't worry. The war is almost over. Guys in my barracks are talking about running away. I'm listening, waiting for the right time. We'll do it together with Léa and Josef. Soon, we'll be home, together, and this will all be in our past." He bent down and kissed Katya on the forehead. "You're going to be a wonderful mother. Tell me again how many children we will have?"

Rose began to cry. She longed for the future André spoke of, yet she had already committed herself to Reinhardt. Her lips quivered as he drew closer and kissed her.

"We're in this together," he reassured her. "Don't worry. I love you, and we'll escape together." The factory bell chimed. He caressed her face, his hands radiating warmth. "I'll never leave you, I promise. I must go now."

"I love you, too," she said, watching him walk away. In her heart, she knew Reinhardt was right—she had to break it off with André—and she was running out of time.

33

Rose

April 1945

At the end of her shift, Rose went to the washhouse to meet André. It was one of their favorite spots—a secluded covered platform on the Müglitz River built with stone columns and a sloped slate roof that shielded them from prying eyes. Sunlight sparkled on the water, and purple and white crocus poked up from the banks on either side.

It had been ten months since the terrible day Reinhardt had made his proposal, forcing Rose to choose who would live or die. She'd delayed as long as possible, hoping for a year with André. In her heart, she knew there would never be room for anyone else. She needed to make this year of love last a lifetime.

She spotted him first. Running across the bank leading to the washhouse, he whistled a familiar French tune she recognized from the radio. Her gut churned a mix of emotions at the grenade she was about to launch into his world.

Something in his movements made her hesitate. It was that irresistible lightness she'd found so attractive on their first date, strolling around Place du Martroi. She felt a pang of regret and doubted her strength. Then she went through the reasons why—the aerial bombings, Katya growing fast and nearly ready to crawl at seven months, Léa and Josef in love, and André, having already lost his father, deserved to be happy with someone else. One recovers from love but not death. If letting go would keep them safe, she needed to go through with it. She forced herself onward.

He jumped onto the platform and smiled, holding out his arms. She went to him, and he brought her close, stroking her back slowly and quietly. Every part of her body quavered under his touch. She would remember this moment and all the other moments. He was the man she loved more than any other, which is why she had to let him go.

"It's good to see you," he said. "Assembling time fuses for bombs makes me dead inside. Then I come here and you bring me back to life." He leaned close and kissed her. She let herself kiss him back because she knew that after today, she would never kiss him again. *I love you. I'm sorry for what I'm about to do.* She pulled away, stepped back, and turned toward the river.

"Is everything all right?" he asked.

"It's been a busy day." Her voice was taut. She wished André knew her better than Reinhardt, could see through her and probe, make her confess her deal with Reinhardt, then talk her out of it, say she couldn't stay, that he had a plan and she would marry him. Then everything would be fine. That was the dream. Reality was the paper she'd signed. She belonged to Reinhardt. The ring in her pocket reminded her. She had to forge on.

"I'm still grieving Nadiya," Rose said. "Poor Katya to have lost her mother like that."

He stroked her arm slowly and softly. "You and Léa are filling in so well for Nadiya. You'll both make sure Katya leads a good life."

He stepped behind her, wrapping his arms around her waist, and held her. She loved his chest, solid and sure against her back, ready to catch her if she fell. She took a deep breath, steeled herself, and pushed his hands away.

"Whoa, what's happening? I can feel the tension in your shoulders. Did the Meister yell at you today?"

"No. Sorry, I feel different . . ."

"Rose, what's wrong?"

"I told you, I feel different."

He turned her around to face him. "About?"

She looked down. He put his hand under her chin, lifting it to look at her. "About us."

He winced as if he'd been stung by a bee. Hands akimbo, his mouth gaped open. "Come on," he said. "Stop joking around."

"I'm not joking."

Silence. His mouth pinched.

"Do you want to tell me what's going on?"

"I'm just having second thoughts, is all." *Do it.*

"About me and you?"

"Yes."

He ran a hand through his hair and, glimpsing the man she'd fallen in love with outside the cinema in Orléans, she couldn't bear to look at him and turned away.

"Yesterday, we kissed and talked and held on to one another like we'd never let go." He shook his head. "I thought we were solid. I—"

"There's nothing wrong with slowing things down for a while."

"You saved my life. I thought you and me—"

"Let's be friends for a while. Then after the war—"

"Rose, I don't want to be your friend."

It was so hard. But her love for him was strong enough to lie if that would keep him safe and bring him home. That's all that mattered. Not some idea of romance. Kissing in a cinema. She'd been infatuated. God, she sounded like Léa.

He came and stood alongside her. They were both looking out at the river. The water was calm and shallow. She could see the pebbles on the bottom, the way the sunlight hit them. It was what Léa had told her about Josef. At least Léa would have Josef. André would find someone. He was young, handsome and so loving. Reinhardt was right. She had to let him go.

"Are you saying you don't love me anymore?" he asked.

"I'm saying I don't know. And because I'm not sure, then it's not fair to you that we keep on like this."

"I can't understand how this has happened." He pulled her close. "Tell me what's really going on."

She stiffened, and he let her go.

"You mean it, don't you?" His voice quavered.

"Yes, I do." She held his gaze. She could see the force of her words settle like a weight on his shoulders and into the curve of his mouth.

He stepped back and looked away. "I see."

"I don't think we should meet in the afternoons anymore. I've got other things I need to do."

He turned around, unbalanced, grabbing on to the stone column to hold himself upright. "Whatever you want."

"Are you all right?"

"I'll be fine. Take care of yourself, Rose."

She yearned to pull him close, feel his warmth, kiss him. Yet, she restrained herself, fists tightly balled, knuckles white. "You should go now," she said, her voice trembling, holding back tears. If she could survive this moment, she could survive anything.

"I'm going."

Closing her eyes, she went back in time to when she'd asked Maître Mallon to write to André. It felt like a whole lifetime had passed since then. Now, listening to his footsteps on the wooden floor moving away from her, she wished for him to live a long and happy life and to find someone deserving of him to share it with. Rose had made her pact with Reinhardt, and for her, there was no turning back.

34

Léa

May 1945

On the first of May, Léa, Josef, André and Rose gathered around the radio in the sick bay, listening to the broadcast: *the Führer has fallen at his command post in the Reich Chancellery, fighting to the last breath against Bolshevism and for Germany.*

"The war is over?" Léa asked, her voice hopeful as she gently rocked Katya in her arms.

Josef held up his hand, continuing to listen, then turned off the radio.

"They've appointed Admiral Dönitz as his successor." He looked up at Léa. A ball of dread gathered in her stomach because she could see he was worried. "They're putting on a brave face. The Soviet army seems to be in control of Berlin; they just haven't announced it yet."

"We must leave," Rose said.

"Where will we go?" Léa asked.

"To the Allied side," Rose said. "We don't want to be here when the Soviets enter."

"How far is that?" André asked.

"West of the Elbe River," Rose said.

"How do you know that?" André's tone was sharper than it needed to be, tight lines around his mouth.

Rose looked down. Léa could see her sister wincing inside but trying to hide it. Usually, she and André stood next to one another, sometimes holding hands if it was just the four of them. Not today. They were miles apart. Something had happened between them.

"Herr Reinhardt told me." Rose looked up. "He warned that if we're here when the Soviet army arrives, they won't permit us to leave."

"They can't hold French citizens. He could be wrong," Josef countered.

"He knows better than we do. He has contacts—"

"In the Gestapo," André interrupted. "Do you hear what you're saying?"

"I know better than you who he is." She swallowed. "But without him, you'd still be in Berlin. Now, he's willing to help us get to the Allied side." She turned to Josef and Léa. "He's arranged a car and driver for tomorrow morning at seven."

André stepped forward. "Why would a Gestapo officer help us?"

Léa saw a faint flicker behind Rose's eyes. She had the same question. Why would Reinhardt help them? In these last days of the war, wouldn't he only care about saving himself?

"He wants to make amends for the horrible things he's done."

"He'll have to do that in prison," André scoffed. "Preferably hanging by a noose."

"Is that true?" Josef went to Rose. "What did he tell you about the car?"

"I believe—"

"You *want* to believe it." André glared at her.

Léa noticed that Rose had been acting strangely over these last weeks. Had she and André argued? She'd been so busy looking after Katya, keeping a close eye on her now that she was crawling and able to grab things and put them in her mouth. It wasn't safe to leave her in the sick bay unsupervised. She hadn't had time to speak with Rose. She regretted that now. She also had the sense that Rose was avoiding her. Either her sister was up to something she didn't want Léa to find out about, or she and André were fighting. Either way, she would talk to her tonight.

"What Rose proposes is our only option," Josef said. "I support it." He put his arm around her. "I'm grateful that you've thought this through. We've all been so busy with the sick bay. Thank you."

"It's best for everyone," Rose said.

"Josef and Rose are right," Léa added, turning to André. "What do you think?"

"A group of men in my barracks left yesterday. No one stopped them." André shrugged. "I guess we don't have anything to lose by trying. A car will be a lot faster than going on foot."

"We need a weapon," Josef said.

"I can get a gun." André leaned forward. "Guys in my barracks have them. They've been stealing them from the guardhouse in anticipation of this day coming. In other towns, rumors circulate that the meisters running the factories are shooting the foreign workers before they have a chance to shoot them."

A few nights ago, Léa heard gunshots and thought it could be the Soviet army, but the next day, when they didn't arrive in town, she realized it was likely a dispute between a farmer and his workers. Order was breaking down. Standing still made them a target; movement provided safety. She turned to Rose. "Is there enough room in the car for all of us? I'll put Katya on my lap."

"The driver and Josef in the front; the three of us in the back." Léa heard the edge in her sister's voice and reached out to touch her shoulder.

"Is something wrong?"

"No, I'm fine. Let me take care of Katya. I'll put her to sleep tonight—it will give you a much-needed break." Rose cradled Katya, kissed her forehead and walked away. Rose's love beamed over the baby, but why then had Léa heard a faint sob from her sister's throat?

* * *

Sometime during the day, while Rose described their plan of escape and Josef stocked the few remaining supplies of food and water for the two patients he would leave behind, Léa made a decision. Tonight, their last night in Glashütte, while Rose had Katya, she would stay with Josef in the sick bay. It no longer mattered what Lagerführer Klein thought. They didn't have to hide anymore. She wanted to be with him. She wanted to listen to the soft vibration of his voice, feeling the pressure of his hand on her waist. He brought sunshine into every room. When he wasn't with her, she felt the world was in shadow and longed for his light. Tonight, they would make time for one another. Who knew how their journey would unfold tomorrow? But they had tonight. Josef had given so much of himself to others; now she wanted him all to herself, selfishly, maybe, just one night to keep him close. When she told him her plan, his eyes sparkled like rays of the sun, warming her heart.

They pulled two beds side by side. Léa settled next to him. She could tell something troubled him. "What's wrong?"

"I feel guilty leaving my patients on their own."

"There's nothing more you can do for them. We're out of medicine. There's hardly any electricity. If you're here or not, it doesn't matter."

"It still feels like I'm abandoning them."

"You've sacrificed all your time to look after them, saving so many lives. Now, it's time to take care of yourself."

He tapped her on the nose. "You and Katya are who I want to look after now."

"Are you upset we're not going to Prague?"

"We can't go with the Soviet army there. I promise one day to bring you and Katya to my magnificent city." She loved how he'd readily accepted Katya into their lives and never questioned the promise she'd made to Nadiya. He turned to face her. "Do you think I'll be able to get a medical license in France?" He took a beat. "It almost seems like a dream, too good to be true."

"To live in France?"

"To live with you and practice medicine. It's all—"

A truck rumbled outside. They listened. For the last days, German troops had been moving through Glashütte, making their way south to the border. Then the quiet returned.

"Everyone is getting out before the Russians come." He looked at her, his eyes reflecting the uncertainty of what would happen tomorrow. "We're doing the right thing, aren't we?"

"Do we have a choice? The German women are frightened about what will happen when the soldiers arrive. They've been told they're animals who want vengeance. We can't risk staying."

"Come here," he said, pulling her close. "How did we find one another in the middle of a war?"

"I want to tell you something."

"Yes?"

"I've never been with a man before."

"And?"

Why was this so hard to say when every part of her body longed for him? Her heart had been shut, he'd opened it, and now she wanted him to open it more. "I'd like you to be the first."

He took her hands in his. "I'd like that too." He leaned in, his mouth near, his breath warm on her skin, but his lips did not touch her. Instead, his finger traced a line from her forehead down the side of her face, curving around her jaw, along her neck to the indent at the base of her throat. She felt the power of his touch, a doctor's healing hand radiating the warmth of the sun, giving life. She lifted his hand to her mouth and kissed the palm. "I love you," she whispered.

"I love you, too." Now his mouth touched her mouth, and her fingers slid through his hair, soft as feathers. She closed her eyes and felt herself unraveling under his touch.

"Léa?"

"Yes?"

"Look at me."

She opened her eyes. The room was gray and misty, but specks of light danced in the air between them.

"When I said we found each other, I mean you've opened something within me. I don't know if another woman—"

"Could have torn you away from your patients?"

He laughed. "It's more than that. You dragged me out of this long tunnel of despair I'd been walking through. I'd forgotten about love, light, warmth. The world isn't a cold and dreary place; we don't have to be alone—we can make the world what we want it to be. You've given me that gift. I want to spend the rest of my life looking into your beautiful eyes, getting lost in them, finding your eyes in our children." His hands cupped her face, and she felt he was holding her whole world inside him.

"Will you marry me?"

"Yes."

* * *

In the morning, she awoke entangled with him, her head against his solid, warm body. She smiled, unable to believe that she would spend every day of the rest of her life waking up like this. She had found her home in Josef's arms, and she could see their future stretching before them, the sun shining beautiful and bright. Today, their future would start and if all went well, by afternoon, they'd be on the other side of the Elbe River, safely in the hands of the Allies.

Josef said goodbye to the patients, reassuring them that the Soviet army would have a doctor to care for them. André arrived at six-thirty, a small bag over his shoulder. Rose was the last one, carrying a backpack.

"Come on, Rose, we're going home," Léa said.

A bird sang. Rose put her arms around Léa. "I love you," she whispered.

"I love you, too, little sis," Léa said, noticing that Rose stood unusually still and quiet. An uneasy feeling crept over Léa. Then she realized Rose had forgotten her drawings.

"You must bring your sketchbooks." She'd spent hours drawing portraits of the Russian women in the sick bay. Léa thought they were her best work.

Rose blinked. "Yes. I'll ask the driver to stop by the barracks on the way."

A car engine sent them outside. It was one of Reinhardt's men driving a two-door cabriolet Opel. Though he was dressed in civilian clothes, a Gestapo officer's hardness in his face and eyes remained. The driver tapped his watch, hurrying them along.

Josef sat in the front. André, Rose and Léa settled in the back, with Katya sleeping on Léa's lap. The car started. Rose leaned forward, asking the driver to stop at the barracks. He nodded. Léa thought it odd that he didn't complain since he seemed to be in a hurry. Maybe it was because they would be taking the road north that led out of town. When they arrived at the barracks, Rose slipped a note in André's hand, and whispered, "Don't read it until I return." Then she jumped out. The driver kept the engine running.

The ground beneath them trembled as a deep *grrrr-grrrr-thud* thundered through the air. Up ahead, a Panzer tank, heading south, was about to pass them. Every door and window in the Opel rattled. The car shook, like a boat on water, buckling against the force of the tank. Léa's skin vibrated, as if it was sliding away from the bones on her face. Katya opened her eyes and cried.

"Hush, little one," Léa cooed. "Your aunt will be—"

The tank commander, towering, stood up in the open hatch. He glanced down, and the driver saluted. A grinding, metallic clatter continued as more Panzers followed, heading south. Léa could taste the acrid diesel in her mouth; the stench of oil and exhaust burned her nose.

Then the Opel was moving. Léa thought it was the force of the half-dozen tanks propelling the car forward, but the driver was shifting gears.

"Stop," she shouted, trying to be heard above the deafening noise.

"Go back," Josef yelled. "Stop the car!"

"We don't have Rose," André called out.

The car rolled on, the driver's arm pulling the gearbox back, as he took the tight turns fast.

Léa held on to Katya, panic ripping through her chest. Why had Rose put her arms around Léa and said she loved her? The metallic taste of fear was on her tongue. Rose wasn't going with them. "Josef, make him stop," she screamed. "Now. He must stop." Unhinged, she shook the seat in front of her with one hand. But he was driving too fast, and she had to use both hands to keep Katya from falling.

"He stops . . . I'll jump out . . . go back," André shouted.

Léa saw the same fear and panic churning in his eyes that she felt hammering in her chest. Something warned that the driver had no intention of slowing down. And what if Rose wasn't here because she never intended to come? Maybe she hadn't forgotten her sketchbooks, but left them behind so that she could leave the car.

Josef must have had the same thought because he turned around, his dark hair knocked sideways by the wind. "We won't leave her. I promise."

35

Léa

They drove for an hour on roads teeming with people. Small groups of men and women dressed in rags or shabby uniforms, pulled carts with all their possessions. They looked like vagabonds, aimless, wandering, stopping to rest on the side of the road. The driver swore at them, shouting that they should get off the road. Outside of Dohma, a line of cars stood at a roadblock. Men in plainclothes pointed rifles, asking questions. The driver clicked his tongue, tapping his fingers on the gear shift.

André opened the note and read it, then folded it and held it to his heart. He glanced at Léa, his eyes burning with tears.

She wanted to ask what the note said, but the driver, grinding the gear into reverse, suddenly backed up, nearly smashing the car behind, then turned and sped off. Gunshots hit the metal trunk. André pulled Léa down, bending over her and Katya.

"Are you all right?" Josef asked, turning to the back seat.

André sat up and checked Léa and Katya. "We're all fine."

"Where are we going now?" Josef said.

"Valley roads." The driver crunched the gears. "Main roads too dangerous."

"Let's return to Glashütte," Léa said, reaching for Josef's hand.

"No. You go to the other side of the Elbe," the driver said.

Josef held her hand. "One of us will go back with him and find her."

For a moment, Léa believed him. She wanted to believe that Rose had made a simple mistake that anyone could have made, like getting off at the wrong tram stop.

They veered off the main road, skidding on the asphalt as the car turned onto a dirt track, driving up a narrow, steep passage. At the top, a small town stood on the hill overlooking the valley below. Léa stared at the church and castle as they passed them in the square, everything painted pale white and blue. Then the car went down the other side, an expanse of green fields and forests as far as the eye could see.

Crack! The car jolted to a stop. Léa, thrown against the back of the driver's seat, clutched Katya to her chest as they both fell into the footwell. Her forehead burned; something warm and thick trickled down the side of her head.

"Léa—" Josef called out.

Crack! Crack!

Josef crumpled down, blood deep ruby red all over the seat. Léa screamed. André reached for his gun, but another bullet shot a hole in his neck, and he collapsed on the footwell next to her. A sea of blood. *Josef? André?* She could still see them as they'd been seconds before. They were going to cross together to the other side of the Elbe, where it was safe. Clutching Katya close to her heart, Léa's senses were heightened—everything came at her in fragments, shattered by fear and blood.

"There's a woman," a man called out in German with a heavy foreign accent. He stood outside the car, hovering over Josef, pointing his Karabiner in the air.

"Are you German?" he said.

"I . . . am French." A viselike grip squeezed her throat.

"We want the car. Get out."

She struggled to draw in air. *Josef, please stand.* We'll go now. She wanted to touch him, but feared the man would shoot her if she tried. Josef's head twisted at an unnatural angle. His hands, palms facing the sky, speckled with blood. Léa started to cry.

"Shut up." The man lowered the Karabiner. "Get out or I will shoot you and the baby."

Trembling, she took the bag, climbed out of the car and stumbled onto her knees. Other men were making their way through the grass toward her. She stood, legs wobbly and unstable. *Walk.* She was numb. The world had gone black. Holding on tight to Katya, Léa ran into the woods.

Her arms throbbed, but she couldn't stop. In her mind, she kept seeing the man with the Karabiner glaring down at her, holding her in his sights. The forest was thick with oaks, and she brushed past their rough trunks, scraping her arms and legs. Her muscles ached.

Katya cried, and she did her best to hush her. After a while, maybe an hour, when Léa felt she was deep inside the forest, she stopped and listened for footfalls, voices, the metallic clunk of a gun. All she heard were softer sounds: birds hopping from the tree to the ground and the wind rustling the catkins hanging from the branches. She was alone, not safe—she would never feel that again—but not in immediate danger.

She gently put Katya on the forest floor. The baby was covered in blood, as was Léa. Josef's blood. André's too.

She needed to be alone. Moving away from Katya, she walked as if she might walk into another life. Then she collapsed on the ground.

In her heart, she screamed and howled at all that had been lost: Josef, André, and earlier, Rose. All gone. A primal fear held her back from calling out. She didn't know who or what else awaited her. Three shots she'd never seen coming had torn her life to shreds. Who were those men? Why did they have to kill so swiftly without saying a single word? None of it made sense. Her hands were still shaking from the shock. Fearing other men like them were nearby, she had to be small and quiet. Rolling on her side, she curled up in a ball and closed her eyes.

Josef, she whispered, sinking her fingers into the forest floor. The ache inside grew. Why had the man with the Karabiner let her live?

Katya whimpered.

Léa rolled over on her back, staring at the canopy, the pale green, soft new leaves in bunches, and beyond, the bitter gray sky. She was tired and weary, like a soldier after battle. A voice inside told her to get up and move. But she'd lost all strength. Wouldn't it be easier if she stayed on the ground, letting her body sink back into the earth? Disappear. Everyone she loved was gone. What was there worth fighting for? One day she too would die. Why not now?

Katya cried.

She turned and sat up, looking out over the undergrowth. Two tiny fists reached out in the air, trying to find something to hold on to. Léa drew her knees up and rested her head on them. She couldn't go on. It was too much. Where was Rose? She'd lost Rose and Josef on the same day. The two people who had known her the best. She lifted her head and saw the blood splattered on her clothes and over her hands.

Katya wailed, legs kicking.

Léa saw the baby's curly hair sticky with blood. Hadn't Katya lost everything, too? A father on the battlefield, a mother giving birth, all the grandparents, aunts and uncles she would never know. And yet *she* had the will to go on. Life was all questions with no answers, chance moments that decided one's fate.

Léa had the sense that Katya was urging her to get up and move. But she had no strength and turned away, tears streaming down her face. She wasn't sure she could do this. And then Josef's words from last night came to her. *We can make the world what we want it to be.* Isn't that what she'd tried to do but failed? Was she meant to keep trying, not give up? If she'd survived, maybe she owed it to those who hadn't—Nadiya, Ewa, André, Josef—to keep going.

Katya howled, inconsolable.

There was something sad and lonely in these woods. The light didn't enter and a chill clung to the air. She could feel the dampness in her bones, and she knew she didn't belong here. She had wanted somewhere to hide, to get away from the man with the Karabiner—but now it was time to go. She wanted to step out of this dark, lonely place and into the light.

Katya bellowed, gulping for air.

"I'm coming," Léa said. She stood and wiped the tears from her face. She brushed off the leaves and twigs on her clothes and pulled her hair back and away from her face. She opened the bag and removed one of the bottles—there were only two.

Katya was hungry. Léa was grateful for something so simple. She could go through the motions of feeding a child, and that would propel her forward. And after she fed her, she'd bring her to the stream—she'd thought she'd heard water rustling nearby—and clean and wash as much of the blood away as she could.

Léa went to her. Katya's eyes were tightly closed, limbs flailing, face red, mouth trembling. Léa watched her for a moment, then lifted her. The baby went still, opened her eyes and listened.

"Yes, I'm here," Léa whispered. "I know you're hungry. I'm sorry, I just needed a bit of time on my own. I'm here. Come, feed."

Sucking on the bottle, Katya's deep, dark eyes watched Léa as if she knew she was her whole world. And in return, Léa was grateful because for the few moments it took to care for her, she forgot about Josef, Rose and André.

After Katya fell asleep, Léa—wrapped her in the sling on her back—picked up the bag and started walking. She stopped at the stream and collected water to wash the blood away. Then she dried Katya and herself with one of the towels in her bag. She had a compass and used it to find north, then she started walking, determined to reach the Elbe.

Soon, she was out of the forest. She stayed away from roads, preferring fields and walking paths. Whenever she saw people drifting in bands, she slunk back, keeping her distance. Dusk dangled in the sky—pale blue and white clouds, a golden light floating in between. She had never seen such a beautiful sky as the one that appeared before darkness fell.

Farmhouse up ahead. Needing milk, she knocked on the door. A man came out with a Karabiner aimed at her. He shouted that she should go away but his wife, seeing the baby on Léa's back, took the gun out of her husband's hand. She motioned for Léa to come forward.

"We have cows. I will give you milk. But don't stay here. Keep moving."

"How far to the Elbe?" Léa asked.

"Five kilometers." The woman gave her a piece of bread. "You're close."

"Thank you."

She took the milk and bread and continued on her way. The one question that coursed through her like the blood pumping up to her heart: would she ever see her sister again?

At nightfall, she arrived in Prina. The town was eerily quiet. A bridge up ahead, the Elbe flowed under it. She would cross that bridge, and on the other side, she'd be free. A jeep rolled alongside her. Two soldiers with American flags on their sleeves sat inside. They stopped. "There's a curfew. No one is allowed out after dark."

She told them her story. Luckily, they understood a few German words. The moment she uttered *Zwangsarbeiter*, forced worker, they nodded and helped her and Katya climb into the back of the jeep. Finally, Léa crossed over the bridge to the Allied side.

36

Rose

Rose watched from the window: Léa in the car, Katya on her lap. It was Reinhardt's plan. He said the driver would wait a few minutes, then leave. *Easier to have them all in the car. They can't refuse to go without you.* The Panzer tanks rumbled past. The driver revved the engine, and Léa leaned forward, trying to stop him from driving off. When she realized she couldn't, she turned back, her eyes stricken with panic. Rose had done everything Reinhardt asked of her, except for the note she'd slipped into André's hand on which she'd written: *I love you. I always will.*

She shrank from the window of the barracks. How could she have been so cruel? Léa had spent her entire life sacrificing to ensure she was fed and housed, only to have Rose betray her. Maybe she would think it was an accident, that Rose had truly forgotten her drawings. But Léa was too clever not to see it for what it was: a cold, calculated plan designed to separate the sisters. Rose had made a pact with the devil, and now she had to live with it. Taking the ring from her pocket, she slipped it on her finger.

The next four days dragged on as Reinhardt prepared for their new life. He told her they would have different names and live on a farm outside of town, up on the hill. *There will be no trace that I was in the Gestapo.* She couldn't figure that out since everyone in Glashütte and Dippoldiswalde knew him. He worked relentlessly, and she had the sense that far from being despondent about surrendering to the advancing Soviet troops, he wasn't giving up but preparing a new attack in a battle he waged in his mind against the enemy.

"Do as you like now because after the Soviet army arrives—"

"What will happen?"

"If I can help it, no one will touch you. But it means you will not be able to leave my sight."

"For how long?" She remembered when he'd spoken of the Soviet army's blind rage.

"We shall see, but likely a very long time."

She visited the patients left behind in the sick bay, helping them to get out of bed to use the toilet, and providing them with water. If Reinhardt gave her an egg or a sausage, she shared it with them. Since most of the country's rail tracks had been destroyed, no food supplies were shipped in, and all that was left were the rutabagas and potatoes from last year's harvest. It was still early for the allotments to be producing. Many people wandered around with hungry ghost-like eyes.

Restless, she too wandered, staying clear of the main road as plenty of fighting was still going on in the Müglitz Valley. At night, she was mostly alone in the barracks, though there were a few Polish women on the ground floor, unsure of what to do and waiting for someone to tell them. She could hear shots around town, and the Panzer tanks still rumbled through, heading south; Rose wondered if there was still fighting in Prague.

During the day, she visited the places where she and André used to go: the forest, the old washhouse by the river, the allotments above the village. The factories were all shut; most of the foreign workers had fled. Down at the river, the meisters, whom Rose had only seen on the factory floor shouting about production quotas and threatening to dock pay, now tracked back and forth bringing files and papers from the offices to throw in the Müglitz River. There was neither coal nor wood to burn, so they relied on the water to swallow and hide their misdeeds. On the second day, the river became clogged with all those files, and the dam at the entrance to the town overflowed. She had heard that the Müglitz joins the Elbe, and she wondered if any of those papers might reach that far.

Rose had her own misdeed to throw in the river. She lifted the square paper she'd been carrying deep in her pocket for months. Unfolding it, she looked at the house André had drawn. *How many children do you want?* She could hear his voice as if he were standing next to her, whispering the words in her ears. She wondered if he had read the note she'd given him, and hoped with all her heart that he would forgive her for hurting him, and that he knew her true feelings, feelings that would never die. She realized then that she couldn't throw his drawing and his words into the river. It was a piece of him she would keep forever. She put the paper back in her pocket.

On 7 May, Reinhardt told her he was ready. They walked to the edge of the town, taking the forest path up a steep hill. It was one she'd never used before, a switchback that smoothed out the sharp bends.

"How long is it to reach the farm?" she asked, breathless, halfway up.

"One kilometer." He smiled. "No Soviet soldier will run up here by mistake."

"What about the winters?" She couldn't imagine walking this in thick snow.

"There are sleds and snowshoes at the farm. But we will have goats. I hope we can become self-sufficient."

"We will live off goats?"

"Chickens, too. Nothing commercial. Just enough for us to get by. You will see."

At the top, the view was magnificent—the entire Müglitz Valley, with its mountains and rivers, extended in all directions. Not far from the path stood a small wooden house with a sloping roof, set off to one side and nestled against a hill. Next to it a small barn. There was a porch outside the house.

"What do you think?" he asked.

"It's fine." She thought of André's house. The olive tree in the courtyard, the windows that opened to the outside like doors. And it suddenly struck her what sort of life she'd given up.

Luckily, there were two bedrooms. Rose was grateful that he honored their agreement. That night, she went to bed, the window open, the sound of the wind whistling through the trees. She awoke to a full moon shining its bright light into the room. And she thought of drawing the white and gray light radiating from the moon.

She sat up. It suddenly struck her that she'd left her drawings and sketches at the barracks. She'd been so torn apart by sending André and Léa away that in the four days she'd waited for Reinhardt, she'd not taken them. She felt a stabbing at her chest at the possibility that someone would find them and throw them out. They were her only reminders of Léa and André and all the women she'd drawn at the sick bay. She couldn't abandon them, but she couldn't go down to get them either. But maybe she could go to the barracks.

It wouldn't take that long—a few hours. Reinhardt would still be sleeping, hopefully not even realizing she'd been gone. And no one would see her in the darkness. She could take a candle to light her way, though with the full moon, she wasn't sure she needed one.

Rose stood and quietly made her way across the wooden floorboards. She changed her clothes, took the candle from the holder next to her bed, along with the matches, and slipped them into her pocket. She went out on the porch, where her boots waited. The air was fresh and clear—no trace of burning coal like in the center of town. Moonlight struck the ground like a torch. She found her way through the clearing to the path without needing to light the candle. Not wanting to carry it, she left it by the side of the path, reminding herself to pick it up on her return.

She navigated the switchbacks slowly, recalling tree roots that crossed the path in certain spots and which she could easily stumble over and fall if she wasn't careful. Tiny steps carried her down. The church bell rang once, signaling the half hour. She hadn't checked the time before leaving; she didn't even know where the clock might be in the house. She guessed it must be three or four in the morning. But by the time she reached the street, the sun was already over the horizon, the town enveloped in a fuzzy gray light.

No one was on the street. The only sounds were the rustle of the river nearby. It was so peaceful that Rose found it hard to believe the war was still ongoing. Reinhardt was convinced it would end today or the next day. When she'd asked him how he saw that happening, he'd shrugged. "You'll have a front-row seat," he'd told her.

Arriving at the barracks, Rose took the steps two at a time. She wondered if all the Polish women had left. On the top floor, she found her four sketchbooks under the bunk bed. She put them in a cotton bag, along with the pencils and charcoal, which she slung across her body. Then she went back down the steps and outside.

The sky had changed. Blue shadows washed out the gray, and between the clouds, a strip of copper flowed like a river. She thought about Léa, André and Josef. Five days had passed. Surely they would have reached the Allied side by now. Rose touched the ring on her finger. The war was ending. Why couldn't her promise end, too?

She glanced in the direction of the forest path. If she returned to Reinhardt, she'd be trapped, unable to get out. He'd told her she'd be in danger after the Soviets arrived. But what was keeping her here now, while one world was dying and the new one had yet to be born? Today might be her only chance to escape. It would be too risky for him, a Gestapo officer, to come after her. She smiled. All his carefully laid plans would be for naught. Everything was possible and in her grasp, if she only dared to reach out and take it. *Go!* She turned away from the forest path and toward the train station.

Rose heard a low-pitched roar, like the pistons in the machines on the factory floor. An early morning convoy of Panzer tanks? But the ground was still. She began to run, willing herself to go faster. After she passed the train station, she'd be off the main rain road and could take a side one. The sound became more precise. She recognized the rumble of airplane engines. Pulse thumping, she pushed the panic and dread aside and ran.

Whee-oo. Boom. A violent wave of air snatched Rose up, arcing her through space as if she was as light as a twig before dropping her hard on the ground with a thundering snap. Shards of glass and stone pummeled the ground around her. She tried to breathe, but her lungs felt like they were all pressure, but no air.

Rose attempted to stand but could only stagger up on her knees. Her ribs seared with a white-hot pain. She glanced at the factory on her right—a bomb crater in the middle—blown to shreds. Her head weighed like an anchor, pulling her down. No sound. She was underwater. Wobbling, unsteady, she saw the plane making a second pass, a machine gun poked from the window. She slid low to the ground, huddled behind a rock, and covered her head with her arms. A whoosh of hot air. Strafe hit the ground. Dust and dirt in her mouth and nose. Her lower leg burned, a searing pain like knives slicing her spine. She blacked out.

* * *

Rose opened her eyes. She was in the farmhouse, in the room she'd left when the moonlight shone through the window. Her body ached, her leg wild with pain.

"Would you like water?" A young woman's voice.

"Yes." Her mouth was dry, and her lips chapped.

The woman moved away, then returned. A hand behind her head lifted her, but her ribs stung like they were on fire. "Ouch."

"Yes, they're fractured. Nothing to be done but rest," the woman said.

Cool glass on her lips, she drew the water in and down her throat. But even swallowing pinched her ribs. The woman gently put her head down, and Rose closed her eyes.

The next time she woke, all was black. The room, sky, her heart. She shivered in the cold. She could feel every part of her body except her leg. She drifted in and out of sleep. Usually, someone was there by her bedside. She sensed a presence. Heard women whispering. Felt the cool breeze enter when the window was open.

"Do you need anything?" a woman asked.

Rose opened her eyes. "Who are you?"

"My name is Johanna."

"Are you always here?"

"I come every night."

"Just you?"

"Oh no, all of us. It's safe here." She took a breath. "And we look after Hans."

She remembered he'd changed his name. What was hers? She didn't care. She would leave. The war was over. So was her promise.

"Do you know what happened?" Johanna said.

"A bomb dropped."

"Yes. And after?"

"No. I don't have any memory. Just falling and waking up here." She swallowed. "How long has it been?"

"Three months."

Rose looked outside. It was nearly twilight but the coppery glow she'd glimpsed before had gone. The sky was now as gray as an old tin pot. She could feel the crisp air coming in through the open window. She'd missed summer. Had she also missed her chance? "How did I get here?"

"Hans brought you."

"He found me?"

"Yes. Would you like to speak with him?"

No. She wanted to be free and far from him.

"I'll get him," said Johanna, taking her silence for assent.

She raised her hand, but it was too late. Johanna had gone. Why not tell him? Once she was well, she would go.

He would have to let her. Now, she knew his secret. *There will be no trace that I was in the Gestapo.* She could do to him what he did to her.

"Hello?" There was something different about his voice. She turned to the door. Johanna held his arm, guiding him. Was something wrong?

"Hello, Hans," she said calmly.

"I'm glad you're talking. I was so worried." He turned. "Where's the chair?"

"Let me bring it closer to the bed," Johanna said. "There you go. Here's your cane. Is there anything else you need? I'll be in the next room. Just call."

"What's happened?" Rose sat up a little.

"He lost his sight when he went through the fire and smoke to get you out."

Rose looked down at her arms, wrapped in thin white gauze.

"Yes, and legs both badly burned." Johanna sighed. "The doctor said it was a miracle you survived, and if it had been minutes later the smoke would have killed you."

A throbbing deep in Rose's throat. She looked at him. His eyes were no longer blue but covered by a milky film. His gaze drifted, unable to meet her own, and ribbed burn scars marked his eyelids.

"I'm sorry you were hurt," she said. "I didn't know."

"All that matters is that you're safe." He sobbed. "I thought I'd lost you."

You almost did. She had been so close. But her timing was off. Too late. Why hadn't she gone earlier?

He leaned forward, gently reaching out his hand until he found the ring on her finger. "You're everything to me. I couldn't survive without you."

Keep a good heart. Her sister's mantra and her mother's words came to her. Even when everything is lost? *Yes,* a voice deep inside answered. Rose glanced at the bandages on her legs and arms, and then at his hand on her ring finger. She understood that of all the healing that awaited her in the months and years ahead, the physical wounds would be the easiest to mend. He'd done terrible things that she could never forgive, but nor could she forget that she wouldn't be here now without him and the price he'd paid to save her.

Rose turned to the window, the leaden sky behind torn white clouds. She couldn't deny the bond that existed between them. Not the bond he wanted, but a fragile thread that she couldn't break because that would mean breaking a part of herself. She didn't know how long it would take, but she would be patient and wait for the coppery light to return.

Epilogue

Dearest Rose,

I can't believe it's you. After all this time? Forgive me, but I had almost given up hope of ever hearing from you again. And then Paulette forwarded your letter, and when I saw your handwriting, the decades fell away as though it had all happened yesterday.

It's hard for me to talk about that last day after you got out of the car. Even now, the memories are still raw. The driver, avoiding a roadblock, took a country lane. A man appeared out of nowhere—he shot the driver, and Josef and André. I believe they died instantly and didn't suffer. Three lives over a car. The man spared me and I fled. At least I was able to save Katya, and, as I would learn later, the baby growing inside me, Josef's daughter.

You asked about Katya—she's now a mother with two teenage boys. She's also a professor of modern French history at the Sorbonne. She's a remarkable woman and Nadiya would be proud.

Eve, my daughter with Josef, is a surgeon at Hôpital de la Pitié-Salpêtrière in Paris. She loves her work and has never married—says she doesn't have time for love. Her eyes are the same as her father's. It's truly astonishing.

I won't come to Berlin. I'm happy the wall is being torn down and you now have your freedom. But we can't go back to being the way we were, not after everything that's happened. I don't know why you stayed behind—perhaps it no longer matters. Everyone else has forgotten the war. I want to forget it too. I've spent too much time living in the past.

Léa

* * *

Dearest Léa,

Thank you for your letter. My heart broke to learn about Josef and André. For me, they had never died, and so they lived and died all over again as I grieved them the way you must have at the time, and am sure, still do. Can you tell me if André read my note before he was killed?

Katya and Eve sound like wonderful young women, and so accomplished. They obviously take after their mother. I do remember Josef's eyes—you once said they resembled the color of the pebbles at the bottom of the stream outside the barracks. Do you remember? And Katya, does she look like Nadiya? What have you told them about their parents? Do they know about me? About everything that happened?

Please can you write again and tell me about yourself? How did you end up in Paris—that is the return address on your letter. Tell me what you did. Maybe we don't get to choose who we save; some hand of fate decides on our behalf, and then our lives spin off in a different direction.

I accept your decision, though I still hold out hope that you might change your mind and come to Berlin. In any case, we can't lose touch again.

With all my love,

Rose

* * *

Dearest Rose,

France was impossible for me after the war. I had trouble in Orléans—people called me a "collabo" because they knew I'd been in Germany. They were looking for women with any connection to Germany. I guess it was easy to blame us for what happened, as if our actions would have made a difference in the war.

When the baby started to show, I was accused of carrying a Nazi child. I was desperate, and unable to find work, so I fled to Paris, where no one knew or cared who I was or where I came from. I enrolled in nursing school and then worked in a clinic to support the girls. I retired a few years ago.

Both Katya and Eve know their parents' stories. I've told them everything I can remember, trying to keep Nadiya and Josef's memories alive for us all.

I'm sorry but I don't think there's anything you could say that would change my mind about coming to Berlin. For years I tried to find you through the Red Cross until they said there was no trace and you'd most likely perished and I've lived with losing you for all this time. You can tell me it's fate or you had no choice, but in the end, you took the decision to stay. I'm not judging you and

I don't want to hurt you, but it is what it is. You can write and tell me more about yourself, if you'd like.
And yes, André read your note.
Léa

* * *

Dearest Léa,

I'm so sorry for what happened to you in Orléans. It must have been terrible and you made the right decision taking the children to Paris.

I'm sure you were a wonderful nurse. I remember how happy you were tending to the patients in the sick bay. It seems our time with Josef marked us both.

Dreadful things happened to women here, too. After the Soviet army arrived, the soldiers did as they wanted with the women. All the women, no matter their age. The men were dead or away. Those who got pregnant were too ashamed to tell anyone. So, I became a midwife. It was out of necessity, and seeing you deliver Katya gave me the courage to try. After I delivered the first baby safely, many women came to me for help. They knew I wouldn't judge them because I carried a secret too. Some didn't want their babies, so I would find the children a home, sometimes caring for them myself. I suppose that was why I never had any of my own.

If there is still some tiny part of you that hopes we might reunite, come to Berlin. I don't think we'll have another chance.

Please, if you won't come for me, then come for Katya and Eve. I have something for them.

You might need to forget the past, but your daughters likely want to know more, and we're the only ones who can tell them.

With all my love,

Rose

* * *

Léa's woolen scarf flew around her face in the bitter wind as she walked along Unter den Linden in East Berlin. She looked up at the bare-branched linden trees, unable to remember them being there. Maybe they'd been planted after the war. Beyond, the sky was gray and threatening rain. Despite the weather, people were out on the streets. Many had come from the West, like Léa and her daughters, crossing over for the day to take photos and point at the bullet holes left in the buildings from the war.

On the day she'd been released from the displaced persons camp near Prina and put on an American army cargo truck for the five-day trip to the repatriation center at the Gare d'Orsay in Paris, she'd sworn she would never step foot in Germany again. But now here she was in Berlin.

"Maman, what could she have for us?" Katya's arm looped through her mother's, holding her close.

"I don't know." Léa's voice was weary. She hadn't slept all night. She kept tossing and turning, wondering what she would say to Rose. It was all so long ago. A part of her just wanted to leave it in the past. And yet, underneath her anxiety, she longed to see her little sister again.

Up ahead, recognizing the side street where the Kaffee Post had been, she stopped, unsure she could do this.

"Shall we sit on a bench?" Eve pointed to a spot across the street. "And give you a moment?"

They crossed the street and settled on the bench; the rigid wooden slats dug into Léa's back.

"Maybe she won't recognize me and I won't recognize her," Léa said. It was fine when it had just been letters, and she could slip back into the person she'd been forty-five years ago. But so much had changed. She wasn't that person anymore.

"I know it's not easy for you," Katya said. "But maybe it's hard for Rose, too."

Léa feared that the love she'd felt all these decades for Rose would no longer be there when they met again after all these years. As long as Rose stayed in her memories, she could hold on to the past—and not have to face the present or how they'd both changed. "I'm sorry. It's silly, we've come all this way . . ."

"You don't have to meet her if you don't feel ready," Eve said, squeezing her mother's hand. "If you want, Katya and I can go for you."

"You'd do that?"

"Yes, Maman, we will," Katya said.

"What will you tell her?"

"That you need more time." Eve put her hand on her mother's shoulder. "She'll understand."

Léa feared she'd never be ready. She just couldn't do it.

Katya stood. "She's been waiting all morning. You stay here, and we'll come back."

Léa watched her two grown daughters—Katya, taller and older, Eve marching with that determined stride of hers—cross the street and walk toward her sister.

* * *

Friday morning. Rose had been waiting four days. She checked her watch—nearly twelve. She'd promised herself that she would wait every morning for the whole week, but she couldn't bear to continue sitting in this café alone. If Léa was coming, she'd have been here by now.

How could she have imagined that Léa would want to see her again? She had her own life with two daughters, a bright and happy life—why would she want to reunite with Rose and relive those terrible war years? Rose glanced at the sketchbooks on the table—the covers still stained with the faded marks of her blood. Her leg ached from the cold. *Go home.*

If she left now, she could still catch the two-thirty train and arrive in her apartment before nightfall. She would make a cup of linden tea. It was better than the terrible *Kaffee-Mix* served here, which was more roasted peas and barley than coffee. It was time to put the past behind her, and accept that she'd lost her sister the day she stepped out of the car. Forty-five years was too long.

Rose slid the chair back. She heard the door to the café open, as she was returning the sketchbooks to her bag. She stood and rechecked her watch: noon. Time to go. She reached across the chair for her cane.

She was stepping away from the table, the bag over her shoulder, when two women approached. Rose's throat tightened. They were tall, confident, and beautiful—as if summer itself had walked into the café. She gripped the edge of the table, bracing herself as her head began to spin. It was them. Léa's daughters.

"Rose?" the taller one said.

Rose recognized Nadiya's deep, dark eyes. "Katya?"

"Yes. How did you know? This is—"

"Eve, Josef's daughter," Rose said, her voice catching in her throat. The memory of him brought sudden tears to her eyes. She stared at the girl. "Your mother's right—you have exactly the same light in your eyes that your father had."

Eve stepped closer with a bright look and a smile across her face. "Tell me about him."

"He was a wonderful, caring man. He loved your mother very much." Rose couldn't take her eyes off the two women and kept glancing back and forth between them, noticing bits of Josef in Eve and Nadiya in Katya. "Won't you sit down? Would you like a drink?"

They pulled out their chairs, Eve taking the one on her left, Katya on her right.

"We can't stay long," Katya said, tilting her head toward the door.

"I'm glad you've come." Rose leaned her cane against the table. "I've something I want to give to you both, something I think belongs to you, not me."

"Photos?" Eve leaned forward. "Maman doesn't have a single one of Papa. I'd love to see him."

Rose pulled out all four sketch books from her bag.

"Photo albums?" Eve asked excitedly.

"I'm sorry, dear, no," she said, arranging them by order—the most recent on top of the earlier ones from Orléans. She handed the first one to Eve.

"Is that . . . blood on the cover?" The young woman's finger traced over the faded stain on the cardboard surface.

"Don't pay attention to that—it's not important." She motioned to the book. "Open it."

Turning back the cover, Eve let out an involuntary gasp as her eyes traveled over the portrait. "It's Papa, I know it," she said. "I can see him the way Maman always talks about him. Round glasses. Broad shoulders. Those eyes. Is that the office in the sick bay? Look Katya, the typewriter!"

"The Hermes?" Katya leaned over to get a better look. "Maman told us about it and says that she still knows the keys by heart."

Eve looked at Rose, her eyes welling up with tears. "Maman said you were an artist, and it's true. You've captured . . . it's better than a photo . . . thank you."

Rose put a hand on her shoulder. "You're welcome, my dear. The first five are all of Josef. He'd sit in his office, writing the patient notes that your mother later typed into reports. While I waited, I'd sketch him." She smiled. "He was so absorbed in his work, I don't think he ever knew what I was doing."

Eve quietly turned the pages, wiping a tear from her face. "What were you waiting for?"

Rose swallowed. "Not important. Look, do you recognize her?"

"Maman?"

"Yes." Rose looked down at the sketch—the only one she'd made of Léa and Josef together.

"I thought it was all so terrible in Germany—Maman said she hated it. But here, she looks happy."

"It *was* terrible. And we hated it, but we were also in love."

"You too?" Katya asked.

"Yes." Even though it had been so long, Rose still felt a thud in her heart when she remembered André. "But I have something for you."

Rose lifted the sketchbook off the pile, opened it, and pulled out a faded green card with a black-and-white photograph on it. She gave the card to Katya.

"*Arbeitsbuch*," Katya read, "*Nadiya Solodowa*." One hand covered her mouth, while the other, with a slight tremor, held the card carefully.

“This was your mother’s work permit issued in Germany,” Rose said. “The photo was taken on the day she arrived—she was four months pregnant with you.”

“I never knew her surname. Is the date her—”

“Birthday.”

“January 18, 1925.” Katya’s voice quavered with emotion. “She was twenty years old when she had me.” She shook her head. “She died so young.” She pointed to a name written on the card, and read it aloud. “Odessa, USSR. That must have been where Maman came from. I never knew any of these things.” Katya reached over and touched Rose’s hand. “I’m so grateful for this. Thank you. I can’t believe you’ve been carrying it around for more than forty years.”

“I’ve been waiting.” Rose paused. “To give it to you.”

Despite dreading their reply, she took a breath and said, “Where’s your mother? She’s not coming, is she?”

Eve looked at Katya. “She’s outside, across the street.”

“Maman’s afraid,” Katya said.

Léa afraid? “Your mother’s the bravest person I know. She was caught smuggling wine by the Germans and sent to an internment camp, and she delivered you not knowing what she was doing. Your mother isn’t afraid of anything. She’s just—” Rose stood “—overthinking.” She picked up her cane and made for the door.

“Aunt Rose, I—”

Rose waved a hand in the air, cutting Eve off as she pulled open the door. The wind hit her. She’d left her coat back in the café. Never mind. She walked as quickly as she could to the end of the lane, leaning heavily on the cane for support. She was here to see her sister, and Léa was here too, so why on earth was she sitting on a bench outside?

* * *

Léa saw Rose across the street, one hand wedged in her skirt pocket, the other holding on to a cane. In the pit of her stomach, something large and heavy settled. Everything narrowed and magnified as if Léa was viewing Rose through the gunsights they'd spent those years in Germany assembling. Rose crossed Unter den Linden.

Léa stood. She couldn't speak. She could only stare at Rose's gray hair, the lines about her eyes and mouth, her limp—what had happened to her? In Léa's imagination, Rose had never changed. She'd always been the twenty-one-year-old sister she'd last seen getting out of the car. Why hadn't she realized that she too would have aged, just like Léa? She stepped closer.

Léa didn't know what to say. It was Rose, but it wasn't her, either.

"I'm sorry," Rose started, "please forgive me."

Léa's fears crumbled to dust. The love she'd always had for her sister, the bond that had endured the twists and turns that took their lives down different paths, welled up in her chest. It hadn't died and withered. She took one last step, arms outstretched and held her.

"We must forgive one another." Léa sobbed and buried her head on Rose's shoulder, and the sisters stood like that in the cold under the linden tree holding on to one another for a long while as the weight of more than four decades finally lifted.

Acknowledgements

I want to thank the entire team at Embla for your professionalism and support in shaping this book. Your insightful feedback and attention to detail have made all the difference.

To Heather Steele, at the non-profit World War II History Project, thank you for accompanying me to Dresden and Glashütte, for translating during interviews, for your passionate research support and for answering my relentless questions about German history.

To Camille Fauroux, I'm grateful for the extensive research you put into writing *Produire la guerre, produire le genre, Des Françaises au travail dans l'Allemagne nationale-socialiste (1940–1945),* which shed light on the forgotten and obscured stories of the French women who 'volunteered' to work in Germany.

To the talented writer Nola d'Enis, a million thanks for brainstorming plot points at all hours of the day and night and for encouraging me always.

With love, to my husband, Ivan, thank you for being my most important reader.

A Note from the Author

While researching *The Pilot's Wife*, I read about Glashütte, a small watchmaking town in eastern Germany. During World War II, three thousand forced laborers, including a handful of French women, worked in armament factories there. In October 2024, I traveled to Glashütte to interview people and see what I could find in local archives. During an interview with the Director of the lovely Watchmaking Museum, I told him I intended to write a story about two French sisters forced to work in Glashütte during the war. He immediately corrected me, saying that no French citizens were forced to work in Germany. Other nationalities such as Poles, Russians and Hungarians were forced, but the French were all volunteers. His response left me shaken and it made me rethink the story I wanted to write.

Out of the nearly 12 million foreign laborers in Germany during the war, the largest group came from the Soviet Union—4.7 million people rounded up during the invasion of Russia and sent to Germany. The second-largest group came from France, with 2.3 million volunteers. Many of these workers were POWs who changed their status from prisoner to worker, or they were young men sent by the Vichy regime under its Service du Travail Obligatoire (Forced Labor Service) instead of military service. According to Camille Fauroux's research, 80,000 French women 'volunteered' to work in Germany. I had never heard or read about these women.

In her memoir *The War*, Marguerite Duras writes that in 1945, while she was at the Gare d'Orsay, a repatriation center for people returning to France, she saw women sitting on the platform. They were called 'scum' and threatened with six months in prison because they'd just returned from working in Germany. According to Fauroux, many of the women who returned from Germany were targeted by those who wanted to shave their heads and humiliate them in public for 'collaborating' with the Nazi regime.

Most of these women came from modest backgrounds. To protect themselves, they kept their time in Germany a secret, and their stories were lost and not passed down to future generations.

This novel is my attempt to work through the nuance and complexity of the Nazi occupation of France while giving voice to the thousands of young French women who went through the experience of working in Germany during the war.

I learned a lot while researching and writing this story, and I hope you've enjoyed reading it. If you did, I'd be grateful if you could take the time to write a review online. Your review can help other readers find my work.

If you'd like to get in touch with me—I love hearing from readers and speaking at book clubs—you can find all my contact details and book club guides for my novels at cynthiaanderson.co.uk. You can also sign up for my newsletter to learn about what I'm reading and to receive a notification when my next book is released.

About the Author

Cynthia Anderson was born in California and has degrees from the University of Colorado and the London School of Economics. She is the author of *The Pilot's Wife* and lives in Switzerland with her husband and their labrador.

About Embla Books

Embla Books is a digital-first publisher of standout commercial adult fiction. Passionate about storytelling, the team at Embla believe our lives are built on stories – and publish books that will make you 'laugh, love, look over your shoulder and lose sleep'. Launched by Bonnier Books UK in 2021, the imprint is named after the first woman from the creation myth in Norse mythology. Embla was carved by the gods from a tree trunk found on the seashore; an image of the kind of creative work and crafting that writers do, and a symbol of how stories shape our lives.

Find out about some of our other books and stay in touch:

X, Facebook, Instagram: @emblabooks
Newsletter: https://bit.ly/emblanewsletter